T0037335

BINGE KILLER

CHRIS BAUER

Severn River Publishing
severnriverbooks.com

ISBN: 978-1-64875-500-2 (Paperback)

ALSO BY CHRIS BAUER

Blessid Trauma Crime Scene Cleaners

Hiding Among the Dead

Zero Island

2 Street

Scars on the Face of God

Binge Killer

Jane's Baby

with Andrew Watts

Air Race

Never miss a new release! Sign up to receive exclusive updates from author Chris Bauer.

severnriverbooks.com/authors/chris-bauer

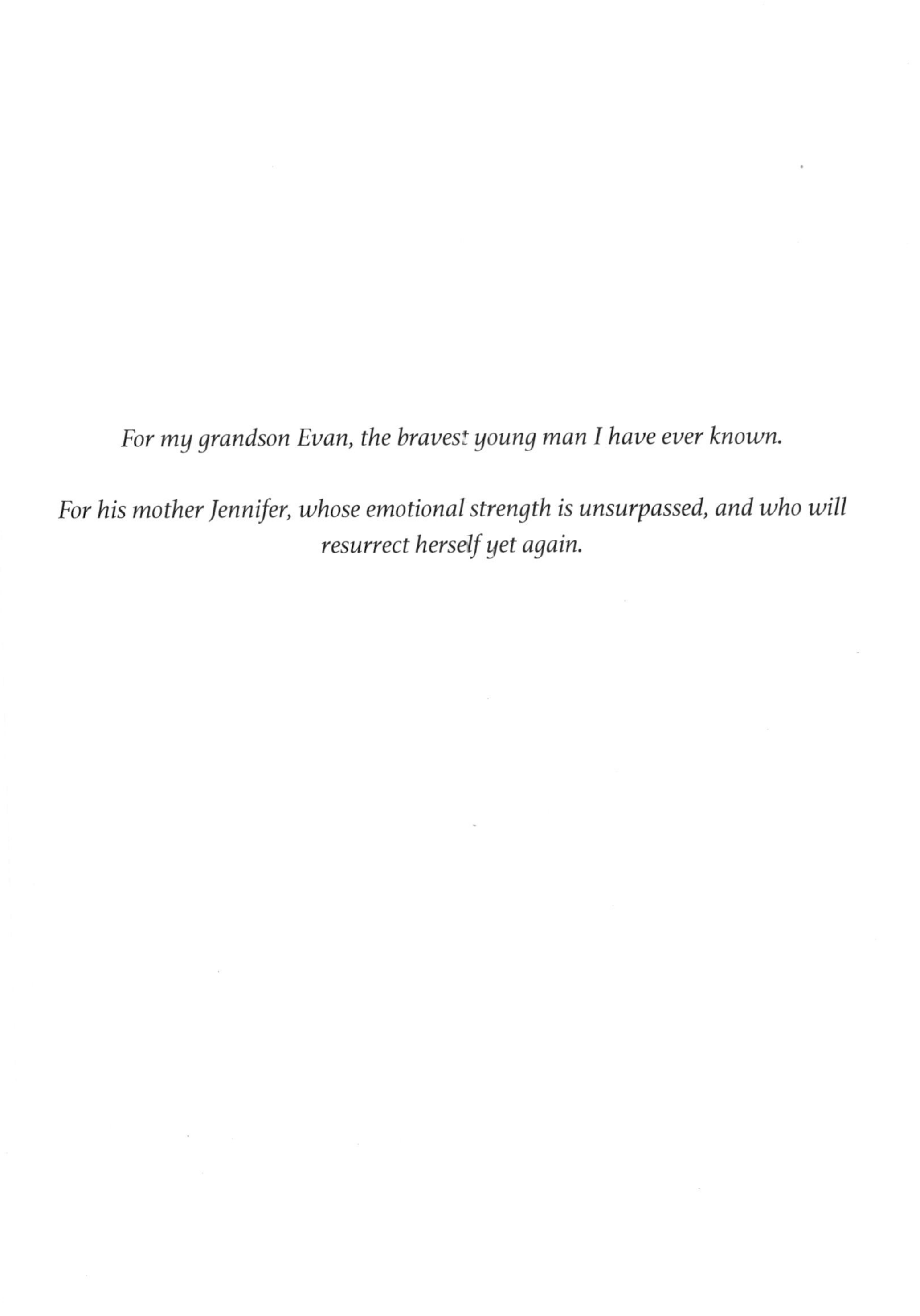

For my grandson Evan, the bravest young man I have ever known.

For his mother Jennifer, whose emotional strength is unsurpassed, and who will resurrect herself yet again.

JUNE 1962

Rancor, Pennsylvania, the Poconos

Maurice Prudhomme stood in line at the bank with a gentle hold on his young son Andy's shoulders, his pay envelope jammed into his coal miner's uniform shirt pocket. Andy, five and three-quarters years old, had dressed himself this morning with no prodding from his mother. Today he'd picked out a striped polo shirt, paisley shorts, white socks, and black high-top PF Flyers. An oversize blue baseball cap rested above Andy's eyes, covering the tops of his ears. Maurice, like the other coal miners in line, was dirty from his Friday night shift, his pale face blackened by coal dust and dried sweat. The other men cracked wise with each other as the line advanced, made suggestive eyes at Kitty, Maurice's sister, a few places ahead of them. At 9:15 in the morning young Andy was working on a wad of baseball card bubble gum that had secretly grown since they'd entered the bank. He snuck another stick into his mouth.

"Andy, kiddo, that's enough," his father said. "Give me the rest."

"Aw, Daddy..."

Three men in Army surplus fatigues with canvas backpacks, leather gloves, and rubber Douglas MacArthur masks stepped inside the bank's double-door entrance. None of their skin was visible, but their weaponry was: two handguns, a sawed-off shotgun, and a Thompson submachine gun.

"Good morning, folks," the one with the Thompson said. Heavyset, his gloved hands rested the gun across his protruding belly. He gave orders in an elevated but calm voice.

"This is a robbery. Now is the time to remind yourself that it's only money. Everyone put your hands behind your heads."

The thug with the handguns left the lobby with the bank manager, a gun to the manager's back, their destination the vault, the robber barking at anyone in his way to either move or get shot. The gunman with the sawed-off shotgun hopped the counter and commenced physically and verbally manhandling the tellers.

Which left the thug with the submachine gun to start at the beginning of the lobby line, forcing people at gunpoint to drop their cash into an open backpack he slid along the floor with his foot.

Andy's dad pulled his son closer and focused on the guy with the Thompson. Andy poked his head out, prompting his dad to firmly guide him behind his legs. His father raised his hands, put them behind his head, and kept them there as instructed.

The gunman moved down the short line. He reached Kitty, a coal company secretary in her late twenties, who mouthed "you bastard" when told to drop her pay into the open backpack. The gunman slid the canvas pack forward then gestured with his weapon to Maurice to make it snappy. Maurice removed his pay envelope from his shirt pocket and dropped it into the bag then returned his hands behind his head.

"That's my daddy's money," Andy said to the gunman. "Give it back, mister."

"Andy," Maurice was stern, "be quiet."

"I'm just borrowing it, young man," the gunman said, a flip assurance with a hint of amusement. He jabbed the Thompson at the next person in line to hustle him up.

Andy pushed. "No, you're not. You're stealing it."

The thug turned back, lowered his head with the rubber MacArthur mask in close for an imperial glance at Andy through the eyeholes. The nose holes contracted a few nasal breaths, more from arrogance than from his ample girth. "Heh. Isn't he precious."

Maurice pulled his son back into him, against his leg, raised his hands again. The lingering robber moved past them.

Andy, undeterred: "You're a liar. And you're fat."

The robber wheeled, clamped a gloved hand on to Andy's chin and squeezed. "Listen, you wiseass little punk..." He raised the butt end of the machine gun.

Maurice drilled a fist into MacArthur's chin, a short, crisp punch that dropped the fat man to the floor on his back. He picked up the machine gun and pointed it at the dazed thug, his finger on the trigger. "You piece of crap—he's just a kid—" In a crouch, with Andy behind him, he swiveled toward the bank counter.

Greeting his face were both barrels of a sawed-off shotgun. The close-range blast blew him and Andy off their feet, Maurice bouncing once then coming to rest on his back, his face shredded by the buckshot. The sepia-hue pearl-marble floor turned into a river of arterial red. Andy crumpled to the marble, still conscious, at the feet of the man with the shotgun wearing a pair of PF Flyer sneakers just like his.

Bleeding from his shoulder, Andy sobbed for his daddy. The two thugs dragged their semiconscious partner and his backpack along the floor then shoulder-shoved their way through the glass doors, out of the building.

Andy's aunt Kitty kneeled, lifted her nephew off the floor, and cradled him in her skirted lap. "Andy. Stay with me, sweetie. Andy, honey—"

1

Present Day

Rancor Savings and Loan's lobby was old-school cavernous, with shiny chrome stanchions, glistening glass partitions, cloth chairs in aquamarine, warm pastel walls, black pens, silver chains, and a swirled-pearl-marble floor. For Andy Prudhomme, the lobby was also a minefield. Fatherless for over fifty years, and Aunt Kitty-less for over a decade, he shuffled forward in line, his and other footsteps echoing. Voices—his father's, his aunt's—and scuffling noises—and the most paralyzing mind echo of all, a shotgun blast, lay in wait each time he visited the bank, the childhood trauma ready to suffocate him with horrific images beginning in bright red soon followed by a deep-sleep black.

A part-time psych nurse at the state hospital in nearby Scranton, Andy was also a full-time local business owner, his trips to the bank for his business frequent enough that they should have bothered him a lot less than they did. He looked younger than his fifty-six years, hair mostly brown, some gray, was tall, "hot" according to his women friends, hotter yet in his nurse's uniform. His half-lidded eyes remained unfocused, directed at the floor, seeing little, remembering too much. To his right, a stretch of marble all too familiar to him forced him to blink through his private horror.

Behind him a young man in creased khakis and a touristy Hawaiian shirt spoke up. "Yo. Buddy. You're up."

Andy smelled the blood, its metallic sweetness, could sometimes see it rivering away from his father on the floor, a wound to his head that was completely incompatible with life, as real today as it had been those many years ago.

The man behind him nudged him with a tap to his shoulder. "Hey. Let's go, fella. Today, already. Move."

When Andy failed to move, the guy reached at him again to get his attention, grabbing his bicep. Andy shuddered, snapped his hand up in a reflex that gripped the guy's pinkie finger and bent it back in a well-executed move. The bozo groaned and dropped to his knees. The woman behind them intervened.

"Andy—it's okay, honey, it's okay. Stop, Andy, relax..."

Dody Heck, burley and blonde, had no trouble inserting herself between Andy and his newest acquaintance. "You're not from around here, are you?" she said to the tourist, her outstretched arms separating them. With her arm pushing at Andy's waist the PTSD moment dissipated, Andy's breathing returning to normal. The complaining tourist found another line.

Andy and Dody did their banking in succession at the same teller, two close friends, one small town, and many unspoken thoughts between them.

They exited the bank together. Across the street, a news photographer framed the bank's entrance in his camera lens. Stately white columns, tall first-story windows, three stories in total, white stone steps. He depressed the shutter, held it down through multiple clicks. Andy and Dody, the bank, the mountain ridge behind it, a few parked cars, and a long and low, etched-black granite memorial all made it into the photographs.

* * *

Andy collected his delivered newspaper bundle and magazine subscriptions from his Rancor Bed & Breakfast walkway and mailbox at dawn. In the pile, Sunday's edition of the Scranton *Times-Tribune, USA Today, People* magazine, *B&B Quarterly,* and *Small Business Owner*. Inside the parlor he clipped open the baled bundles and walked the guest room circuit, dropping a copy of the newspaper at each doorstep. He returned downstairs on creaky hundred-year-old steps to read copies he kept for the parlor.

A few minutes later he was done with the newspaper. He found the *People* magazine. The pictures on the side inserts for the front cover hit him like a sack of coal in the solar plexus.

Rancor Savings and Loan Bank. Two photos, both from the same vantage point. One was present day, in color, a wide-angle shot, and was meant to contrast the second photo, a black-and-white Polaroid from five decades earlier. The words on the magazine cover adjoining the pictures: *The Safest Town in America. Rancor, Pennsylvania, 1962 and today.*

Andy focused on the magazine cover, his jaw clenching. “Sonovabitch.”

A shit-storm was coming.

2

Randall Burton and his landlady Loretta Spezak exited the Sands Casino's parking garage in Loretta's car. Loretta vouched for the '61 Chevy Impala's low mileage.

"Nineteen thousand six hundred miles is accurate, Stephen," she said, addressing his alias, another in a succession of many, all of them chewed up and spit out over the years like sticks of chewing gum. "With a beast of an engine. Four hundred nine cubic inches. My indulgent daddy bought it for me before I was old enough to drive. Garaged ever since."

He'd heard about her attachment to her beloved car many times. Today he'd been invited to drive it. First time ever. He'd queued up a few other firsts in his mind for the day as well.

Randall, age forty-five, was often mistaken for sixty, older if necessary, all except for his sex drive. Mark Twain/Santa Claus handsome. Premature white hair and a gray-white beard contributed to his image. He wasn't complaining; the coloring came in handy. He could go full senior in seconds. For Randall, life was good, excluding one part of it: he was dying.

He'd felt crappy. Tired, out of breath, and with a persistent cough. A clinic diagnosed his anemia first, then they handed him his death sentence: Stage 2 pancreatic cancer, at the moment still localized. Without aggressive, cutting-edge procedures, it would progress. Procedures he couldn't afford, at least not as a free man. Procedures he might expect to get in prison, considering this was where he would probably end up. Guinea pig medicine or the death penalty: one way or another, prison would cure him.

As a boarder in Loretta's suburban Allentown rancher, one year now, he'd never been invited to drive her precious car. It took two months of chatting her up before he could ferret his way into her personal space, first as a bingo player, then as a bridge partner. A month more to gain her trust in minor matters like cashing her small third-party checks to use for their shared house groceries and her prescription co-pays. Another month of weekly late afternoon and evening trips with her to the Sands Casino Resort in Bethlehem, where he'd bankrolled her almost as often as she'd bankrolled him. He'd also gained the trust of her senior women friends, banging two of the friskier ones when the opportunities presented themselves. And the last two months he'd spent stealing Loretta's identity. Last week, he drained her bank accounts. Then he got the cancer diagnosis.

He had most of her savings now. Added to this was this little matter of a new charge for attempted rape of a minor, the trial scheduled to start tomorrow. His grandfatherly demeanor and appearance convinced Loretta he couldn't possibly be guilty of the accusation. The time was right for splitsville, but not without leaving a significant impression here like everywhere else he'd lived, because this was what he did.

One thing Randall hadn't counted on: the despair that came with the diagnosis, and his pressing need to find one of his women, sixteen years absent, and the child she was pregnant with when she left. Regina, an exotic dancer, barely legal. Small-town girl from a burg outside of Scranton. He'd convinced himself there would always be time to find her—them. His long game: settle somewhere in the middle of nowhere, forget about his past life, then track her down and bring her and her kid—his kid—back with him. However difficult this might prove to be, connecting with her amicably would be almost impossible, considering someone shot him in the face and left him for dead when that someone spirited her away. She wouldn't want to be found, at least not by him.

He would arrive in Rancor, near Scranton, by nightfall today, and start his search. His interest in her personally bordered on zero. His interest in her child was now his reason for living.

Loretta beamed in the seat next to him, feeling giddy from Pink Squirrels and the adrenaline high that twelve hundred dollars in casino winnings had given her. He'd talked her into letting him drive her car for the short leg home.

"I'm glad you like it, Stephen. Driven only by, yes, this little old lady, to the grocery store on Fridays and to church on Sundays." A vivid yellow headscarf, some Marilyn Monroe sunglasses, and the massage and facial she'd made him wait for had telegraphed her mood. "Except today, I'm not feeling very old."

With the Chevy's top down, the wind in her newly rinsed blonde hair, and an attentive man at her side, she for sure felt like a million bucks and decades younger, the day ahead full of possibilities.

"And right now," she said, her drunk smile greeting Randall's glances, "I'm not feeling all that ladylike. And I was never little in two places that count, as I know you've noticed."

Her warm eyes looked at him expectantly. She moved closer to him in the seat, dragged a pudgy, red-manicured finger sensually up and down his forearm. Her hand went to his lap, creating a stirring in his pants.

He willed his arousal to cease. This would happen on his terms, and his terms only.

Home at her place in fifteen minutes, he reminded her. "It'll be worth the wait," he said.

In her bedroom, he delighted her by the largesse of his package in both length and girth, but her delight wasn't how he intended their intimacy to end. Their second time would all be about him. She screamed in panic as he choked her with his belt. He punched her unconscious after he climaxed. Randall dragged Loretta to her garage, secured her wrists and ankles together with plastic cable ties, then duct-taped her mouth. He lifted and dropped her into the Chevy's trunk, banged her up a little on the way in, slammed the trunk lid shut. If she were found dead, her body left in her house, he'd be the prime suspect. With the both of them missing, the wheels of justice would take longer to turn. Now he went about gathering up his packed clothes and garment bag and arranged them in the back seat of the Chevy, all of this premeditated. In his pocket was a prepaid cell phone with double minutes. He tossed an unzipped gym bag onto the front seat, the bag filled with stolen IDs, fake credit cards, a laptop, a handgun, another prepaid cell phone, and yesterday's issue of *People* magazine. He pulled out the magazine and put it next to him on the seat, its front cover facing up.

* * *

The last exit on the northeastern extension of the Pennsylvania turnpike was Clarks Summit, near Scranton. Coal country. Loretta was making noise in the trunk; Randall chose an exact-change lane to avoid attention. He dragged her out of the trunk behind a convenience store and crushed her skull with the car's tire iron. Her body went into the store dumpster.

Meticulous about these things in the past, he was no longer being careful. It was obvious, even to him. He was dying, for Christ sake, so why do otherwise.

3

In this business, if you run, you're guilty.

So there was this certain jackass, Vonetta told me, who bolted on an Allentown arrest for attempted rape of a minor. He was charged and jailed, made bail, then ran, just before his court date. Finding and returning Mr. Stephen Linkletter to the legal system was worth a thousand bucks to me, two grand to Vonetta's bail bond company, and five grand, maybe even her life, to the woman who arranged his bail. Like the bail-jumper himself, the woman was missing.

Midmorning, and I was headed north until my van ran out of turnpike, the Allentown-Bethlehem interchange up next, the Lehigh Tunnel after that. A pleasant drive, little traffic, the sunroof open, tousling my pixie cut newly rinsed in an espresso brown. Hills, trees, farms; overpasses; an occasional billboard. My K9 deputy Tess snored on the floor in front of the van's passenger seat, my other deputy Fungo doing likewise in his crate in the back. I had a loose grip on the steering wheel, a firmer grip on my takeout coffee. The name scribbled on the front of the cup was *Cuntsel*, not Counsel, the male barista at the counter capitalizing on my Tourette's outburst. Another perk of this disease. Difficult for everyone afflicted, but worse for a woman.

The name on the cup put me in full contemplation mode.

My hands were pre-arthritic marvels, their bones set and reset too many times, one knuckle scarred and bulging bad as popped corn. Too many rash decisions over the years, mostly from a bad temper and ballistic reactions to other people's ignorance. About women who could handle themselves. About women who were different—women outside normal expectations. About women who had Tourette syndrome. It was tough fighting against society's expectations all—the—damn—time.

By the time I turned sixty I would need help toileting. And today, like so many days, I noticed my fingernails the most. Ragged in spots, with me trying to get past a few days where I didn't nervously shred one or more of them. Multiple stops at salons for acrylics, whenever I felt like pampering myself. Never better than a C in Health Habits all eight years of Catholic elementary school, and a target for the nuns. Strong female types were like lepers to them. Yes, I had a chip on my shoulder. My voice, my attitudes, sometimes I just didn't give a fuck, but all the time, I was aware. None of it matched the veneer, which was easier on the eyes than my cynicism would ever admit.

My dogs and I were powering through a two-hour-plus ride into Pocono country. Where the turnpike ended, it would be ten miles west to Rancor, Pennsylvania, my new center of the universe, until I caught my bounty, if he was still there. Call it kismet, but Rancor had just received some national press, a significant mention in a *People* magazine article open on the seat next to me:

People's Top Ten Safest US Towns List, Lowest Crime

#10, Glens Falls, NY...

#2, Rockingham County, NH

and #1, in the Pocono Mountains, small-town venue Rancor, Pennsylvania...

Snapshots of Rancor surrounded the list. A bowling alley. Side-by-side photos of Rancor Savings and Loan Bank fifty years apart, showcasing identical breathtaking views from the bank's perch atop the town's highest elevation. I had parts of the Sunday edition of a suburban Philly newspaper fanned out under Tess's butt on the floor. In it was a teaser front-page sidebar reference to *People*'s "Safest Towns in America" article plus a second curiosity, a page-seven story on a cold Philadelphia suburbs case, "Whatever Happened to Bunyip Deveraux?"

I already knew Deveraux's story. The Bunyip was a pissant pimp with kangaroo ears, a platypus face, bubble nose, and scraggly brown hair. Nuclear-accident ugly. His "Bunyip" namesake had been a mythical 1950s local Philly TV hand puppet. Deveraux hung out his pimp shingle in the Philly suburbs, stayed out of the police crosshairs, played up the Bunyip angle by branding his girls with a distinctive tattoo: the bunyip puppet's head. Rumor was no girls ever quit him alive, a rumor he'd started himself, to keep them all in line. When he went missing a few of his women did report it. Lots of whore and drug traffic for a few years running and then poof, he was gone. Poof into fairy dust or a black hole, or cement shoes, or another pimp's blade, no one in the business knew for sure, but he ceased to exist as a player on Philly's suburban streets or elsewhere.

For the record, I never did drugs, and I never smoked. I liked to drink, and I only liked men, having done both in excess after my divorce. Each pursuit dulled my senses when I needed it to. Trying to limit my intake. Too many indulgent lapses.

Tess's tail stub wiggled. She had a sixth sense in her Bull Terrier blood, especially when it came to me.

Yeah, I'm looking at you, Tess, you head case.

In Tess's dog brain: *Ditto, nut job.* She climbed onto the passenger seat.

With my other deputy in the back, it was a lot less complicated. An intense eighty-pound black-and-tan German Shepherd, Fungo stayed crated for road trips and liked it that way. Stayed in the crate even with its door open, was always leashed; the leash was short. Crate and leash were nods toward his previous living arrangement: chained night and day to a doghouse outside a Levittown, Pennsylvania, home, protecting a crystal meth operation. He had to be tranquilized when Animal Control liberated him. Aside from his crate and leash as security blankets, Fungo liked four things: food, family, fucking up criminals, and fucking in general. He wasn't fixed.

A lot of *F*s in that last sentence. Alliteration. I often went off the chart when it came to my uncensored subconscious expressing itself, barking orders because of the Tourette's. When the pressure built between my ears, my diuretic mouth opened to relieve it.

Lucky for me, relief was in the seat next to me. Tess's ears felt silky smooth between my fingers, which she started licking. All better now.

Tess was a law enforcement veteran like me, a working dog, part of the Pennsylvania State Police's K9 Unit, and my partner. When I retired I bought out her contract so she could retire with me. Cost me twelve grand, which approximated what the force would need to spend to train a dog to replace her. Money well spent for me, her being a combination apprehender, heat-seeking missile, and therapy dog rolled into one.

She and I rescued my shepherd Fungo from a shelter. I bailed him out after discharging a gun loaded with blanks near his cage, to see how he'd react. Other dogs in the shelter went berserk. His look at me said, *What else you got?*

The rest of the *People* list's footnote: *As a bedroom community to Scranton, Rancor earns the top ranking for the following anomaly, a testimony to small towns everywhere: No—repeat, NO—violent crimes have been reported within its jurisdiction for the past fifty years.*

I hoped things would stay that way, except for the one promise I'd made to myself about Mr. Linkletter: his apprehension would include a tune-up that might border on the criminal. With me, this underage shit was way personal. A brother-sister thing, my older brother doing the protecting, and me doing the watching and the wincing, too young to fully understand the depravity and the sacrifices he'd made on my behalf.

* * *

We passed the Wilkes-Barre, Pennsylvania, interchange.

What my bounty Mr. Stephen Linkletter didn't know was that the red-and-white classic 1961 Chevy Impala he'd helped himself to had a GPS tracker on it. Law enforcement might not have had the time to track him down, but his bail bondsman did, hence the reason why said bondsman—bondsperson—and premier State Police trooper pal-o'-mine Vonetta Posey bugged the cars her clients had access to. I got a call from Vonetta yesterday, me catching some rays in a tank top and cutoffs out back of my house, a rancher on a small lake outside Philly. Mr. Linkletter had missed his court date, which was troublesome for Vonetta.

In response to my hello:

"This, my pathetic, white, piece-of-shit, retired canine sergeant honey, is Vonetta."

"Woof, Sergeant Posey."

"Woof, Sergeant Fungo."

More beer.

My full name is Counsel Abigail Fungo, née Drury. Retired sergeant, Pennsylvania State Police. Something Vonetta and I had in common, both of us busting our balls to make that rank. And yes, I named my stud male dog Fungo after me, the difference in our sexes be damned. It was early in my civilian narcissistic period, begun right after my twenty-and-out state trooper retirement. Unlike my well-honed trooper narcissism, my civilian narcissism was a work in progress. People, men in particular, told me I was already good at it.

After Vonetta put in her twenty, she and her husband bought some pastureland upstate with a few goats and cows and whatever other animals a person needed to have property taxed as farmland. The civilian world was Vonetta's oyster. For me, the civilian world was more like the fish I forgot to bring in from the car.

Back to her call. She'd asked for help. I'd never heard of Rancor, Pennsylvania. I worked mostly in and around Philly and Willow Grove, thirty miles outside of Philly, near the naval air base the feds had closed.

"The landlady's vintage Chevy is up there somewhere, Counsel. She came to me for Linkletter's bail. We bugged both cars, his and his landlady's. Hers moved, his didn't. His trial was supposed to start today. He didn't show, and now the Chevy's on a road trip. The dude's got this thing for minors. Right up your, you know, alley, so to speak. Sarge? Fungo? Counsel, honey?"

Fungo, Sarge, Counsel; I normally answered to them all. Some dead air hovered between us after her comment about minors. Vonetta knew a lot about me; she took liberties. I let her hang a little.

"Counsel. Sweetie. You gonna help me here or what? Miss Fungo? Hello?"

When Vonetta stepped into any of my personal minefield crap I usually let her leave with all her limbs and our friendship intact. The next bit of dead air filled with the neurologically defective mental asshole bullshit baggage that I carried, in rapid-fire, head-spinning fashion.

"—shit-fuck-piss, you need to look at this.

—cock-a-doodle dance gonna twerk it on your pants.

—shit-fuck-piss, you need to look at this..."

If some other woman ever had thoughts like this, they'd never make it out of her mouth. With me, an embarrassing difference. I repeated this declaration three, maybe four times before I was able to stop myself. "Sorry, Netta," I told her. The apology wasn't needed. Not with Vonetta.

I told her I'd take the case.

"Great. Glad to hear you're still as gifted as ever, Sarge. Music to my ears, hot stuff."

Far from music; my crosses to bear. Diseases with unpronounceable words. Coprolalia, or compulsive profanity, and copropraxia, performing obscene gestures. A double-C psycho-cocktail subset of Tourette syndrome. I wished I'd never heard of them.

It ran in the family. My brother Judge Drury, eleven years my senior, was similarly afflicted.

"Yes, still occasionally thrilling the general citizenry. Send me the bounty's info and I'll get on the road."

* * *

As a teenager I tried to keep my mouth shut and my hands in my pockets. An impossibility, and the reason my hands were so buggered up. Being an afflicted young woman—a *big* afflicted young woman, who became an even bigger afflicted adult—sometimes meant physical confrontations. Our introductions, with Vonetta and I billeted next to each other as trooper cadets at the State Police Academy, escalated with the first words out of our mouths:

"Vonetta Posey, Bethlehem, Pennsylvania."

"Counsel Fungo, Philly. Nice to—*nigger nigger suck a trigger*—meet you."

Vonetta demanded an apology, said she'd knock my tits through my shoulder blades if she didn't get it. I knew how to box; a physical response to her threat might have cost her a broken jaw. My verbal apology was what she deserved and got. She and I became close; the best of friends ever since. A testament to the State Police and to her, not to me. She was an aggressive woman when it came to strays and lost causes. For me, friends were a rarity. I almost moved to Bethlehem because of her. Regardless, I wanted to live near Philly, where I spent my childhood, difficult as it had been.

I learned the hard way not to be the aggressor when it came to people making fun of me. A few schoolyard assaults, giving and receiving, became suspensions. I graduated high school a year late, enlisted in the army before the Tourette's took hold. Got me some armed services discipline after almost washing out of basic training. Put in four years, did two tours, decided that was enough.

Early summer in the northeast, and I had the crotch rocket in tow behind the van. A red Suzuki Hayabusa 1300. Livin' large at age forty-nine. Mr. Linkletter's mug shot and newspaper accounts of his arrest were with me for the road trip north. A female Allentown cop posing as an underage runaway at a bus terminal had reeled him in. After jumping bail, Mr. Linkletter now had his landlady's car. The landlady was also missing.

Coming up on the last exit of the turnpike, Clarks Summit, an hour and a half north of Allentown. A bit more highway, then we would head into the Pocono woods.

About the dogs. I had one as a child in our home in Bryn Mawr. Mom took in a stray when I was five. Dad, at that time only a corrupt Philly union official, "got rid of it" a few days later. Fast-forward to basic training and my drill sergeant, a compassionate SOB who used some of his Zen/Dalai Lama mojo on me. When I told him about my afflicted brother's success as a marine MWD K9 officer, he agreed to try the K9 unit as a placement for me. Military working dogs became my army life—detection, deterrent, detainment, sometimes destruction—and canines became my salvation.

I wished I'd known as a teenage girl how therapeutic pets were. For me, at least. For the bounties I chased, not so much.

* * *

A concrete bridge tall as a western state's railroad trestle finished off my turnpike travel. We curled around to the tollbooths, curled some more before we slid into traffic on a four-lane strip in Clarks Summit, only minimally commercial. Ten minutes later we were inside Rancor town limits, cruising Rancor Boulevard. Woodsy, dense, hilly. A feed store, a landscaping business, a John Deere outlet, a Greek diner. A post office. A single-story cinder-block bingo hall and the aforementioned bowling alley. There were three or four bed-and-breakfast establishments in the region, but one B&B was all I needed. A big B&B fan. Just another thing I had in common with my brother, like bounty hunting, working dogs, and Tourette's.

I'd always been a soft touch for comfy beds and homemade food; the fugitive recovery business supported my B&B habit. Too many stakeout meals while I was on the force, too much diner food later, after I lost my ex-husband, who'd remained a good friend.

We pulled into the Willow Swamp Farm B&B. Two other vehicles in the lot. The inn was a restored Victorian on three acres per the website, with tall ladderback rockers and a two-person swing on a wraparound porch filled with wicker. Full breakfast, afternoon tea. The clincher: pets were welcome. My new home until I found Mr. Linkletter.

I walked Fungo and Tess, cleaned up after them, gave them some water, and put them back in the van for now, windows and sunroof open. Fungo moved into his crate. Tess sat in the passenger seat stiff and observant, would stay that way and not leave her post. A custom conversion in black and gold, the van was designed for fugitive recovery, not tourism. Leg irons, handcuffs, waist chains, a baton, leashes, dog harnesses, Kevlar, night goggles, some weaponry. An open concept interior that looked like a traveling BDSM wet dream. No bulletproof glass or other barrier separated the bucket seats from the cargo area; that would have been too confining for the dogs. We typically caught and held our bounties until I could call them in. I let the experts handle transport.

I hefted an olive-colored duffel with wheels out of the van. Standard road trip stuff, jeans, pullovers, underwear, toiletries, some skirts and blouses, and two handguns. Tess inched over to an open window in anticipation. I cupped her sweet brown-and-white Bull Terrier face in my hand. Her expectant look encouraged me to give a good account of myself when I got inside. *My hope as well, Tess, my hope as well.*

4

Andy's croissant appetite was gone. His stomach acid churned from his last sip of coffee. An eighth grader from an inner-city elementary school in a tough section of Philadelphia was the reason for his focus on the *People* article. To'Nay Witherspoon's entry in the magazine's nostalgic "What I Did Last Summer" essay contest had taken top prize. According to the "Safest Towns" piece Andy was reading, her entry was what had opened the eyes of the *People* editors.

Is Rancor, Pennsylvania, for real? read the title of the magazine piece.

He had it open on the B&B's secretary desk in the parlor, with him leaning over the desktop while he read. A cheerful article with good intentions, and it accompanied the safest-towns list along with excerpts from the girl's contest entry. Brutally honest feelings about gang-terrorized urban life eloquently stated by a thirteen-year-old, showing her extreme yearning for, and appreciation of, the closeness and the safety that this small town in upstate Pennsylvania had embodied for her during multiple years of girls' summer camp there. To'Nay hailed from Philly's tough inner-city projects, one of a number of minority kids bused in to commune with kids in upstate Pennsylvania for two overnight weeks in July each of the past three years. The camp showcased events and games with positive themes, team-building sports, and creative crafts, but of most interest to her was the coal mining folklore around the campfire, and children's silly stories of guardian angels and benevolent boogeymen. Bullies, parents behaving badly, an occasional domestic spat, mischievous teens: in Rancor, per local lore, they'd all be taught lessons, have their tables turned by anonymous spiritual zephyrs who evened scores when necessary, and made kids and their families feel safe. Even a boogey*bitch*, the Rancor kids mentioned to To'Nay, this whispered nickname generating snickers and rib pokes from eleven- and twelve-year-olds sitting on tree stumps eating s'mores and other gooey marshmallow treats around the campfire. The essay was an impressionable at-risk child's perspective about growing up scared and anxious versus her need to feel safe and protected.

To'Nay hadn't flinched at the harsh language her essay had related. *Bitch, f******* bitch, motherf****** and worse were all part of her own vernacular, all "street," yo. No, To'Nay had been more intrigued that there walked among these fabled Rancor equalizers an empowered, superhero woman delivering beatdowns whenever and wherever the need. A need that was infrequent, incidents often separated by years, yet they had fostered the campfire folklore. In her essay, To'Nay harbored hope that someday the women in her neighborhood, in all neighborhoods, would rise up and do the same. That, plus she liked the handmade crazy quilt each camp attendee received as a gift, courtesy of a local Rancor quilting club.

To'Nay's words compelled the magazine's editors to look closer at Rancor for their top ten safest towns article. They were blown away: Rancor had no reported violent crime in five decades—*"and with a police force of one!"*—the italics theirs. Rancor, according to *People*, had a capable, persistent town watch, a robust self-defense program, a tough coal-mining heritage, and generation after generation of close-knit families. A town that relied on word-of-mouth exchanges at pie-eating contests, bowling alleys, and bingo halls as much as on Google searches. A 1950s-America throwback.

The stairs behind Andy creaked. A couple on their way down the steps was getting an early start to their day. He straightened up, greeted his guests, and closed the magazine.

Guardian angels and altruistic boogeymen: the long-time Rancor residents let these campfire legends coexist along with the town's less spiritual, more practical history, a history that had an Aunt Kitty, an incendiary kind of woman. Its crime-free legacy began with her, with the bank robbery trial's miscarriage of justice as its catalyst, after which Kitty had decided to make a difference.

* * *

Andy eventually learned the clandestine history about his aunt. In the beginning, after the trial for the bank robbery and murder, Kitty Buchinsky née Prudhomme had been a one-person equalizer. Equipped with a no-bullshit attitude, a few small caliber antique guns her hunter father had left her, a robust sexual appetite, and a body men found appealing, she used each of these tools to even the odds and right wrongs. Aunt Kitty hadn't been just any boogeybitch, she was *the* boogeybitch from whence the myth was born. Near her end, however, her age and hard living had taken their toll, and her boogeybitch vigilantism died with her.

Squeaky springs on the B&B lobby's screen door protested its opening then snapped it shut after a woman entered. Andy's mosey down memory lane ended.

"Good morning, Andy."

"Hi, Ursula."

At seventy-seven, Ursula was a town mainstay with generations of Rancor family history preceding her. Spry, spandexed legs, a summer blouse, and a rinsed white perm with a black hair bow dead center, Ursula exuded an active older adult persona, all except for what she carried: a quilt and a quilting supplies bag, the quilt ready for final embroidering.

"Your mom joining us today, doll?" Ursula asked him.

He'd forgotten. Today was a quilt-finishing session on the enclosed side of the B&B porch, where Ursula and his mother, members of the Piece-Makers Crazy Quilt Club of Rancor, would stitch themselves silly, entertained by an old TV and fortified by a few afternoon manhattans and martinis.

"I'll bring Ma out in a minute," Andy said. He tucked a side chair out of the way, clearing a wheelchair path for his mother. Ursula stepped outside the lobby, onto the front porch.

Ursula and Aunt Kitty: the best of friends while Kitty was alive.

The town's no-violent-crime legacy in the earlier years had remained intact because Kitty had no respect for criminals, and was also pretty much a cheat when it came to dealing with them. Her brand of justice: the end justified the means, don't play by the rules, and do so as invisibly as possible.

5

"Do you know her?"

Lunchtime at a strip joint in Scranton. The two pictures Randall showed the hostess were all he had left of her. The first was a glossy glamor shot, Regina at twenty-one. Tits with no-quit cleavage topping a rock-star-thin body, and a cute pout-and-a-half face, the photos taken pre-Randall. Also pre-Randall: casting couches, drugs, and some rather tasteless skin flicks. Nothing she could ever show her hometown friends. The photo shoot had cost her all her money after her arrival in Philly, as in it ultimately put her in a homeless shelter for women when things hadn't worked out. When her money dried up, as her story to Randall went, she'd been too embarrassed to admit defeat and go home.

Each dancer he asked said she'd never seen her before.

In the second photo, Regina wasn't smiling because she wasn't happy, and she wasn't happy because she was more than a little strung out. But what she was those many years ago was *alive*, and Randall could take credit for that. He'd been every bit her protector—her savior. Food, shelter, new clothes. Money. Drugs. And a new life—for her, and for the baby growing inside her. Except her opinion of him on many of those nights they were together had been extremely south of flattering.

One night, everything went sideways. Masked gun- and bat-wielding strangers ambushed him behind a Bristol, Pennsylvania, pub. They spirited her away, a liberation that was, for her, apocryphal, but for him, apocalyptic. Regina had bit the hand that fed her, had dimed herself out. A triggered pump-action shotgun left him and his upper torso, including his face, to bleed out on a sidewalk. The attack and his convalescence retired him as a player on the street. He, too, then disappeared into the night, and when he reemerged he'd reinvented himself—new identity, new face, same big dick, same charm, but now always on the move; also now terminally ill.

The dancer on the stage was in midsquat, her gyrating lady parts inches away from the top of his drink glass. Some guys got off with so suggestive a positioning; Randall wasn't one of them. She straightened up, tucked his folded ten-dollar bill into her G-string, did a slow twirl for him, told him to put away the pictures.

"For a girl to admit"—her hips seesawed—"that she knows a girl like the one you're describing"—another twirl—"the guy doing the asking"—a slow bend at the waist, her hands on her knees, with ass then taint thrust eye-level to him—"needs to be asking someone who actually gives a shit." A tousle of her bottle-blonde hair and her direct eye contact ended with her bouncing away from him, over to the next bar customer, her stilettos click-clacking on the stage.

The translation: *pay me, old man, and maybe I'll give the shit you want me to give and answer your questions.*

On her return spin, Randall asked, "How much?"

"A hundred bucks gets you an answer, nothing else, tiger."

She leaned over, advertised ample cleavage that her barely-there dance top showcased, a suggestion that the nothing else that he wasn't going to get might be worth paying extra for. Randall knew better, that it wouldn't be worth it, considering she was the oldest dancer on the stage—someone who had a better chance at having a longer memory.

He hadn't been the kindest of boyfriends to his prospective baby momma. He knew this, but that was the nature of his street persona. In his heart he'd loved her, something he thought Regina knew. She apparently hadn't, so when the cavalry arrived those many years ago, a trio of masked avengers, she ran.

The money changed hands.

"She got a name, sweetie?"

"Regina Briscoe," which was what her driver's license showed when Randall took it from her. Could have been a fake; Randall had multiples for himself, too. Except she'd been a teenager with no money; it was likely her real name. "Her stage, screen, and street name was Juicy Luster."

"Cute name, but no, never heard of her," the dancer said. "And I know 'em all around here, at the other clubs, on the street, everywhere. If she's twenty years old in that picture, she's never been one of the girls in play anytime during the past ten to fifteen years. How about you, lover? You got a name?"

He'd had many. "Things are complicated. Maybe some other time."

He experienced the same zero luck at a second club in Scranton as he'd had at the first, other than to learn that his real destination, nearby Rancor, was a wholesome family town with a small population and no similar risqué outlets. If Regina was alive and living nearby, she was no longer in that life.

The strip club visits had stirred his juices. The question was, what now to do about it. Find another whore? Not appealing at the moment. He craved something a lot younger.

One block away, Cheesus H. Christmas, a holiday-themed, franchised pizza restaurant popular for kids' birthday parties, open year-round. Shitty pizza, beer, wine, kids' amusements, and parents who often weren't paying attention.

* * *

The *People* article had closed the deal: no reported violent crime in over fifty years in this small town in upstate Pennsylvania.

He'd rebuffed the Scranton dancers, instead acted on opportunity and impulse by molesting then strangling an unattended little girl at the pizza restaurant, and stuffing her boney birthday-girl body into a restaurant toilet. Randall was now in need of a good muscle stretch, some greasy bar food, and a pint of whatever Irish beer the Rancor bowling alley bar had on tap.

Randall studied the *People* magazine on the seat next to him. He was parked near where the pictures on the cover were taken. Inside the article was a photo of the bowling alley, the alley shiny from a sun not quite directly overhead, the sky a cobalt blue behind the building's marquis of sequentially flashing Vegas-style lighting. He climbed out of the car.

"That's a lot of fucking lights," he murmured midstretch. "Podunkers and their bowling. Made for each other."

He checked out a white message board's boast at sidewalk level beside the bowling alley's front door: *Mon-Tue-Wed, Day-Evening Senior Leagues. New in Pocono country: Dollar slots!*

Anything between eight and eighty, blind, crippled or crazy. A cliché he'd heard as a horny teenager; his motto for the last thirty years. Yet now he typically stayed at the farther ends of the motto's spectrum: defenseless kids, defenseless senior women. Considering his diagnosis, the more defenseless, the better.

He knew the psychology of it; he wanted to get caught, just not until after he found his kid. The trail left in his wake so far—Loretta, and now the innocent little birthday girl—said as much. Except now that he'd arrived in Rancor, the thrill had returned. The safest town in America. A thrown gauntlet just too damn good not to pick up.

Senior women, slot machines, hopefully his ex, hopefully their child, who was hopefully a boy. If so, and if Randall could make the connection, he'd die a happy man.

He eyed the classic Chevy. Old and beautiful, but too conspicuous once someone found Loretta's body. He needed to get rid of the car.

6

It hadn't taken long. Ninety seconds, a hundred cobblestone feet, a set of porch stairs, and one sentence.

The proprietor had led with "You must be Miss Fungo," when greeting me as I entered the B&B parlor, his comment suffixed with a killer smile. Attractive guy.

Yes, my nod told him. Then I opened my mouth and entertained him with the bane of my existence.

"*—I'm on the hunt please kiss my cunt, on the hunt, kiss my cu-cu-cu...*"

An embarrassment, sure. Sad to say not my worst, but all too common regardless. And subconsciously not embarrassing enough for me to not repeat it at least four more times before I squeezed the fuzzy dog keychain hanging from my belt loop. My frequently opinionated left hand and rat-a-tat brain needed to stay occupied. The fuzzy keychain helped, a life hack courtesy of my older brother, that eased me away from many a meltdown.

No "Excuse me?" or "I beg your pardon" from the proprietor, not even a flinch. Now he was waiting me out, giving me a chance to redeem myself.

"Tourette syndrome," I said. "I'm so sorry. If you're uncomfortable having me stay here, I'll understand."

He studied me, studied my face, my eyes. He didn't blink. "Andy Prudhomme," he said. "I fill in at the state psychiatric hospital in Scranton as a nurse when I can." He smiled, letting the coincidence sink in for me. "Your secret's safe with me, Miss Fungo, although I'm sure it's anything but. You're checked in. Tomorrow's breakfast menu is posted on the chalkboard on the porch."

I exhaled, my tension gone. He did good. He did real good.

Six-one or two, with a dark complexion that set off his indigo eyes. Wiry. Flat stomach, lanky, smartly trimmed light brown hair. Could make it as a T-shirt and jeans model. On the B&B website there'd been no reference to a proprietor wife or partner.

I needed to quit my gawking or I'd embarrass myself again. My fingers stroked the keychain. Over his right shoulder, on the wall behind him, a framed vintage WW2 poster read *Coal is good for America.* Other coal posters and prints hung elsewhere in here, this parlor serving as the B&B's lobby.

"You're in room five, Miss Fungo," Mr. Prudhomme said. "It has fewer antiques and less chewable trinkets. I ask that you keep your dogs leashed if you bring them inside the parlor, and when wandering the house and grounds. Do you need two keys?"

"No."

"You're good to go, then. We'll serve tea and lemonade and some homemade snacks around three or so. Hope to see you then. Otherwise, I'll see you at breakfast. Enjoy your stay."

* * *

Room Five. My guns stayed in the duffel. Guns for the room and guns for the van, plus I carried a Glock semiauto .45 in a holster against the crook of my back, covered by my untucked tee. I moved my clothes from rolling duffel to drawer and closet. My bag of toiletries and other necessities went to the bathroom. I was unpacked; took all of thirty seconds.

I paged through a scrapbook on the antique white bureau. It gave some stats about Rancor, a population of twelve hundred, its elevation, seasonal festivals, etc., but it was filled mostly with pictures of coal miners and former coal miners, some I recognized from the B&B website. Stills in black and white from the late nineteenth century through the 1970s, the more recent shots as good as anything I'd ever seen in *LIFE* or *Look.* If you lived in this region, you and your family had taken your lumps, no pun intended. Mining was its staple, generation after generation, unless it killed you. Depressed, dirty, and dangerous. No new news here, discounting a recent anniversary of sorts for Centralia, Pennsylvania, a half-hour drive away. Fifty-plus years ago a fire started in the town dump and moved into the rich coal veins near the surface, then it spread deeper underground. It was still burning. The streets of Centralia, what was left of them, were buckled and hot to the touch. Fifty-plus years. A few of the Centralia residents refused to leave.

Three non-mining pictures. One of the old Rancor police station in black and white, taken in the fifties. Beside it, a photo of it now as a bingo hall, in color but barely. There was only so much you could do with gray cinder blocks and windows crosshatched with iron bars. A wooden crucifix was affixed to each of the hall's two front doors. A repurposed real estate sign planted on the lawn read *St. Possenti's: Bingo Mon-Sat.* Six days a week was a lot of bingo, even for a church. The third photo was of the new police station, now an unimposing, small storefront next to a barber shop in the middle of town.

Bingo and bowling. Rancor was one fun-loving, rockin' town.

One other picture, black and white and grainy, stood out, not much more than a stereotype: a head and shoulders shot of a coal miner. Sweat-stained with a coal-dusted face, his eyes half-closed but their whites pronounced because of the grime around them, a pickax resting on one shoulder, a shovel on the other. No smile. It was special because it was the only labeled photo in the collection.

Maurice Prudhomme, 1928–1962

I headed back out to the van to make sure my belongings were secure and to bring Tess up to the room. Fungo would come up later. He needed more time in his crate now that we were stationary.

Maurice Prudhomme. Dead at age thirty-four. An icebreaker for my next contact with Mr. Andy Prudhomme, B&B proprietor.

7

A new alias for Randall: Howard Isaacs. His suggestion for Mr. Nap Napoli, a fortyish Tiparillo-chomping greaser used-car dealer, was a straight-up trade, the 1986 Buick Electra sitting front and center on his car lot for a classic cherry 1961 Chevy Impala convertible that, unfortunately, sat broken down eight miles away and just off the road, not far from Glacier Pothole State Park in Rancor. Randall had called for a cab then had it drop him off at Nap's dealership.

"Breathtaking," Randall-alias-Howard offered to the greaser, for this tourist to see a hole, the park's glacially formed pothole, that large, that deep, up close, visible for seventy-five feet or so into its mouth because it was a bright day. Beyond that, dark and creepy. Who knew what was at the bottom, Randall blathered to Nap.

Too much info, or info Nap already knew, Nap's nod told him.

Sure was, Randall knew. All part of the con.

"So, Nap, is there any way we could maybe complete some of the paperwork here, grab the keys and some temp tags, then take the Buick out for a spin to see my trade? If you like what you see and you can get the car started, we can finish everything up right there. I could follow you back to make sure it doesn't give you any trouble. The car title's in the glove box. I know, I know, I shouldn't keep the title with the car. Old habits die hard, Nap, yes they do..."

"Look, Mr. Isaacs—"

Nap studied this white-haired, friendly grandfather-type, was debating the proposal, was close, just wasn't quite there.

"Howard. Call me Howard," Randall said, flashing another gosh-golly, harmless old-guy smile.

"I, ah, suppose a vintage Chevy on my showroom floor wouldn't be a bad thing. You seem like a nice guy. You are a nice guy, right, Howard?"

"Last time I checked, Nap," Randall said, adding a chuckle. "A nice guy looking for a good new home for a great classic car. So can we make this work?"

Nap Napoli's gaze was piercing; he was still deciding. Then, "Fine. Why not. It's not like I get a shot at owning a sixty-one Impala every day. Let me grab some paperwork, we can fill out some things here, then we can drive your new car out for a look at your trade."

* * *

Here they were, off to the side of a two-lane road adjacent to another two-lane road leading to the state park with its heralded pothole. Tall trees, leafy canopy, heavy underbrush that served as a shoulder all made the area darker, even at midday. Nearly nonexistent traffic. Randall smiled internally when Nap had trouble containing himself, the dealer's eyes flashing excitement at his first glimpse of the Impala.

The Impala's hood up, Nap reseated the distributor cap. The car started; the 409 engine purred. The only thing still needing Nap's inspection was the trunk. Nap leaned under the trunk lid, came out with the tire iron, gave it the once-over.

"What's this, Howard?" Nap said, eyeing some smudging on one end of the lug wrench. It was brownish-red and sticky.

"Hmm. I dunno, Nap." Randall extended a beckoning hand. "Here, let me have a look at it."

8

Tess and Fungo were squared away in my room. Time to do some reconnaissance on the bike. First stop, Thunder Wonderland Lanes.

The alley's flashing road sign was trying way too hard, the size of a drive-in theater screen, said *look here, look at me, don't pay attention to all those dead coal miners and abandoned holes and strip mines dotting the countryside*. On the marquis, a continuous loop of sequentially lit bowling balls scattered pins that crisscrossed and turned into a big red X then erupted into Double Bubble pink and Wrigley's Spearmint green fireworks. The pins regrouped and readied themselves for the next sequence. How fucking dandy. I removed my helmet, shook out my pixie haircut, and headed inside the building.

Forty bowling lanes on the left. On the right against the wall was a huge room full of video poker and dollar slots. In the room next to it, a plush toy crane, kids' video games and three Skee-Ball lanes. A shoe and cashier counter was middle of the alley on right, a springlike deodorizing scent lingering on the surface. Farther down, the counter became a full-service bar with café tables in front. A carpeted kiddie play area was deep right, far end.

Red flag. A children's play area this close to an exit, even if the exit was alarmed, was just plain nuts. It made no difference that this Pollyanna of a hamlet was on a safest-towns-in-America list. They were tempting fate with this arrangement. This wasn't Mayberry.

Soon as the guy behind the counter saw me in my leather pants and coat he moved toward the alcohol-dispensing part of the counter. On his way there he shoved a pair of multicolor bowling shoes onto a shelf below the counter.

"What can I get you?"

I checked the red stitching above the pocket of his white shirt, something that could have passed for a barber's smock. I did a double take on the name: *Floyd.* Christ, right out of TV Land's central casting.

Cashier, bartender, bowling-shoe guy, Mayberry namesake; Floyd here was multitalented. Mustachioed, not tall, maybe five-eight, maybe late fifties, but was maybe nothing else like Mayberry's Floyd the Barber because he was maybe really chunky. Over his shoulder was a chalkboard menu bolted into the wall. The menu items were hand printed, the letters all straight-edged at the bottom.

If you're also the cook, Floyd, you'd better be washing your hands. A lot.

I copped a feel from my fuzzy dog keychain because I felt the need.

"Bacon cheeseburger," I told him. "No pink, with fried onions if you have them, plus onion rings, and a draught Guinness."

Floyd grunted. I didn't know what the grunt meant, but he grabbed a wide-mouth glass, shuffled down the end of the bar, got busy drawing my brew.

The wait for a Guinness was worth it if the bartender drew it right. Room temperature glass, forty-five-degree tilt. *So far, so good, Floyd.* Floyd left the bar, entered the kitchen while the draught settled, returned to finish it off with a fill to just above the rim. The foam drooled down one side like in a beer commercial. Floyd seemed like an observant, capable guy who actually had his shit together. I'd be able to talk to him.

I leaned against the bar, sipped the Guinness and waited for my food.

Bastard. Not a Guinness. A deep black beer with a tan head, but it weren't no Guinness. I called to Floyd. "Bro. 'Sup with this shit?" I held up my glass.

"Around here, you ask for a Guinness, you get a Yuengling Porter. You don't want it, don't pay for it." Another grunt. He folded his arms, finished with, "bro."

Floyd didn't budge.

Fine. Free beer.

I got a few raised eyebrows from the lady bowlers. It was the leather, my aging body still looking okay in it. I was occasionally good for a lingering look or two, women included, but aside from Floyd and one other guy munching nuts and sipping a can of Mountain Dew a few bar stools away, there were no men in sight. All women, all older, all bowling, and most of them festooned in silky team bowling shirts that ran the Crayola gamut. None of the looks I got from them was a smile. I let this fact settle.

"Helen will have your food up in a minute," Floyd said. "Don't mind the poor reception. We've had a few out-of-towners drop in today. Some with badges." He stared, his smug face looking for a reaction.

First, I was happy about the division of labor between Floyd the bowling shoe guy and Helen the fry cook. And second, fuck you, Floyd, you'll get a reaction when I'm ready to give you a reaction. I ignored him, sipped my beer and watched the bowlers. He got tired of waiting, headed toward the shoe counter. I slapped a print of a mug shot on the bar loud enough that he had no choice but to retrace his steps. I slid the eight-by-ten over.

"You seen this guy?"

Floyd gave a good show of studying the picture. "The guys who badged us had the same mug shot with them. Can't say that we have."

"'We'...?" I asked, not following.

His chin rose, pointing it in the direction of the swinging doors to the kitchen. "Me and Helen, the cook."

Fine. "These guys—their badges said they were what? Cops? Feds? What?"

Floyd hesitated. It was a simple fill-in-the-blanks, Floyd. They badged you. There weren't that many law enforcement agencies to choose from.

I needed to hustle him up. "Look, short of you telling me it was Fresh Prince and Tommy Lee Jones, I promise I won't be scared."

Another stare from him, him not liking me now, but he answered anyway. "FBI. They were FBI."

There. That wasn't so hard. Except this surprised me. Then again, maybe it shouldn't have. This would, however, require a phone call.

The food arrived. Helen was a rock star in a black T-shirt, fitted and with long sleeves, with a silhouetted headshot of Jeff Bridges's The Dude in white on it. Or maybe it was Jesus. Festooned with neck ink, a rave-blue hair rinse, and a safety-pinned face, she was trim, with no thickness around the middle like you'd expect on a fry cook at a bowling alley, and midthirties, my guess. Helen slid the plate over to me, tucked the greasy check underneath it, and repositioned a squeeze bottle of Heinz so I couldn't miss it. Her parting glance at me said *eat your shit and get out*.

She left a second lunch plate for the bar-leaning customer nursing the Mountain Dew. Young guy. UPS uniform, summer brown. He bit into a ketchupy onion ring, pulled it back to get a better look at it, exaggerated a grimace. An Academy Award performance. He tossed the half-eaten onion ring onto his plate.

"These are awful, Helen," he said. Helen was on her way back to the kitchen, kept walking. "Taste worse than Ore-Ida. Ketchup ain't helping worth a shit. No marinade today?"

I looked at my onion rings. Hand-battered in so much beer I could smell it. And big. I took a bite; excellent. The UPS guy's onion rings looked like orangey mini donuts with burn spots from a bake sheet.

"We've been through this, Carl," she said, then pushed her way through the swinging doors. She finished with a raised voice from the kitchen: "You're in recovery."

"Yeah, well, they suck," he said, the *suck* loud enough to impress her even at this distance. He followed it up with more raised-voice griping at his absent target, a cord in his neck popping while he delivered it. "And I ain't paying for them neither. Ain't paying for none of it. It all tastes awful. But I'll tell you what I will pay for." Carl leaned over for a look into the kitchen at Helen, through the swinging doors now settling. "Yessir, I'll pay for some of *that*."

Floyd's interest in me evaporated, but he didn't get a chance to move. Helen burst through the doors, marched past Floyd, pulled Carl close with a fist full of UPS shirt, and cold-cocked him in the face with a straight right, knocking him off the stool. She winged the paper plate of ketchup-drenched orangey onion rings at his head, followed up with the burger plate to his chest. "Get the fuck out, Carl. Now, before I call your supervisor."

Carl picked himself up, kept his distance. She glared at him, daring him to protest. He cursed under his breath on his way out.

Helen to Floyd, on her way back: "Use FedEx from now on."

The doors to the grill area swung closed behind her. "So tell me," Floyd said, his beaming face blanking out again, "badge-wise, what are you?"

I handed him a business card. "No badge. Just a friend of a friend, asked to perform a public service." The card announced my name, my state trooper rank at retirement, what I now did for a living, and my contact info. "Keep the mug shot," I told him. "If this guy shows up, give me a call." I dropped two tens on the bar for my food and beer, then I dropped a third, making a production out of it. Then I decided to show some manners. "Please."

Floyd wandered to the other end of the counter to hand out a pair of women's size tens. One of the bills I gave him went into the register, a second into a tip jar. He tamped the third ten into a slit atop what looked like an old miner's helmet. A donation to the Maurice Fund, or so said the black indelible marker scrawled along the baby-blue helmet's rim.

* * *

Outside the bowling alley, I cranked up more recon time on the bike. I drove up some trails, over hills and around curves, and down the few major roads that led to scattered neighborhoods and a number of large properties. I didn't get lucky.

Nice small town. Some lunchtime drama in the bowling alley, sure, but not my business.

Coming up on two o'clock. I needed to call this off and head back for a dog walk, maybe take a break with some of Mr. Andy Prudhomme's tea and sweets on the B&B porch before I came back out for another round of surveillance.

Things got done, the bail jumpers and other bad guys all got caught based on my schedule, no one else's. I was in the bounty business for the thrill, not the money. Mom's stock market portfolio gave me the luxury, relegating my state trooper pension to a rounding error. For some folks, that could come across as too laid back. I didn't give a shit.

Mr. Linkletter, wherever he was, best behave himself for the time being.

9

Ursula and Andy's mother, Charlotte, embroidered their crazy quilts on the B&B's side porch, providing finishing touches for gifts to this year's Rancor Summer Camp middle-schoolers. The oldest members of the Piece-Makers Quilting Club sipped their drinks in between their stitching. Next to the TV, the liquor cabinet's doors were open, its bottles vibrant with pick-me-no-pick-*me* colors and labels, clamoring for renewed attention.

In concept, crazy quilts were abstract arrangements with asymmetrical fabric pieces randomly shaped and sized. Not quite true of Charlotte's offering. Most of her patches were circular, overt representations of bowling balls in fluorescent silks, satins, and velvets, in pinks, greens, yellows, and blues, complete with embroidered finger holes. One and only one round patch was glossy coal black, and next to it, one and only one round patch was flaming red, the color of Charlotte's hair. Her artistic signature. These two side-by-side patches, Andy knew, were as sentimental for his mother as two hearts with an arrow carved into a backyard elm.

Ursula picked up the TV remote, changed the channel to CNN. Coincident to the channel change, Andy made a visit to the porch. He topped off Ursula's martini from a pitcher sitting atop the cabinet and he dropped a few additional fiber-fortified Triscuits onto a plate within reach of the women. Charlotte's manhattan needed no similar assistance.

"Ursula," Charlotte said.

"Yes, dear?"

"How did you do that?"

"Do what, Charlie?"

"Use the clicker to get another drink?"

Charlotte had been oblivious to Andy's entrance, was also oblivious to his presence behind her. At eighty-one Charlotte remained an incredibly smart woman, but dementia had been making inroads. So far the disease was more inconvenient than invasive, with her needing only occasional reminders of names, dates, places, and times. Andy hung around a moment to see how Ursula responded to the bizarre question from her lifelong friend.

Ursula held up the TV remote for Charlotte's inspection and offered a straight-faced explanation. "New technology, Charlie. A single remote for TV, DVR, stereo, and liquor cabinet. Press this button right here and voila, more booze. What won't they think of next, right, love?"

Humor was how the two best friends handled her occasional dementia lapses. Charlotte's parry would typically be an off-color two-word retort, but today she showed no recognition, having already moved on, unfazed. She lifted her quilt in both hands and held it aloft in triumph. "All done," she said, her face aglow.

While her mental sharpness had suffered, her hand dexterity and muscle memory had not. Her hands always knew their way, in bowling, quilting, and as a board-certified surgeon, her fingers as nimble as ever and entirely capable of the intricate stitching needed for the quilting masterpieces she produced. The women started today's session with only one finishing touch needed for each of their individual quilts, their embroidered message *SAFE AND SOUND*, which every quilt received. Andy and Ursula admired Charlotte's handiwork, her quilt raised next to her perky, proud face, the message in a silky gold thread.

"Nicely done, Ma," a proud Andy said.

Their smiles dissolved. Over her mother's shoulder on the TV, a reporter standing outside a kid's pizza restaurant delivered a sobering, breaking news story.

"That's Scranton," Ursula said. She remained expressionless, her eyes fixed on the screen.

A young girl's body had been found stuffed into a toilet at the Cheesus H. Christmas pizza restaurant. There for her ninth birthday celebration, per the report, she was discovered missing only after the police arrived to break up a brawl inside the restaurant.

The reporter: "The restaurant serves beer and wine to its adult customers. The police believe alcohol contributed to an argument that turned into a melee with multiple participants. The little girl's disappearance went unnoticed until police arrived. Authorities are now reviewing interior and exterior video for leads."

The story, dramatic, frightening, and nearby, had them rapt. Ursula, eyeing Andy's tight-faced interest, went for levity. "I've been to that restaurant," she said. "its policy is a two-beer maximum per customer, but they don't enforce it well. One time I saw a man passed out in the plastic ball pit with his kids."

Andy was stiff and stoic, and went right at what was on his mind. "I'll get Dody to find out what happened. The Scranton police owe her."

Ursula's face soured. "Scranton isn't Rancor, Andy," she said, her tone chiding.

"Yeah, but it's close enough," Andy said. "We need to know what happened."

Ursula pushed. "Andy, please, let the Scranton police handle it. It's not our problem."

"Not our problem *yet*," Andy said.

10

The Buick Electra idled, Randall inside, a bit nicked up. The Electra faced the Impala head on, French-kiss close. The Impala's convertible top was down. The new body Randall had put in its trunk would stink up the interior less that way, until he was ready to move it.

Nap the car dealer was one of those wiry pint-size Italians with genes that had to come from a bricklaying or cement-working father from the old country. He didn't go down with the first tire iron shot across his face, instead came at Randall like Rocky fucking Marciano, wading in with his fists up and his head all bloody, dazed but still looking to land that one good punch that would put his attacker into a fist coma. The second tire iron shot Randall put on him dropped him flat on his back in the brush, but not without Nap landing a clean, solid right to Randall's ribs first. After a few minutes Randall's breathing had returned to normal and left him hopeful that none of his ribs were broken. His few-minute respite gave him time to think about what had just happened. Nap had raised himself from the dirt after the second thump from the tire iron, spit into Randall's eyes, blinded him with blood, snot, and chunks of teeth, and just kept coming. If Randall hadn't had the Beretta, Mr. Napoli might have gotten off that one punch he'd been so willing to take so bad a beating to deliver. Judging from his loss of breath from Nap's first punch to the ribs, he was glad he hadn't had to deal with a second.

The pancreatic cancer was showing itself, starting to wear him down, and was one reason why he'd decided to go out on his own terms after finding his kid. He'd have fun with an unsuspecting population, soil up this small town's reputation but good, then pack it in. Except he'd been sloppy, again. The gunshot to Nap's face took care of it.

The park closed at seven. Randall intended to rest a few minutes more, take the Electra out for a spin then come back to the park after it got dark to move the Impala.

Christ, that wiry little bastard could hit.

11

"Call me Charlie," she said.

The side porch of the B&B faced a stand of Pocono pine that ran uphill, toward a mountaintop. I was there with my two dogs resting next to me, having tea with one other guest, the mother of proprietor Andy Prudhomme.

"Hello, Charlie. I'm Counsel Fungo."

"Pretty name, Counsel is," she said.

"Thank you."

Mr. Prudhomme popped back onto the porch to check on his afternoon tea participants. "Everything good, Ma? Miss Fungo?"

A yes response from me, a nod from Charlie. The two of us sipped our freshly pressed Earl Grey double bergamot. Far as I could tell, Charlotte—Charlie—was the only other B&B guest. She boasted she was eighty-one, had an apartment nearby, and because her son Andy owned the place, boasted that she had a room here, too.

"I have to tell you, ma'am," I answered, "women who call themselves 'Charlie' usually like pounding back shots and chasing them with Pabst Blue Ribbon. The name doesn't fit a person with your elegance."

She blushed. Her son left the porch satisfied his guests were getting along with each other. He returned shortly with homemade brownies and cookies, placed them on the wicker table between the wooden rockers the two of us occupied. I couldn't help it; my glances between the two of them were overt. An incredible mother-son resemblance, discounting the gender and Mr. Prudhomme's salt-and-pepper hair.

My interest led to some uncut, uncensored verbalizing. "You're both so fuh—fuh—"

The ears on Tess, she at rest beside me, perked up. She stood, lowered her chin onto my lap. A few pets of her silkiness and I was able to contain myself.

"—so fuh-*freeeaking* handsome," I said on the exhale. "Sorry. That could have been a lot worse."

Charlie's face lit up at the praise. "Sorry for what? Comparing me to my gorgeous son? Nonsense." She gave me the once-over, chuckled at herself. "A put-together woman like you, thinking I'm the handsome one... How nice. But sorry, Miss Fungo, I'm already taken, a few times over, it's been now."

"Not into women, ma'am," I said, smiling for her, "so you're in the clear."

Her son inserted himself into the conversation. "Let's keep this clean today, Ma, okay?"

"My Andy here, he's another story. Married a major bitch. Andy, honey, take a good look at this woman. Easy on the eyes, right? How about you two—"

His mother fit the elderly senior mold, a heart-on-your-sleeve type who didn't care about speaking truth, the way she saw it, to power. Fungo, my German Shepherd, saved the awkward moment by pulling hard at his leash toward Charlie. Fungo recognized the territory; older folks were pushovers.

"Charlie, this is Fungo, my deputy. You can pet him, just no quick moves please."

Charlie massaged his black-and-tan head, her French manicure be damned. The dog's ears were back, looking borderline orgasmic. My Bull Terrier, Tess, stayed sprawled at my feet, only vaguely interested.

"I used to be a bowler, Miss, um..." Charlie said, then she looked at me, suddenly puzzled. "What's your name again?"

"Call me Counsel, ma'am."

"Miss Counsel."

"No, ma'am, Counsel is my first name. My name is Counsel Fungo. Call me Counsel."

"You're named after your dog?"

And this was how it went for much of the conversation, Charlie lucid one moment, a bit confused the next. Her hair was perfectly coiffed, tinted a flaming Ann-Margret orange-red. Her perky cherry cheeks were only slightly rouged, and the skin on her neck taut, her chin aristocrat thin. Such grace and beauty. She looked incredible for her age.

"Mom's retired from her medical practice," Mr. Prudhomme volunteered. He'd already warned me that Charlie wasn't firing on all cylinders, also assured me that despite her new challenges, she still had an agile medical mind. "But I'm sure you'll be hearing more on the other topic."

"When I wasn't bowling, I was performing surgery," Charlie volunteered. "When I wasn't in surgery, or being a mom, I was bowling." Her eyes twinkled, the comment getting a rise out of her as she delivered it. "A person's got to have some priorities, Counsel. I knew pro bowlers Dick Weber, Don Carter, and Earl Anthony, and I bowled with Paula Carter, Don's wife, in some pro-am tournaments. And I'm still very close to the dearest of the dear, Bert Carbone, the Carbon County Carbine."

Mr. Prudhomme had taken a seat in the worn fan-back wicker chair across from his mother. The Bert Carbone comment seemed to trouble him.

The names Charlie dropped I recognized from the seventies and eighties, when the pro bowler tour ruled late Saturday afternoon TV, right up there with ABC's *Wide World of Sports*. I was pretty sure his double take was because all these people were dead. Which made his mother's current friendship with one Bert Carbone, apparently the county's top bowler, somewhat suspect.

"Mom is such an incredible surgeon," he said, redirecting. "General surgery, trauma. Reconstructive surgery is her specialty. She still has the steadiest of hands."

"And a one-eighty-six bowling average, Andy, back when I could really bring it, yes indeed." Charlie's eyes brightened, my nod and smile at her the reason.

Charlie's chin lowered to her chest, and just like that she dropped off for a nap. A wayward brownie crumb sat outside the corner of her red lipsticked mouth. Mr. Prudhomme reached over with a napkin and brushed it away.

"Charlie has survived a lot, in and out of medicine. She likes the salt-of-the-earth types, and is happiest when she's at a bowling alley."

"So she's still practicing?"

He'd used present tense to describe his mom's vocation, past tense to describe her as a bowler. Fair question, I thought, no hidden agenda, considering his mother was on the slippery slope dementia-wise.

"Oh no, of course not," he said. "That wouldn't be wise. Sorry, Miss Fungo, a slip of the tongue. Charlie hasn't been in a hospital in years, other than for her own medical challenges."

Charlie stirred, awakened, was groggy but apparently aware. "She's named after her dog, Andy. Isn't that strange..."

"Yes, Ma, strange."

"'Counsel,' Mr. Prudhomme," I said. "Like I told your mom. Call me Counsel."

Charlie again, rallying a bit: "Counsel, you can call him Andy. Short for Andrew. Andy, call her Counsel. There. Settled."

Charlie nodded off again. Fungo bobbed and sniffed at Charlie's side, gave up on her, moved to her son's hand and nudged it. He picked up the petting where his mother left off.

"Counsel is an interesting first name for a person."

"My father had high hopes," I said. "Wanted me to be an attorney. Then I showed symptoms."

"As a child?"

"Late teens."

"Taking any medication?"

"Antihypertensive agents. Clonidine works best."

He nodded. "Good results, in my experience. Your parents must have had a time settling on a treatment for it. No medication works universally."

"Not my parents. My mother. She did all the heavy lifting. My father wasn't quite as interested."

"Sorry to hear that."

"No biggie, but thanks, Andy—short for Andrew."

Okay, fine, so maybe that was me flirting. So what. It elicited a nice smile from him.

"Bert Carbone died in January," he said, serious again. "His death affected my mother deeply. When she's on top of things she accepts it, but then she drifts away."

"Were they a couple?"

"There were rumors. Mom was a young widow. We lost my dad. It happened during a bank robbery. He died"—his smile was self-conscious—"protecting me. She never remarried."

"Wow. Sorry."

"Yeah. Tragic. Thanks."

"Anyone caught?"

"Yes. They tried them, in western Pennsylvania. Publicity concerns made them move it there. The bastards got off."

He laid it out. "No guns were found. The only one who could identify anything about the shooter was me, a wounded five-year-old in shock. I got a close look at the shooter's sneakers. Same brand as mine. Unreliable and not definitive enough, the defense attorney said. The jury agreed. Our town was devastated.

"The torch my mother carried for my dad never went out. But just look at her. She's still gorgeous. If she sought comfort somewhere, I'm sure there was no shortage of offers."

A horrifying story. I did the math, connected some dots. "The bank robbery. Was it here in Rancor?"

"Rancor Savings and Loan."

I mentioned the squat, silver-etched black granite memorial that I'd seen on the corner of the bank property; Rancor's tribute to its fallen miners. "That's quite an inscription. 'The dust, the dark, the deep, and the damned. We stand tall against it all.'"

I held my stare, hoped he'd get my drift.

"You saw the *People* magazine article," he said.

"Sure did."

"Look—Counsel—we're proud of this town and its independence, it's no-serious-crime record. We're upset about the spotlight the media's shining on it."

Fungo nudged Andy-short-for-Andrew's hand again with his nose, an attempt at getting him to follow his head down to the porch floor, with Fungo looking to stretch out and still get massaged while doing it. He lost out as hand and dog head parted company, Andy intent on concentrating. He addressed my next question before I had a chance to verbalize it.

"The robbery and murder were Rancor's last reported violent crimes. My father's name is on that memorial; his murder prompted its construction. Since then, fifty years of safe streets and relative obscurity."

I nodded. "That scrapbook album in my room. There's one picture in there I wondered about. Is that—?"

"Maurice Prudhomme. My dad." A slight pall crossed his face. A sadness he couldn't hide.

"I see. And the Maurice Fund? I had lunch at the bowling alley and saw this helmet..."

"Him again. A local charity. For deceased miners' widows and orphans. The town set it up when he was murdered. The helmets have been donated over the years by families touched by one mining tragedy or another." He paused. "There are a lot of helmets out there."

He changed the subject. "So it was lunch at the alley, then. Helen's a great fry cook. She marinades everything in Yuengling. Burgers, chicken, onion rings, fries."

"Then I suppose you could say I went double-down."

"Ah. A draft porter to go with a marinated burger and beer-battered onion rings. The locals call that the Thunder Wonder Combo."

I nodded again, then fished out a business card. "Look, I'm in private law enforcement and I'm tracking"—cough, swallow—"*ack-ack-ACKING!*—tracking someone. I work with bail bondsmen."

Andy-short-for-Andrew didn't wince at my oopsie. He read the card, netted out the info for himself: "So you're a former state trooper who's now a bounty hunter."

"Yes." I pulled a flyer from a pouch in Fungo's harness and handed it to him. "Here's the fugitive I'm after. He may still be driving the same car you see at bottom."

He studied the flyer. "A face and beard like Santa Claus. He's here in Rancor?"

"Him or the car or both. Or were. He jumped bail on an attempted rape charge. He might have kidnapped an older woman in the process. If you see him, don't confront him, just call me."

"Interesting. So you want me to bypass our sheriff."

"What I mean is—"

"Look, we're a one-lawman town here. The sheriff's not particularly fond of extra-law enforcement factors roaming around, like bounty hunters. Just let him handle things. That's why we elected him. Do that, and maybe you'll get that call afterward."

Great. A town where the law was elected and hadn't had to deal with a felony in over a generation, and me the former State cop slash current fugitive recovery agent who'd been taking down felons for over twenty years, being told to take a back seat. Except something behind his stare said this was non-negotiable.

Fine. But Mr. Andy Prudhomme here was a nurse and a B&B owner. If I didn't stand down, it wasn't like he'd ever know.

"Sure. Of course. Safety first. Nine-one-one is the way to go, then call me. Please."

Tess was up now, nudging my thigh. Pee time. Charlie snored, Tess whimpered and got pushier, and Fungo rose to all fours, the two ready for their walk. I tightened my hold on their leashes. Time to go.

Andy collected the plates. "Charlie will nap out here until dinner. Tonight she'll be at the lanes with the bowling team. A team," a sly smile to himself, "of nurses and doctors who expect to prevail in the alley's spring Senior League Mixed Doubles semifinal."

Fungo pulled hard, nudged Andy's mother for one last pet. Charlie mumbled and responded with a weak scratch of his head. She dozed off again.

"Mom could have used someone like you back when our lives were turned upside down. Still, in the grander scheme of things, the men who killed my father did pay for their crime."

This got my attention. "Paid how? Bad karma, fate, what?"

"Someone tracked them down and executed them. One in a motel just over the New York border, the other two in Ohio."

The inference hit a nerve. "Just to be clear," I said, "I'm paid to return people who skip out on the crimes charged against them, not execute them."

"Sorry, Miss Fungo—Counsel—my bad. I'm not implying—"

"No, no, of course not, my bad, where are my manners?" I needed a redirect. "You were wounded. That's something I never experienced in two decades with the state cops. Unless you count dog bites."

"I don't remember much," Andy said, "other than the same shotgun blast that killed my dad wreaked havoc on my shoulder. He took the brunt of it. I lost a lot of blood, but I recovered quickly, so to speak."

So to speak. A deference to a to-be-determined outcome. Quite a burden for a kid to carry.

"Physical wounds heal," I said, waxing philosophical. "Emotional wounds, from traumatic events, are different. I've been there, unfortunately. If there's anything I can do..."

"Thanks, appreciate it, but we're good."

12

Outside the B&B on the back lawn, Tess and Fungo took care of their business. The chat over tea had been invigorating, for me and my deputies both. Interesting discussion with an interesting woman and her son. That, plus my German Shepherd got a nice massage without making a scene, considering massages usually gave him wood.

Hell, not a fair assessment on my part. They were more than interesting. The mother became a surgeon, the son a nurse. Impressive, and after so terrible a loss. Strong woman, assertive child, little drama. Two kick-ass, in-your-face responses to having your heart ripped out. It helped when you were able to relate. Andy seemed less the sexy beast here, more the gentle caregiver and survivor.

I had a firm hold on each of my deputies' leashes, but that often meant they were as secure as a lasso on a twister. When they weren't on a mission, a leash served the civilian population and my dogs well. At other times their training and their eagerness to please me controlled them, not these pieces of leather.

I loaded them into the van and headed for a hiking trail that the internet said was pet friendly and pro level. Time for me and my team to get in some fieldwork.

* * *

Ballast, cinder, crushed stone, and hard-packed dirt formed a trail wide enough for two cars to pass side by side. Abandoned railroad tracks paralleled it. At one time rail lines were popular in this part of the state, the tracks laid more than a hundred years ago to haul coal to other railway systems. When the mines closed, these short railways closed with them. Still, they spawned some serious hiking trails just like this one.

The three of us were out here in the late afternoon heat, Tess doing fine without the leash, Fungo trotting next to me, his leash dragging. Tess darted in and out of the brush going after whatever interested her, had no trouble keeping up despite her digressions, blessed with some serious acceleration capabilities and an incredible vertical leap to go with them. At home, for squirrels who decided to hesitate on a tree trunk, a huge fail. If they didn't get their rodent asses farther up the trunk, and quickly, I'd be cleaning up regurgitated squirrel guts in my living room later on.

I stopped for a breather, bent over, hands on my knees. Fungo stopped, sat next to me. Tess was up ahead at a rise in the trail, waiting for us.

I didn't like Tess's look; she was going to run. "Tess, come," I called, my voice stern.

She looked over the rise, looked back at us, and was gone.

Fungo and I trotted to where we saw her last. In the distance, Tess circled a large oak, her squirrel prey thirty feet up and well into its routine of scolding its pursuer from the safety of the treetop.

"Bad dog, Tess, bad."

She cowered, lowered her ears, and tucked her tail stub where I couldn't see it. It was an act. She was remorseful, but more so because squirrel notch number twenty-eight or more had eluded her. I called her again. She slinked her way back to me, her head still bowed, hoping I bought into her act.

"You know the drill. Drop and give me twenty."

She slid down into a crouch. I dropped to the grass next to her and assumed the push-up position. Tess, her stubby tail moving nonstop like a car wiper in a hurricane, hopped her fifty-plus pounds onto my back and found her balance. We pounded out twenty push-ups in under half a minute.

"That'll teach you," I said, out of breath.

Another quarter-mile down the trail and—fuck—again Tess was gone, this time around a bend. After a moment I whistled. Then it was a two-fingered whistle with feeling. No Tess. After that, I went with the one shouted command that never failed: "TESS, FETCH."

The forest shouted back. Hooting owls, chirps and caws, tree branches on high swaying from the wind, cicadas. Still no Tess. Fungo and I jogged beside the tracks that followed the bend in the road.

Noise, far left. I squinted to focus on an opening in the trees and a path of disturbed leaves that was still settling. Tess. She had another scent. Here the hiking trail and the rail tracks separated. I followed the tracks. Fungo and I jogged into a parting of the trees that the tracks ran through, followed them to where they ran up a slight grade. At the top of the rise, facing us across a dip and underneath a rocky, moss-covered ledge, was a large gash carved into the base of the opposing hillside, the gash dark and shadowy. The train rails led inside.

An old mine entrance. From this distance we saw Tess, on her way in. Me screaming at her, scream-whistle, whistle-scream, did nothing other than piss me off and rile Fungo up. He broke ranks and bolted, his leash trailing, airborne.

I managed a "Fungo, stop!" before the Tourette's started in, rose up my throat, spewing like bile, jerky hand gestures hindering my trot. My mouth was a slave to it, commenced launching its contorted, sick mind-farts. They came hard and fast, and were as welcome to my ears as a runaway nail gun.

"—bile vile doggie style, in the aisle—

"—doggiedick-lemonstick, flick your Bic, flickle tickle fickle, cocka-doodle ding-dong, dippity-do, zippity do-dah—"

Fungo put on the brakes before he entered the mine, did an about face and waited for me to jog up to him. My mouth finished with its shit. When I got there I gave him a quick pat and a chewy piece of jute rope from my pocket as his reward.

"*—good boy, boy-o-boy, ahoy me matey—*"

I caught my breath and puckered up, then I let go a granddaddy of a whistle and followed it up with another "Tess, come!"

Barking floated back to me from inside the mine entrance, the echoes turning in on themselves. Before I moved another step the barking stopped, and now I heard accelerating paw patters from dog toenails that need clipping. They glided across the railroad ties and were coming my way, the nails scraping the wood and the crushed stone that separated them, closing fast.

Tess exploded out of the mine, scrambled up, sat next to Fungo at attention. Her tail stub wiggled while she waited for a pat on the head or a treat or both. "No reward. Not after what you did."

Didn't matter, there was nowhere to put it. Her mouth was full of rat. A big, squirming, meaty all-white rat with black eyes and red drizzle leaking from its mouth.

Tess's jaw closed tighter. More squirms from the rat now, and more rat blood. Then it was no more squirms and a lot more rat blood. She would have crushed it if I didn't stop her.

For what it's worth, she'd abided the fetch command.

"Tess, drop it."

She obeyed, the oversize white rat now at my feet. Dogs with terrier genes and rodents of all species had a long history with each other, although not on a persistent personal basis, considering one did the chasing part and the other did the getting caught, ripped up, and eaten part. Not this time. Tess held back, was as interested in this thing as I was. I'd seen white rats before, but not outside and not this big, this one the size of a toy poodle. She nudged it. Its mouth ack-acked, then it shuddered, then it was gone for good. I pulled her back by her collar before she could get at it again and I sat her down, her back and neck muscles straining against my grip. She whimpered; I quieted her with a raised finger. Another scolding, another twenty push-ups. We pounded them out one more time together, more stressful for her this time than for me because I made her do it right next to the dead rat, with her fucking knowing better than to break ranks while we did it.

* * *

White rats in coal mines. They were in my head on the jog the whole way back. At the van I toweled my two deputies down, deposited them inside, and moved to my phone, which still had a signal. I did a search.

Superstition: A white rat in a coal mine is a sign of a cave-in. Hell, not all that different than rats leaving a sinking ship. Nothing new there, like the canaries that miners took with them into mines to detect carbon monoxide.

I ran across a different spin from an early twentieth century newspaper entry: *White rats are common in the deeper parts of an active coal mine. They live on what miners, careless or otherwise, leave behind. A rat's life span is two to three years, so multiple generations might never see the light of day if they're given enough to eat...*

An active coal mine? Hardly. Yet the idea of something living in there, even rats, with nothing to feed on but rocks, dirt and coal was a real stretch.

Another search result. A warning of sorts: *The next time you go into an abandoned mine may be your second to last trip underground.*

I let that search result have the last word. It was almost six o'clock. The sun was below the ridgeline, a mountain mist starting to creep in. Time to get back to the B&B to feed my posse their dinner then grab something to eat as well. After that, we'd need to go looking for that classic Chevy.

13

Andy arrived, parked out front, grabbed his equipment bag and slipped it over his shoulder. St. Possenti's didn't so much look like a bingo hall or a building named after a Catholic saint as it did a cinder-blocked fortress reminiscent of its former life as a police station.

He retrieved his membership ID; the smiling senior at the entrance waved him through. "You're good to go, Andy," he said. "Have fun."

Once past the vestibule he passed a few occupied booths, found one that was empty and rested his bag in it. He unfastened the clasp, pushed some of the bag's contents out of the way, and searched inside. On its flat bottom sat an antique handgun in an equally antique cracked black leather holster, vintage items both. The gun wasn't in his bag so much for protection as it was a reminder to him, daily, of his aunt, Kitty Buchinsky.

Aunt Kitty had bequeathed him the 1890s Colt, a six-shooter Kitty's father had given her as a child. A "squirrel gun," her father called it. At close range it was as deadly as it needed to be, but because it was a smaller caliber it did the job without ravaging the meat the hunter intended to eat. Andy lifted the antique gun out of the way, continued rummaging in the bag and each of its side pockets.

Dody Heck arrived alongside, dropped her bag next to his. Andy persisted in his agitated search. "What didn't you bring?" she asked.

"Eye protection."

"I've got a spare pair."

"Thanks. So what did you find out?"

Dody, Rancor's chief of police before the job became an elected position, had connections with the Scranton police department and law enforcement agencies in other neighboring towns, relationships she'd fostered from nearly thirty years as a cop. They were further solidified by her husband's brutal death while on the job in Scranton, a crime the police never solved. Kinship among cops, feelings of guilt; these both begot infrequent favors and information requests the Scranton police chief granted Dody when she'd occasionally asked. Today had been one of those occasions.

"Morgan Higgins is the little girl's name," Dody said. "Sodomized and strangled while her parents were preoccupied in the restaurant brawl. Nine years old, in a white birthday dress. Her partially clothed body was crammed into the toilet like a roll of paper towels. There's DNA, and there's video inside and outside the restaurant. Right now their person of interest is a guy driving a sixties Chevy convertible in urban streetwear. A maroon hoodie with airbrushed pictures of blunt-smoking cats."

"Gangster wannabe," Andy said.

"Nah. Older white male with thick white hair. Grandfatherly type, but he could be younger according to one of the restaurant's employees."

"Any chance the Scranton chief will let you see the film from the security cameras?"

"He already has, sweetie. When we're done here I'll pull it up for you. But Andy, honey, the person who did this could be anywhere by now."

"Anywhere includes here."

They strewed the contents of their bags around the side-by-side personal booths lined up against one end of the building's well-lit open area, a space the size of a small auditorium. Piece by piece they costumed themselves, colorful vests, pinned safety badges, wraparound safety glasses, and noise deafening headgear for ear protection, initially draped around their necks. They stepped into their individual booths and activated their sessions with a push of a button.

Andy moved the headgear into place. Deep and vibrant, reverberant guitar chords from the bingo hall's sound system warmed him, a sensual song and a favorite of his, Chris Isaak's "Wicked Game." He wrapped his hands around his nickel-plated firearm, raised his arms eye-high, and emptied his head of peripheral thoughts. One eye closed while he spread his feet, lined up the sight and steadied himself. He squeezed the trigger six times, discharging the contents of Aunt Kitty's Colt into the paper target twenty-five feet away. Six out of six hit the head area.

"We have a bingo," Dody said, her voice elevated.

"We have a bingo," other pistol range patrons intoned.

Andy returned the old Colt to his bag, removed a Sig Sauer semiautomatic, found a full clip and inserted it. He waited a moment, watched Dody squeeze off multiple rounds that also demolished her target's head area. Andy reassumed the position for another round, this time with his Sig. Another bingo.

14

Randall enjoyed their attention. The two chatty uniformed waitresses were either married to cheating husbands and were cheaters themselves, or were heavy partiers, or they were shacked up with boyfriends number two or three or ten, and in the market for more.

His mannerly nice-guy routine was smooth. Never a shortage of desperate women anywhere he'd ever lived. One had to be Greek, with thick, naturally black hair, the other he wasn't sure, was maybe Greek, with who knew what color hair under the uniform, but it was definitely not the teased honey-pot blonde above her collar.

His peripheral vision caught the signals: slumped postures that straightened up on their approaches so their ample Greek or Irish Catholic or Jewish Princess breasts were properly showcased. Neither acknowledged knowing Regina when he showed them her photo.

The black-haired one: "More coffee, sugar? Hey, up here, sweetie, eyes north. You want more coffee?"

"Yes, please. Thank you."

He decided the honey-pot babe would be the easiest, although Xena, or Apollonia, or whatever the dark one's name was, was for sure just playing hard to get. He'd come back and make a play for Honey-Pot. Aristotle's Diner looked to be family-owned, so the darker Greek one could have a brother or a cousin or an uncle as its manager or a cook, and Randall didn't need no crazy cleaver-swinging Greek after his ass.

* * *

Randall pulled off the road. Eight p.m. on the Buick's dashboard clock. The Impala was where he'd left it, a quarter mile from the state park, which closed at sunset. Better that the Buick stay distant from the entrance. He'd need to leg the distance only once—the way back. He threw on the gangster hoodie he picked up on one of his trips to the casino, a ghetto brand, the street hustler making him pay double for it, Randall being a cracker and all.

He popped open the Impala's trunk lid, shined a flashlight in. Nap was still there and still dead. He checked Nap's pockets. A wad of cash, a set of keys, a wallet with a condom in it—how quaint—and a phone, still on. He hit a few buttons, pulled up a list of missed calls. The scrolled list was long.

Pictures in the wallet. Nap and his wife with a college-aged son and teenaged daughter. A picture of an elderly couple, probably Nap's parents, a professional shot, for their fiftieth anniversary per the handwriting on the back. An intimate photo of Nap's dimpled, pudgy Italian wife. Definitely doable. Then again, maybe not: he found her Catholic death announcement from last year.

Randall wasn't envious. Being close to people who might miss you was overrated. He hadn't been missed by anyone since he reached the age of puberty. Biological parents? No idea who they were. He was in the state's care until he ridded himself of his last set of foster parents, those Wisconsin dairy farm fucks who died in a suspicious barn fire a week short of his eighteenth birthday. How he'd hated that farm and those fucking cows.

He keyed the Chevy's ignition and put the convertible top up. No lights on the road from either direction. The Chevy was on the move.

At the closed state park he checked out the entrance with the headlights on, wary of the two black, utilitarian wrought-iron gates. They'd be a bitch to push despite their wheels, the gates secured to each other by chains in the center of the asphalt. Headlights off. Out came the bolt cutters and a flashlight from the back seat.

Snip-snap. The chains untangled, and with a hefty swing they ended up in the brush. He strained to push the gates out of the way.

The Chevy entered the park. Beyond the park entrance were the parking lot, a small touristy-type single-story building, and a walking path to the main attraction. The car rolled to a stop in front of two massive boulders. More chains there, bolted into the boulders and joined in the middle by an upright metal sign on a post sunk into a cement-filled bucket. The sign read *No Vehicles Past This Point.*

Snip-snap, snip-snap, chains and sign eliminated.

Back in the car he inched it forward, sizing up the space between the boulders, inched it forward more until the chrome front bumpers kissed the inside of each rock on both sides of the car. He grabbed a flashlight, circled one boulder on foot to face the car's front and get a good look at the Impala's wheelbase, tire to tire. Its full width, including the fenders and the bumper, might not fit through the opening, but everything from the tires on inward would.

He backed the car up seventy-five feet. Lights on.

The Chevy revved while in neutral. The Beach Boys were in Randall's head now, praising the car engine's monstrous, oh-so-fine magnificence. He hummed along. "Giddy-up, giddy-up, four-oh-nine... Four-oh-nine, my four-oh-nine..."

He slammed the transmission into drive. The car fishtailed then straightened out to make its run.

The side fenders and the edges of the front bumper crushed inward, and the bolts the chains looped through in the rock cut jagged stripes from front to rear, slicing both sides of the Impala open. The car's steel panels screamed in protest joining Randall's rebel yell, him knowing what he was doing to the car, feeling the rush, knowing how phallic this was, him jamming himself into something that wasn't ready for him. The speed and his aim and this motherfucking monster engine's horsepower grinded the car through the separation, its peeled steel chunks of fender and rear bumper left to bounce and spark in its wake. On the other side of the boulders he jammed the brakes, the front tires skidding onto asphalt, the rear tires kicking up crushed stone. The car stopped half on, half off a paved walkway.

Visible in the headlights was a chest-high silver pipe railing with chain-link fencing between its posts and rungs. It bordered a thin but reinforced concrete slab that jutted forward over the gorge. The railing snaked an amoebic path around the curve of the huge pothole, the pothole at its widest point the width of two basketball courts end to end. The car lights illuminated both the near and far sections of railing. Between the two was eighty feet of nothingness, a blackness dark as a nightmare, and the reason the car was here.

He grabbed a second flashlight from the back seat for a closer look. One step up put him on the concrete slab, flashlight a-blazing; he reached its edge. Tourists could lean over this railing, and he could visualize them doing this, all trying for a better view into the deep abyss.

Some bodies had to have found their way down there, considering the hole had been thousands of years in the making. Unfortunate folks who either jumped, were pushed, or got tossed in. Still, according to the media, this hadn't been the case, either here or anywhere else in Rancor, for the last fifty or so of those thousands of years.

That would now change.

He leaned over the railing and shined the light in, illuminating the hole's topmost section. How deep it was, per the hype, he couldn't remember, but it was definitely more than a hundred feet, the flashlight showing no more than a quarter of that. What he could make out was its spiral shape, winding and elliptical, the diameter decreasing the deeper it went, like the inside of a funnel cloud. He raised the flashlight, illuminated each section of the iron railing that surrounded the abyss' perimeter. There, at three o'clock, where he'd stood earlier in the day while he reconned this caper, was a section of rail with a wide patch of grass leading down to it from the paved walkway. Room for a car to get a running start.

He was alongside that railing section now with his bolt cutters. *Snip-snap, snip-snap;* an expansive width of chain-link fencing connecting multiple pipe posts dropped to the grass. All that separated Nap's body from a spectacular four-hundred-horsepower, deep-pothole burial in his newest classic car purchase were two thin pipe rails set in dirt postholes.

This will work.

He retrieved his supplies from the back seat, left them in the grass: two bottles of Poland Spring, one flashlight, the streetwear hoodie, and a gas can. Loretta's full-size umbrella moved from back seat to front.

Here we go.

Headlights on high beams, convertible top up, transmission in neutral, and Randall in the driver's seat with a chubber. He depressed the gas pedal, revved the 409, let it idle then grabbed the umbrella and jammed it between the gas pedal and a seat bracket. The throttle opened wide, the car's tachometer approaching orgasm. Randall slid out of the seat, reached back in, and slapped the Powerglide automatic transmission into drive. The car jolted forward.

Enjoy the ride, Nap.

The car accelerated across the walkway, bounced down the wide grassy strip and slammed and uprooted the pipe railing. It jettisoned from the runway into an airborne arc, hesitated at its apex, then dropped headlong from view. Randall followed on foot in the car's wake, expecting fireworks from an exploding gas tank. Instead he heard clanging and banging and crashing of metal against rock multiple times over as Nap and the car somersaulted to their deep grave.

Randall hustled to the concrete slab that reached out across the pothole and leaned over the railing. In the hole's farthest reaches were faint, glowing red specks.

Taillights. The car still had juice.

How's that for penetration, bitch.

He was now horny as hell, but he was also tired. Honey-Pot would need to wait. He'd hoof it back to the Buick and find a place to stay in Dickson City, maybe watch some porn and spank the gorilla, then he'd get some sleep. He'd make his way back into Rancor tomorrow.

Welcome back to violent crime, you deprived small-town motherfuckers.

15

A tabletop jukebox stared me down. There was one in every booth in this throwback diner heavy on chrome and Formica everywhere I looked. I felt for my fuzzy keychain on my belt loop.

I can handle this.

In 1994 I demolished a jukebox in a bar in Hershey, Pennsylvania. A Wurlitzer bubble-top floor model with real vinyl 45s. I made it flash and whirr and choke and puke up the record it was playing. The bar was a five-minute cab ride from the State Police Academy's training facility. I was twenty-two, celebrating my graduation from training with a few newly minted State Police boots just like me, young men and women. Mom attended the graduation ceremony, was proud as hell. She returned to Philly right afterward; I was okay with that. What mattered most was she'd been able to attend, and she was beaming. The US Senate was in session, which meant my senator dad couldn't break away from banging one or more of his aides for the afternoon.

My training buddy Vonetta and I were in the bar with Pennsylvania's newest crop of state troopers, male and female, and we were getting ripped pretty good. Vonetta knew my affliction made me different, but she knew nothing about the other baggage that came with it. Like triggers. Great big, hairy, psycho-triggers. She sidled up to the juke and dropped in her money. Three plays for a quarter. She tripled up on one particular song. A mistake.

"Fortunate Son." Creedence Clearwater Revival, John Fogerty lyrics. By then the anti-war classic rock rant had crossed over to become part of an unofficial US military music playlist. I loved CCR, loved John Fogerty too, but I'd have paid a sizable sum to never hear that song again.

By the third play all the State Police bar patrons were fired up and loving it. Vonetta led them in the lyrics, knew all the verses. They were overly familiar to me too, unfortunately.

John Fogerty's senator fathers had pulled strings to keep their kids out of military service. My senator father did the reverse, went as far as greasing the Pennsylvania governor's hands to make sure the State Police Academy would accept me, to help him wash his hands of me. A favor I didn't need or want, and it put a target on my back in the academy and during my early years on the force.

I was a senator's daughter, yes, biologically. But emotionally, ideologically, morally, he and I couldn't have been from the same fucking universe.

I did not sing along. Near the end of the third play I put a spit-shined shoe heel through the Wurlitzer's bubble top, then a few fists into its guts. I grabbed the offending record and snapped it in my bloodied hands. A shoulder shove tipped the jukebox over; multiple kicks retired it for good. It took Vonetta and two other troopers to subdue me. One night into my release from the academy and there I was in a drunk tank with bandaged hands and a fifteen-hundred-dollar bill from the bar for damages. An alcohol-intake fail on my part, considering the meds I was on back then. I changed meds after that.

Was a Senator's daughter. A past tense distinction, one that sounded so much better.

A waiter appeared at my table now. Cute guy; young. I gave him my order. "Chicken-fried steak, garlic mashed, onion rings, and a biscuit. Gravy on all of it. With a Coke Zero."

The waiter didn't hide his smile, also couldn't hide his dimples. "Coke Zee-rohhh," he mouthed, finishing off my order longhand with an exclamation point on his tear-off pad. "The all-purpose, heart-friendly, dietary equalizer. Got it, ma'am."

The tabletop jukebox playlist was open to more CCR and other early seventies music, some Joni Mitchell, Linda Ronstadt, other favorites of mine. I passed on all of it, ate my food, and further reminisced in the din of Aristotle's Diner.

A warm night in May 1986. I was attending a sports ceremony and celebratory dinner, me a star forward on a Police Athletic League girls' basketball team. League MVP, age sixteen, also an honors high school student at Sacred Heart Academy for Girls in Philly. This PAL dinner was the event that put Dad on notice, when my affliction laid a bold claim.

Mom, Dad, and Uncle Ernest, Dad's disgusting brother who lived with us, were all there, at the ceremony, then at the dinner. Also there with us, seated next to Dad, and unknown to me until he was introduced, was the college admissions director for the University of Pennsylvania. Politicians had this reach; my father was no exception.

The only person I was happy to be eating that dinner with was my mother.

Over salads, Dad, Uncle Ernest, and the recruiter shared jokes, sports, and politics, smiling through all of it while Mom and I ate. Over dessert, Dad poked the recruiter. A cue.

"Counsel," the recruiter began, "your father has told me so much about you. It gives me great pleasure to inform you that the University of Pennsylvania would like to extend to you an offer to join its freshman class..."

My dad, the great Senator Edmond Drury, smiled his authoritarian smile, savoring the moment. His brother Uncle Ernest, with his sick fucking demented visage the same as it was at home, narrowed his eyes, drilling them into mine, same as when he would cram my brother Judge's head into his crotch and make me watch him deliver a blow job, his hands gripping my brother's hair so he couldn't retreat, again, and again, and again, me seeing this at age four, five, six.

My older brother, my savior, taking the hit, always protecting his little sister...

It came over me like a bolt of lightning at the table, all liberating and powerful and mesmerizing and euphoric and Forrest Gump–like, but also devastating, with me unable to control some of my bodily functions.

What my left hand did: flipped the admissions director off with feeling, a full-fisted, bent-elbow, ram-it-up-your-ass gesture, delivered with the enthusiasm of a home plate umpire.

What my mouth did:

"—fuckface, dicknose, up your ass, garden hose/get in there, suck cock, big girl on your cumsock..."

What the off-duty cops from other tables did: subdued me, hauled me out of the room, then pummeled my teenaged hussy ass because I fought them, with them breaking all the fingers in my left hand and a bone in my forearm.

I was held overnight for observation in a Philly hospital's psychiatric unit, where they sedated and straitjacketed me, to shut me up and keep my injured left arm from becoming a nonstop, uppercutting blur.

There was no mystery here. I hated pedophiles and abusers of children. Would never not hate them, would never accept their rehabilitation, and would always associate my Tourette's with me witnessing these unspeakable acts.

A third Coke Zero appeared at my booth. It was a refill I wouldn't touch, next to a dinner I now couldn't finish, next to pie à la mode I hadn't ordered, all delivered by an attractive young waiter with mommy issues who was chatting me up the whole time, and who was now telling me he finished his shift in half an hour, in case I was interested.

I never earned this. The cleavage, a haughty voice, and if I let it grow, a full head of long, straight dark hair that took its color well, all things that drew men of all ages to me. I occasionally took advantage of it, but after forty-nine years I still hadn't earned it. Which was why my chin was scarred, some of my nails were chewed, and my hair was kept short. Compensation. And yet the hookups were always there if I wanted them.

I told him thanks, I was flattered, but I needed to take a rain check.

Back in the van, I checked my phone. No signal. Sixth sense said I needed to talk to Vonetta. The diner had a pay phone, but it also had the waiter I'd just rebuffed. I drove back to the bowling alley instead, pulled up a text from Vonetta when I got there, then lost the signal again.

The text was already a half hour old: *Car is on the move.*

At the bowling alley bar, I waited for Vonetta to answer her home phone. I was on the bar phone dialing her collect, landline to landline, a swallow of beer left. I watched the busy bowling lanes from a barstool. Vonetta picked up, accepted the charges.

"What, you in jail now, Sarge?"

"Phone service isn't consistent up here. And a great big how-the-hell-are-you to you too. Tell me why J. Edgar's feds are here in Rancor."

It had cost me another ten to use the alley bar's phone. I was now apparently persona non grata with Floyd, although the second ten went where the first ten went, into that old miner's helmet marked *The Maurice Fund.* I watched bowling balls from three different lanes each hit the one-two or one-three sweet spots in succession, which gave us thunderclaps of ricocheting, pin-concussed fury. These senior women were serious.

"Are you *bowling,* Counsel?" Vonetta asked, except I could tell it was another pissed-off sneer masquerading as a question. But when I thought sneer I thought snicker. When I thought snicker, I thought snigger. When I thought snigger, the Tourette's kicked in.

"*—nigger nigger.*

"Sorry, Netta. At a bowling alley but not bowling. Tell me about the feds."

Stretch pants, bicycle pants, track pants, sweatpants, up and down all forty lanes. Loose bowling shirts. All women, mostly white, some with significant tans. Their bowling balls showcased the colors of the seasons. One short, thin woman on the lanes stuck out, her large black clip-on hair bow centered above the wrinkled leather of her tanned forehead, the hair bow nesting in a white bouffant perm. She picked up her ball at the ball return. The only all-black ball out there, and in her small senior hands it looked the size of a beach ball. A few jittery steps and the ball was gone, traveling the lane not quite as slow as a two-handed throw from a six-year-old, but straighter. She left one pin.

"Don't worry about the feds," Vonetta said. "No mystery there. Our bounty crossed jurisdictional lines. My offer's still good. You bring him in, you earn the money. The feds... well, you know the feds. They mean well. Any takers on the photo?"

"Not yet. Where's Mr. Linkletter's car now?"

"What do you mean, where's his car?" she said. "That tracking app on your phone should tell you where the car is. I see it on my end. You don't?"

"Collect call for Ms. Vonetta Posey," I sing-songed like a lobby bellhop. "It's these mountains. Reception fades in and out."

"Dude, that's not good. What's the last location you have?"

"Rancor. Somewhere on Layton Road, in Rancor."

"What the fuck I'm gonna do with you, Counsel? That's so five hours ago." Right about now she was going into her Muhammad Ali, curled-lower-lip snarl. "Look, you cheap-ass diva, you need a real five-G provider, not that hamster-powered Sam's Warehouse old-lady piece of shit you have. Or did you stop paying your bills again?"

"I don't need your bullshit, Netta. Next time hire NASA, you deep-pockets fuck. Just tell me where the car is."

"My pockets are deep like your dick is long. Hold on. Here it is. It's in the vicinity of Glacier Pothole State Park, whatever the hell that is, just outside the Rancor town limits. Go get 'im, Sarge. And I'm signing you up for a better service provider, right the fuck now."

* * *

I cruised Rancor Boulevard in the van, a mile away from the Glacier Pothole State Park entrance per a road sign. It was ten p.m. No scenery on this two-laner, and little traffic. The forest looked impenetrable for the past few miles, as dark on both sides as walls of chunk chocolate. Anticipation kicked in, of confrontation and a mounting danger. Along with this, an adrenaline rush. And along with that, excessive mouth action:

"—dark park, dog fart, choco-darts, the dog did it—"

Tess woke up in the middle of my verbal digression, raised her head, felt my tension. She hopped onto the passenger seat, nudged my elbow for a touch that did us both some good, except my subconscious was still in overdrive, spewing its alliterative pearls.

"—diddle kibble, doggie-doodle, doodle-dog, doodle your daughter—"

Tess licked my hand.

"—dickhead, dead dad, dad's a dick, dad's dick is dead—"

The signs were there when I was in my teens. Mom saw them. Dad saw them too, but the bastard passed them off as benign manifestations of female puberty, no worse than bad acne. He expected it, them, all of it, to "clear up." He browbeat my mom into ignoring them.

Signs like tapping my heels to the drum solo in "Wipe Out" by The Surfaris in music class, age twelve. I couldn't stop myself and was sent to detention for it. It continued for two hours, then the detention nun got smart and took my shoes from me to quiet things down.

Then there was a meltdown in the school nurse's office at age twelve for aggressive nose-picking in class. I drew blood, both nostrils, both hands. This episode drove my already low self-esteem to new depths.

At age thirteen, the last day of Catholic grade school, when I said goodbye to a nun and it exploded into a repetitive fine-print disclaimer that she was a soul-sucking cunt. Sadly, she was a nun I adored.

Age sixteen, the college admissions director episode plus two high school suspensions, one for defending myself on the school bus, the other for multiple cursing infractions in the classroom.

My hand was now moist from Tess licking it. We were coming up on something as the van leaned into a curve. A car on the opposite shoulder. Someone in cargo shorts and a logoed hoodie approached the stopped car on foot, a gas container in one hand, a swinging flashlight in the other. My mouth quieted. I slowed the van, received an I'm-good thumbs-up from the guy so I moved on. Farther down on the right shoulder a fawn, alive and motionless in my high beams, was thinking about crossing. I honked the horn and braked. The deer did an about-face and returned to the woods.

And still farther down, the road bent then straightened out. Next up was a pickup truck on the right shoulder, its flashers on, and a man in the glow of the truck's headlights. With a rifle. Also in the headlights was a deer struggling to get to its feet, trying to drag its mangled and bloody hindquarters away from broken headlight glass on the shoulder and into the brush, one leg at an impossible angle. A terrible scene. I pulled alongside, lowered my passenger side window and called out to better my van's engine idle with an offer to help.

The guy called back. "Much obliged, ma'am, but I got this."

I pulled away, and in my rearview mirror I saw him raise the gun and pull the trigger, the gun's report echoing. A chunk of deer head separated from its body. The gun lowered, the man freezing in place for a moment, lingering over his handiwork. There was a good chance he was a hunter, and there was also a good chance his hesitation meant he was rethinking his hobby.

At the left turn to the park entrance, the dogs and I sat a minute staring into the woodsy interior. Two black iron gates were visible under a single elevated floodlight. The gates, taller than necessary, did not abut each other. With the park closed this time of night, my guess was they should have been connected.

My phone signal was back. Some texts were queued up from Vonetta.

Dude I upgraded your phone service. First month's on me

Phone store in Rancor has the order so get your ass over there

You wanna cancel after a month I don't give a fuck you cheap bitch but while you're on this case you need better service. N btw fuck you

"Fine, Netta," I said aloud. "And fuck you too, sweetie."

In front of the gates now. They were open wide enough for a car to fit through. Tess stretched upright in her seat like a prairie dog on high alert, jerked her head left and right multiple times. If she saw something, anything, she'd paw the window. She stayed seated, but she was tensed up. I pulled the van through the parted gates.

No difficulty finding my way. The *No Vehicles Past This Point* sign was knocked over on its side, the chains once attached to it snaking along the blacktop, leaving a gap between two huge upright boulders, a twisted chrome car bumper and other debris scattered there as well. I needed a closer look, so I reached for my door handle. Tess was in my face.

"Sorry, young lady." She gave me some side-eye. "You guys need to sit this one out." No reason to tempt fate with a huge black hole somewhere out there.

Tess bristled when she saw my Glock emerge from behind my back, commenced her pretty-please stubby tail wag. I cupped her face, told her again it wasn't going to happen. After a quick grab of my halogen lantern, I climbed out of the van.

Gravel was underfoot as I walked, then blacktop, then a step up onto a concrete slab. A walk across the slab and I was at the railing. And here was our pothole.

This was one rather large pothole.

My mouth went into high gear, chatting up a Tourette's blue streak, spitting profanities into the dark. The gun went back into my jeans and my fingers found my keychain. Better. I illuminated what I could of the pit with the lantern.

Red lights, deep. They looked like car taillights.

A vehicle down there? *How* in the *fuck...*?

I squinted to get a better read, concluded that yes, there was a car where it shouldn't have been. The chrome bumper mangled near the boulders, 1960s vintage, meant there was a good chance it was the car I was tracking. I texted Vonetta.

Netta I'm in the park

I see you counsel. I see the car on the gps. Less than 50 ft from you. Reel him in

Not gonna happen. 50 ft as the crow flies but another 150 ft down at the bottom of the pothole. Car is history

Wtf? He in it?

How the hell would I know if he's in it? It's 150 ft into middle earth. Fill you in later

I ran the lantern beam around the attraction's perimeter. There—a break in the iron railing that merited a closer look. On my way on foot.

The railing was lifted out of the way. I looked closer at the area behind me. Unobstructed and flat for forty, fifty yards or more. A Thelma and Louise runway. Except I guessed Mr. Linkletter wasn't down there with the car. Mr. Linkletter was a coward. He molested children.

I canvassed the immediate area. My lucky day: an empty Poland Spring plastic water bottle near the edge of the pit. Maybe it would be good for a scent. DNA too, maybe, if it were ever to come to that.

Another look down into the pothole would have made sense, but not from this vantage point, where there was no railing. I moved over to a railed section. Here I got the view I needed. Yes, it was a car, and it was in the deepest section of the pit, the front end not visible, like it had jammed itself or crawled part way into a cave. Aside from the glowing taillights, I saw a blob of white with cherry red against layers of sandstone and shale. White metal, red side panel trim. Looked like what I was after, a vintage sixties Impala, surrounded by jagged gray and brown bedrock and a black coal seam.

White and red, like the bloodied rat Tess had dragged out of the coal mine today. How symbolic. Wait, some movement down there, something scurrying. No shit. Forget the symbolism, it was a rat. And it was white.

What kind of sick fuck did something like this? My only answer was he was a grandstander. This was *The Stephen Linkletter Show*, starring Stephen Linkletter. Bail-jumper, predator, and tourist attraction vandal.

I walked back to my van. In the glow of the interior lighting I checked out the Poland Spring bottle, gave Tess a sniff. Fungo was eager for the same and got it. Tess's ears perked up; Fungo growled. Maybe it was Mr. Linkletter's scent, maybe it wasn't. But whoever's scent it was, they now had it.

We were done here. This late-night trespass, into a closed state park... Interesting, but no bounty. Time for a 911 call. But a point of fact was I didn't know for sure that the car didn't actually have someone in it. I pulled my phone from my pocket.

"You! In the van! Reach both hands out your window so I can see them. Now!"

Tess and Fungo went berserk at the voice, the two of them wanting out of the van. We heard no vehicle, no footsteps. I did as asked while shushing my dogs. They calmed down, but maintained a low growl.

"Stay in your vehicle, please, while I call this in!"

'Please?' *Did I hear that right? Did he just say 'please?'*

"Badge me," I called, so I would know what or whom I was dealing with. In my side view mirror I saw him start slowly forward, his industrial strength flashlight trained on my empty hands still reaching through the open van window as he'd requested. I tasted the sweat collecting on my upper lip. My adrenaline gave him the benefit of the doubt. But this dude was in a world of hurt if he had bad intentions.

He passed through the red glow of my van's taillights. I gauged his size in the side mirror, the glow strong because my foot was on the brake pedal. No bigger than five-six, and he was wide.

He stopped next to the rear tire, his left hand shoulder-high with his flashlight. In his right hand, no gun. Something rectangular; his badge, raised next to his face. It was on a tether, and the tether was still around his neck. I saw the shape of his hat, a wide, circular brim, and sitting back on his head, too big for him.

A park ranger. He couldn't be armed else he'd have had it out by now. And he was nervous.

"I'm Park Ranger Cadet Trevor Stovall," his shaky voice said. "I need to report this."

Christ. Not even a full park ranger, a Smokey the Bear *cub*.

In my head: *Colonel Klink, shrinkydinks, smokey slinky kinky cubby ratfink...*

"Counsel Fungo, Pennsylvania State Police, retired," moved ahead of my diuretic queue. "I need to get out of my van. My dogs—"

"No! Stop. Is there anyone else in the van with you and your dogs, ma'am?" The voice was less shaky this time, more in control.

"No."

"Fine. Stay where you are, please."

Again with the *please*. I humored him, my hands still out the window, his flashlight showcasing them. I took my foot off the brakes. The red glow from my van's taillights dimmed.

I gave the kid credit for getting the drop on me. I heard no car engine, but he couldn't have gotten here on foot. Far as I knew, there was nothing, no homes, stores, nothing around here for miles.

Another tap on the brake pedal told me. The brake lights reflected off the chrome of a Vespa Scooter parked well beyond the boulders, near the front gate. So he was at least old enough to drive. Or sort of drive, considering his transportation choice.

He put a phone to his ear. Someone was verbally kicking his ass.

"... but... uh-huh. No, that's why I called. Uh-huh. But I'm sixteen. But... aw, c'mon, Aunt Dody...."

After I passed some ID through the window, Trevor—or more likely his aunt—let me exit the van without me having to get rude with him.

"Aunt Dody knows who you are, Miss Fungo. She says you were at the bowling alley today."

No shit. Floyd the bowling shoe guy got the word out. Good for you, Floyd. "Your aunt yelled at you for approaching me in the van, didn't she?"

"Well, sort of. Yeah. Look, I just wanna do my part."

The two of us were on the concrete slab overlooking the pothole. We shined our lights in. They illuminated some of the hole, the bottom still shadowy except for those beady red taillight eyes and Mother Nature's glacial handiwork. Impressive.

"Pretty cool hole, huh?" young Trevor said. "Wanna hear about it?"

He rattled off a bunch of wiki info on glaciers that a nerdy park ranger cadet would know. In a nutshell: a melting glacier dripped into an indentation in the bedrock. Rock fragments, sand, and gravel from the glacier spun into the indentation and carved out, after billions of gallons of melting water rushed into it, an elliptical hole through layers and layers of stratified bedrock. A geological masterpiece. This one also had a black coal seam running through it.

"So, Trevor, any chance you saw what happened here tonight? How that car got where it is?"

He shook his head no. "I was at St. P's. It must have happened before I came by on patrol."

"St. P's?" I said, with *trapeze* and *on my knees* on my lips ready to go right behind it, but my face contorted itself while I choked the words back. My furrowed-brow WTF look suffixed the contortion. Combined, they did a good job of blaming him for my not knowing what St. P's was.

"You know, St. Possenti's." He blinked. When I didn't acknowledge him, his next blink was an eyelid flutter. A tell. He'd slipped and said too much. St. Possenti's was probably somewhere he shouldn't have been. His next comment would be measured.

"At bingo. I was playing bingo. But don't tell my aunt, okay, ma'am? She doesn't want me hanging at St. P's. Then I went on patrol. When I saw your van here after dark, I called her."

Bingo. Sure, whatever. I suspected it wasn't like chunky Trevor here would have been covering for a high school flash house-trashing party. Not in his chick magnet Park Ranger Cubby Cadet outfit, and with a scooter. His bingo story was BS, but I gave him a pass on it.

"My lips are sealed. But you called your *aunt*?" My pathetic look hinted at my opinion, which was you're a wimp, kid.

"You don't know my aunt," he said.

Trevor told me about the Rancor Town Watch. They were well organized and proud of Rancor's crime-free heritage. Round the clock patrols. Citizens of all ages participated. And his Aunt Dody—Dody Heck—ran it. She was the last top cop the town had, he volunteered; she was now retired.

I asked him what the Watch would do about someone sabotaging the town's only tourist attraction.

"About the car? I dunno. Nothing, I hope. I kinda like it. It looks cool down there. I suppose they'll look for the person who did it, make him pay somehow. You said it's an old Chevy? Awesome."

I told him the equipment they'd need to haul the car back up. A wrecker, a big one, the kind that could tow a semi, plus a couple hundred feet of strong chain or cable.

I took another look into the hole while Trevor relayed this info to his aunt, him still taking flack from her. I liked him. A teenager with a Vespa; took guts for that to be his ride. I leaned over the railing, lowered my lantern down a bit. Nothing much visible at this distance other than the car's back end and its taillights, still with juice, but faint. It was a miracle the car's gas tank hadn't exploded.

"Plus a cave spelunker, Trevor, or at least the fire department," I called over my shoulder. "Someone sure-footed." One final gander at this nightmarish hole, then I would call it a night.

Maybe not. From deep in the hole, the dimming Impala's brake lights flashed.

* * *

I was an item now. The firemen and the EMTs hadn't wanted to wait for daylight after hearing my story about the taillights. I also met Dody Heck, Trevor's aunt, another bowler, and shaped like her nephew Trevor but bigger. I kept my promise to him: no mention of bingo, whatever bullet that helped him dodge.

The battered Chevy Impala was lifted out of the pothole and onto a flatbed truck. Its white convertible top survived three-quarters of the drop to where the cave spelunker peeled the canvas off a jagged piece of bedrock like a burst gum bubble. Yes, someone was in the car, but not in the driver's seat. In the trunk. A dead someone, his face all beat to shit, half of it blown away from a gunshot. This discovery almost but not quite validated my plea for urgency after I saw the taillights flash. Except the caver found no one else down there, alive or dead, human, rat, or otherwise, and a brake pedal clear of all debris, leaving no answer as to who or what had tapped it. Certainly not the dead guy in the trunk, considering the damage the gunshot had done to his head. The car's front end plugged a hollowed-out coal seam that terminated into cave rubble. No exit, as far as the caver could tell, from the pothole into middle earth.

No way into the hole other than from above, and no other way out, although a geologic survey the firemen brought showed the pothole was once connected to a coal mine. An EMT took my statement. The equivalent of a ghost story or an alien encounter or some middle earth hobbit tale from a woman with no business being out this late other than for nefarious reasons, his expression said, but I stayed with it.

"Sometimes a traumatized mind plays tricks," the young, male EMT had offered, humoring me. "Probably just a malfunction of a battered car, a short circuit or something." He stayed away from me after that. They all kept their distance, like I was a lunatic.

The answer I settled on: it was a rat. Had to be big. Large enough to depress and hold down a brake pedal for at least a half a minute. Except I was having trouble with the half-a-minute part. And maybe the part that it was a rat too.

The road was empty this early in the morning. At four a.m. my dogs were sacked out in the van, exhausted from being cooped up while at the pothole. I was on Rancor Boulevard, heading back to catch a few hours of sleep. My deputies had made nice with Trevor, Tess especially, even let him feed her a treat. His park ranger khakis helped; Tess liked people in uniform. I passed the spot where the pickup truck's gun-toting driver had finished off the deer he hit last night. Bloodstains on the shoulder, but no leftover roadkill, which meant venison steaks for him and his family, maybe his neighbors as well.

Farther down the road I entered the curve where the other car had run out of gas overnight, the car now gone.

I jammed the brakes, did a U-turn, stopped hard on the opposite shoulder and glared at something glistening on the ground inside the periphery of my headlights.

Another discarded plastic bottle of Poland Spring.

I picked it up.

16

A knock on the door to Andy's B&B owner's suite at four in the morning.

"The woman in the room below us," an elderly male guest asked a groggy Andy, "is she all right?"

His mother, Charlotte, was having a rough night, not a new occurrence. Andy let himself into her room, tried to roust her from a dream with a few shakes to her silk pajama shoulder. "Ma. Mom. Charlie—"

His mom's scrubbed, smooth-skinned face was pulled tight, terrified. She uttered soft, contained screams, then one loud one, accompanied by rambling dream-speak. A night terror, the kind that only seniors with long, chaotic memories could conjure. Her ramblings coalesced into coherence, but she was still in the grip of the nightmare. She finally woke up.

"My Andrew. My Andy. The blood—"

"Yes, Ma, I'm here. I'm all healed, Ma. I'm okay. Shhh..."

"Maurice—"

And here was where Andy always stumbled, having to tell his mother once again that this part of the nightmare remained true. He got through the explanation about his father as tenderly as he could, comforting her like she had comforted him during his childhood years. In tonight's aftermath they shared a subdued cry together, side by side in bed, Andy hugging her. His mother's melancholy lifted.

"I told her no, I wouldn't allow it," Charlotte said, fully lucid.

Not a rambling comment. Andy knew where she was going, his mother's face grim. "It wasn't your choice, Ma."

"Too dangerous," she said. "Kitty had no right."

"To her, Ma, it wasn't a right. To her, it was an obligation."

Kitty Buchinsky. His father's sister. Aunt Kitty had survived a don't-fuck-with-me hardline childhood in West Virginia coal country. Their father fought in the 1921 Battle of Blair Mountain. The largest armed rebellion since the Civil War, with striking coal miners facing off first against a detective agency then against a sheriff's department then the State Police then the US Army. A hundred-plus dead, nearly a thousand coal miners arrested, among them Andy's grandfather. When he was released, the family left the state and relocated to Rancor, Pennsylvania, where there were coal-mining jobs from a more benevolent employer, and where Andy's dad Maurice was born. A hunter and a coal miner, and no stranger to firearms, the grandfather taught his children Kitty and Maurice well.

Late fall the year of the bank robbery trials, Kitty hadn't returned to work after the court rendered the not guilty verdicts. To the uninformed, she was on another bender, in perfect character for her. Two weeks on the road, they all assumed, in bars and clubs. In reality, she was on a mission.

The masked bank robber with the shotgun, her brother's murderer, she found in lower New York state. Kitty played the party girl role, never a stretch for her. In a shitty pickle-tickle motel room she trap-doored him into hell's abyss with one gunshot to the head.

The next two bank-robbing men she tracked to Ohio. Two point-blank executions, all business, soon as she got into their cars.

Three bullets, three not-guilty verdicts overturned. Justice served, in the person of one Aunt Kitty.

Her many boyfriends never knew this history; the two husbands she buried never knew it either. No one ever knew anything until Kitty deemed that her nephew Andy was ready for the truth twenty-five years later. Ready also to accept the encumbrance that went with it.

Bravo, Charlotte said to Kitty when she'd confessed to her. Bravo, Andy, age thirty, had agreed. Rightful, satisfying outcomes. Then Kitty told them more: she hadn't stopped with the bank robbers.

1966, four years after the bank robbery. A drifter dishwasher raped a local high school girl. An unreported brutal, sadistic crime, but the traumatized young victim confided to a friend. Kitty heard about it, which begot the dishwasher's execution, this time with no body found. "The Centralia coal mine fire. New back then," she'd explained. "A thousand degrees down there, with sinkholes and other mine subsidence holes," like one behind a Centralia graveyard. After the execution, an anonymous letter and pictures sent to the raped girl, with a plea to remain quiet, informed her of the vigilante vindication.

1972. Severe domestic abuse in a Rancor household, repeat occurrences, life threatening. Unreported by a terrified wife, but she had friends. Kitty heard about it and shot the bastard husband. "Centralia's coal seams, still burning," Kitty told Andy. "More fire in the hole." No body meant no crime. An anonymous letter to the wife, for closure, and another plea for secrecy.

1975. A Rancor Vietnam veteran who lived in the woods was beaten, robbed, doused in kerosene then set ablaze. Never reported missing, but the itinerant coal miner who killed him blabbed. Kitty heard about it. Retribution. Fire in the hole, then an anonymous letter to the homeless man's parents.

A few others since then, all needing punishment. Infrequent transgressions. Kitty heard about them. Centralia's hellish sinkholes never refused the bodies. Again, anonymous letters. The urban legend, that of a mysterious Rancor, Pennsylvania, boogeybitch, had been soundly solidified.

That day, when Aunt Kitty confessed about her deadly moonlighting, she also approached Andy with a plea. "I'm tired. One person is all we need. One discreet person to accept this responsibility for our town, whenever the need arises."

And who more appropriate than you, my brother's son, she'd said to him. For the good of the town, Andy. To deny future transgressions by sending these monsters to hell. To keep the town safe, Andy. *Please,* Andy.

But what about the implications, Aunt Kitty? About getting caught? What about my young daughter, Aunt Kitty? And what about me not wanting to kill another human being in cold blood?

The sting of having lost his father to violence had lessened in the twenty-five years that had passed, though not fully; Andy's emotional scars were still healing. Time, a good life with his surgeon mother, plus Andy's own nursing career and his small B&B: while it remained an uphill battle, all continued to work on dulling the trauma he'd experienced as a child.

Andy Prudhomme, picked to learn from the original by the original, the legend. If he'd accepted, it would have been his cross to bear while he walked among the population and carried a big, retributional stick, silently and anonymously, like his aunt Kitty had.

Charlotte dozed off in Andy's arms, exhausted. Time for him to supervise the preparation of the B&B breakfast; no more sleep this morning for him.

The town remained safe, a wonderful place to live, the safest it had ever been. The benefit of anonymity, and of being viewed only from a distance. With the release of the *People* magazine article, the anonymity was gone.

He tucked his mother back into bed then saw himself out of the room.

Andy was thirty when he'd said no to Kitty, but he did accept her guns.

17

It was Ms. Townsend's fault. Randall's Wisconsin high school music teacher; she, forty-two, him, not quite fifteen. Her fault for him being the way he was, his predawn subconscious told him as he lay in bed in his utilitarian motel room in Dickson City. She introduced him to sex.

They'd handed him a tuba to play in the marching band. After his second music lesson with her she told him how much she liked his sensual, full lips. She wanted to know if he liked hers, and how would he like them wrapped around that schoolboy cock of his?

And he did like her lips just where she'd suggested. He was gifted, she'd told him. Women would love him when they learned what was in his pants, flock to him, would want him to do to them what he'd started doing to her after school three days a week his entire sophomore year. He had, in her words, a magnificently pagan dick. Porn-star quality.

Then, without notice, she quit him. Gave him shit about how he'd started to scare her with his own heightened sexual appetite. After she cut him loose, he couldn't pass her in the school hallways without going rigid and needing to relieve himself in the lavatory. That much sex, with all her screaming, pounding, and intensity, had made it so that he needed new outlets. He took what he could get, whenever, wherever. High school, playground, church, mall. Girls, guys too. Except he wanted the music teacher back. She knew how to do things. And she'd been his first.

One late afternoon after he forced her into a school broom closet, she further solidified her distinction with two additional firsts for him: rape and murder. As luck would have it, the other "last person to see her alive" had been the married high school band moderator whom she'd been banging as well. Motive, opportunity, and a number of people had seen her and Bow-tie Benson flirting over the prior few months. Circumstantial evidence got Mr. Benson twenty-years-to-life for her second-degree strangulation murder.

Her eyes. Oh yes, he loved how they'd roll up into her head during the throes of her ecstasy when the grinding of his engorged cock tickled that sweet spot of hers. Especially that last time. The visual—their whites about to pop as he strangled the life out of her while she fought him—this had really gotten him off.

The dream, her stricken face freeze-framed in terror, her orgasmic death rattle: he was as hard as a rhino horn now that he was fully awake. To the motel room toilet. After that, he'd rub one out.

They would all soon know. They'd find the classic Chevy deep underground, plugging a Pocono cave. They'd find the used car dealer's body in the trunk. Some of Mrs. Spezak's worried friends would have reported her missing. Stephen Linkletter, aka Randall Burton, accused predator out on bail and living with her, and also missing, would become a person of interest.

FBI and state law enforcement. If they hadn't already involved themselves, they would now. All except for the local Rancor police, consisting of one cop. One. Not even a real cop, an elected sheriff. Randall liked Rancor, Pennsylvania, for the same reason he liked so many of his victims: they were defenseless.

Back to Ms. Townsend. Back to big tits and tubas. Oh, how she loved his junk. He was nothing, she'd screamed at him while she rode the knob fantastic, if not for his lovingly large package. God's gift to him, and Randall's gift to women and other impressionable, vulnerable creatures. Sometimes whether they wanted it or not.

His junk made him the man he was. Without it, he was ordinary.

Without it, he was the antisocial, abandoned loser-child who no one ever had any time for. But when they caught him—when he finally let that happen—this would all change. They'd all want a piece of him.

Hail to his junk, long may it live. Long enough to find Regina and his kid. Long enough to know he'd left something of value behind.

18

I dragged myself downstairs, arrived under the wire for breakfast in the B&B dining room. My deputies were sleeping in.

A feast worthy of a Philly longshoreman. Thick French toast soaked in melted butter pecan ice cream then baked until golden brown. Pure maple syrup. Butter. Combined, a day's worth of calories in one forkful. Plus sausage patties and hash browns. Just looking at it I could feel my arteries harden.

Andy the B&B proprietor pushed through the swinging doors from the kitchen, dropped into the chair across from me at a table that could seat ten, today set for only three. I sipped a glass of orange juice, shared with him where I was until four this morning, and rambled about the pothole tragedy with the vintage Impala. He waited until I was finished my story.

"My dad had a sixties Chevy Impala too," he said. "Really loved that car."

Some quiet between us while I ate and Andy remembered. Eyes lowered, he skirted past his dark cloud, followed up his tendered memory with an admission: "I knew about the car in the hole already. Dody Heck called me. She's not taking the park trespass well."

"Makes sense," I said. "She's a former cop."

"It's more than that. Her husband was a cop too. Killed in the line of duty, in Scranton. That's when she decided to retire as Rancor police chief."

"Sorry. Killed how?"

"Street gang. Nothing like New York or California, but they're still a problem. For some of Scranton's young adults, many descendants from old coal-cracking families, the economy isn't picking up fast enough, so they're making poor decisions. Plus New York gang members passing through sometimes look to have fun with the locals. Occasional drive-bys.

"The point is we'll clean up this mess with the car at the park and get on with our lives. It's what we do." He softened his look. "Do you bowl?"

A polite yes nod from me with a small smile that changed my yes to a slow headshake that said no, not really, a nice way of saying that bowling was not at the top of my preferred entertainment list. "Something I never got into. Not that there's anything wrong with it."

A chuckle from Andy. "Dody's ribbing me about tonight's senior mixed doubles championship final. My team against hers. Rancor will be a-rocking."

I buttered a homemade muffin but didn't take a bite, squinting at him. Something on my mind, and asking about it was going to sound rude.

"How old are you?"

He gave me an are-you-for-real look, deciding if I was charming or pathetically clueless. "Was that the Tourette's, or you really need me to answer that?"

"Just working my way to a compliment. Aside from two or three people at the bowling alley yesterday, I saw no one under the age of fifty. How can you be bowling in a seniors league?"

"Anyone fifty-five and over can bowl in the league. I'm fifty-six."

Confusion or appreciation, I wasn't sure what my face registered. "Huh. I mean, really. Huh."

"Good genes," he said, "monster gym workouts. And I only nibble at these breakfasts. No other help."

Preemptive on his part, the translation being, before I had a chance to really embarrass myself, he'd had no cosmetic surgery, except I didn't embarrass easily.

"No surgery then. Good for you."

"Wiseass."

"A relief to hear that, Mr. Prudhomme," I said. "I was expecting 'asshole.'"

"Look—Counsel," his expression said I'd scored some points, "repeat guests call me Andy. I hope you'll be one of them. Only because you're, you know, special, with your Tourette's and all."

"Asshole. I mean fine, Andy."

"Apology accepted, Counsel."

I bit into the muffin then returned it to my plate, could eat no more. Andy pushed himself away from the table, excused himself.

Last call, since we were sharing. "So tell me, Andy, your mother makes your wife sound like the Antichrist. She seems like a great cook. She has to have some other redeeming qualities."

He stood. "The cook's not my wife. I'm divorced." He paused for effect, his smile gone. "You finished with your breakfast, Miss Fungo?"

19

My deputies and I were in my van in a Rancor strip mall parking lot, checking out my new phone service. The bugged Stephen Linkletter Chevy Impala ship had sailed, but I was liking this new toy anyway. I mouthed a thank-you to my absent trooper buddy Vonetta while I keyed "Andrew Prudhomme" and "Rancor, PA" into a search engine.

A sighting on someone's social register pages: *Andrew Prudhomme, Rancor, PA. Staff nurse, Scranton State Hospital... Good Samaritan Award... Dr. Jasmine Prudhomme, CEO and Chief Administrator, the state hospital in Scranton... her handsome husband Andrew Prudhomme at a Rancor fundraiser...*

"Let's look for more on the wife, shall we?" I said to Tess, her head resting on her paws on the front seat. She grunted her agreement.

And yes, here she was again, more pictures of Andy's ex.

Dr. Jasmine Prudhomme, head of the state hospital, with Philadelphia socialite and hospital contributor Joseph Kullard...

Dr. Jasmine Prudhomme was in a gown. Small woman, fake chest.

Dr. Jasmine Prudhomme. Charges of sexual misconduct with young male psychiatric inpatients have been dropped...

Whoa.

Andy's ex was an accused sexual predator, but she'd gotten off. And on her arm in this picture was a younger man, early thirties at best, in a tux.

No way the stud and her weren't a couple. The guy was a main line Philly socialite with money. I agreed with Andy; I now didn't like his wife either.

But there was more. A lot.

Scranton *Times-Tribune*: *Jasmine Prudhomme, MD, former local hospital CEO, found slain in Philadelphia.* Subsequent articles on the attack had followed over multiple weeks in the *Times Tribune* and the Philly *Inquirer*. A more recent article said the murder remained unsolved.

Huh. More violence. Not here, yet it did involve someone from this supposed violence-free hamlet. Add this to what had happened to Dody's cop husband in nearby Scranton. Unnerving.

Ten seconds in ponder mode, then I moved on. I used my new toy to take some quick pics of my dogs. I pointed and snapped one of me puckering, a big smooch at the camera, sent it and all the K9 shots to Vonetta. I got a text back.

Dogs look great fungo. BTW you need to get laid, lady.

I could have texted her back, to confess that I saw the bounty last night, the guy with a gas container. I could have told her how my dogs' sniff test of the Poland Spring water bottles had settled it, that the same person handled both bottles. The gas container was a nice touch on the bounty's part, there supposedly to fill up a white '80s Buick. Yet with no face or head recognition because of the hoodie, I blew the ID. I could have told her all this, but I didn't, to maybe avoid hearing Vonetta say "shithead" four times in a six-word sentence, about how oblivious I was on occasion. I texted her this leading question instead.

You still Catholic?

Does the Pope shit on a bear? Hell yeah I'm still Catholic, counsel. I like the schools here in Bethlehem. Sup with that?

Ever hear of a Saint Possenti?

Because I never had, I told her. Not as a kid in Catholic school or as an adult when I was still practicing. My not knowing wasn't a stretch, considering I pretty much lapsed myself onto hell's doorstep after my ex was gone. I told Vonetta about my new teenage cub cadet park ranger buddy Trevor's mention of this saint in relation to a bingo hall, to give her context. She texted back that yes, she'd heard of him.

St Gabriel Possenti. Not cause I'm Catholic. Cause I'm a gun owner

Not following you, netta

You got a new cell provider. Go look him up. I gotta go. Alleged perps want bailing out

I keyed in the search for a Saint Gabriel Possenti. Thirty-seven thousand results. Catholic votive prayers to Blessed Gabriel, Gabriel of Our Lady Of Sorrows, Gabriel Of the Sorrowful Virgin, plus a long wiki entry loaded with the saint's mid-nineteenth century life in Italy, his calling to the cloth, his miracles, and his early death at age twenty-four from TB. I quit part way through the wiki, impatient. Then I clicked on this: *St. Gabriel Possenti Society.*

gunsaint.com

Patron Saint of Handgunners

A website for gun-wielding Catholics. Their mission was to have the Vatican reinvent this saint in their image and likeness on the strength of a legend: his pre-priesthood skills as a marksman saved an Italian town from marauding bandits in 1860. Contributions to the society were United Way eligible.

Only one actual church listing popped up in the search, St. Gabriel Possenti of the Sorrowful Mother, 150 miles south of here.

I rechecked the search results. Other Catholic churches and parishes in and around Rancor and Scranton, but no St. Gabriel Possenti. Yet St. Possenti's Church had what appeared to be a thriving bingo operation in Rancor, but no church presence to go along with it.

Maybe bingo didn't mean bingo.

A commotion in front of me, outside the Rancor Family Pharmacy. A gangbanger in a Dodgers baseball cap on his way out of the pharmacy in a hurry knocked a young mom and her toddler son on their asses. The banger had enough bling around his neck to choke a pharaoh, with low-riding pants belted barely thigh-high. Hispanic. Couldn't miss the waistband of his white boxers with dancing valentine hearts. A bad stereotype. The dude leaned down to apologize to the woman.

Oops. It wasn't an apology. He grabbed her purse, speed-walked around the corner of the building and disappeared. No way Mr. Dodger could outrun anyone in those low-rider pants; someone had to be waiting for him in a car.

Tess and Fungo growled in unison; it was uncanny how they felt my tension sometimes. Fungo was out of his cage, nudging my shoulder. I grabbed Tess's collar and held her back, then I grabbed Fungo's nose to get his attention. He had his harness on, which to him meant he was already on the job. "Okay, dude, let's do this."

A button on my door panel opened the van's sliding side door. Target acquired, Fungo was gone, his leash trailing him. I slammed the van in gear, my tires squealing. We followed Fungo to the corner of the building, past a white-haired woman quick to help the young mother to her feet.

I liked it when scumbags did stupid shit in broad daylight practically begging for a confrontation. I unsnapped my seat belt.

Mr. Dodger quickstepped to a tricked-out Honda Civic with Jersey plates and someone at the wheel, the engine idling. He lobbed a plastic shopping bag through an open rear window, hung on to the purse, then dropped himself into the front seat.

A purse-stealing perp plus his driver, a hemorrhoid-red custom ride sitting in a loading zone, a loud, rumbling engine idle, and rap music. In addition to the other bad behavior, the music had to be a noise ordinance violation for sure. Plus I hated rap. Reasons enough for this citizen with a permit to carry and her trusted sidekicks to confront these young men. I stopped my black-and-gold van on a diagonal in front of the Honda. The dumbasses were wedged in.

The Honda engine revved, insinuating I should move out of the way. Fungo was already in the driver's face, barking and snarling, his paws on the car's window ledge.

I exited the van and grabbed for my German Shepherd partner's leash. Mr. Dodger and his driver couldn't help but notice my drawn Glock and my Sarah Connor camouflage tee, me straining to keep Fungo under control. Whatever they were thinking, that I was a local K9 cop or State Police or maybe off-duty SWAT, had them paralyzed. There was room for the car to run, but only in reverse.

"Something wrong, ma'am?" the driver said. A pudgy-faced white guy, midtwenties, his words were loud enough to better the noise coming from the car's speakers. Weed smelling sweeter than a freshly mown lawn clouded the car's interior. Fungo sneezed, expelling a huge wad of dog snot;

the timing couldn't have been better. The pudgy-faced white guy cursed while he wiped the snot out of his ear. Mr. Dodger snickered.

"I'm a retired state trooper," I announced. "Show me your hands."

Their hands went up. "Toss the purse out the window—*now*." I heard bystander activity behind me, corner of the building: the old woman who helped the mother with the toddler. White permed bouffant, black hair bow. Unmistakable as the senior who stared me down yesterday at the bowling alley. She kept her distance with her phone in hand, snapping pictures of us.

"The purse or your balls, Diddy. And turn down that shit you're listening to. It offends me."

Fungo sneezed again. This time his dog nails scratched the Honda's custom paint job. Now the driver was pissed. He shoved against the car door to open it. He was either stupid or had firepower or maybe both. Fungo left his feet, nipped at the driver's ear, drew blood. I swiveled my Glock back and forth between their crotches preempting either guy showing a weapon. The car door eased shut. Fungo growled and barked while I backed him off.

The purse dropped to the pavement. I pulled Fungo away from the car door by his harness, no easy feat with him this stoked, but when I told him to sit, he did. I went for my phone. This needed to be someone else's mess to clean up.

The driver wheeled the car into reverse, its tires smoking until it reached the rear corner of the building, then it skidded to a stop. I kept my weapon raised, gripped Fungo's leash extra tight. Pudgy stared at us from fifty yards away. He flashed a huge fuck-you smile, threw the transmission into drive and flipped me off. The car disappeared behind the rear of the building.

Fungo whimpered and twisted me up in his leash, all because we now had company. The white bouffanted hair-bow lady offered me a shake of her hand. I resettled Fungo in his crate inside my van with his piece of jute first.

"I'm Ursula. Thank you, miss, for going after them," she said. Her shake was a bit on the skeletal side, but still firm.

"No problem, ma'am. Counsel Fungo. I'm a retired state cop. Are you all right?"

"I'm fine. My granddaughter will be too, once she gets her purse back. You missed what went on inside the pharmacy." A too-bad shake of her head. "He pistol-whipped the pharmacist unconscious and left with a lot of pills."

The plastic shopping bag. *Shit.* Glad I didn't know. I might have done something stupid.

An approaching siren. Fungo howled, rhapsodizing with the ear-piercing noise. Tess joined him from the passenger seat, her window cracked open. Horrible racket from the two of them, as earsplitting as a Yoko Ono/Tiny Tim duet. Rewards in the form of jute rope pieces shut my deputies up.

"Not to worry," Ursula said, her eyes brightening. "The store has cameras. Plus I took some pictures of their car with my phone."

The pictures might have been useful on some level, but chances were Pudgy and Mr. Dodger were halfway to New York or Jersey by now. When the State Police realized the car or the plates or both were hot, and they would, the case would go cold. Made me wonder if these Rancor folks had taken enough into consideration thinking this whole elected sheriff with no additional cops all the way through. A dead body, felony vandalism, an assault and a robbery, all in the day and a half since I'd gotten here. So much for a crime-free town. Shine a light on something good, the story went, and it wilted. The media would eat this up once they heard about it.

"So someone from the pharmacy already called this in?" I asked her. There was only so much the state cops could do with an incident like this. Within the law.

"Yes," she said, "it's been called in. And the pictures are out there. Someone's tracking down our sheriff."

The ambulance arrived. The EMT techs wheeled a gurney into the pharmacy. I watched the pistol-whipped pharmacist come out, still unconscious, her face bandaged, then I waited longer on the sheriff, chatting Ursula up. I soon ran out of patience. Aside from giving a statement, there was nothing else I could do here. At least the EMTs were quick.

I handed Ursula a business card, told her she could use my name and have their sheriff call me for descriptions and a statement whenever he got around to it.

20

Andy, in his nurse whites, filled in for a flu-stricken nurse who couldn't finish her shift. He tended to patients in the psych ward's large recreation room.

"Nurse Ratched, help me," a patient pleaded. "It's not working."

A nickname. Louise Fletcher played the iconic SOB nurse in *One Flew Over the Cuckoo's Nest*; she won an Oscar. Coworkers referred to Andy this way in front of the guests, where it was expected to, and did, go viral internal to the hospital. Not a harmless joke; a well-intentioned slur. He ignored the patient's parroting, accepting it as part of the facility's monkey-see, monkey-do atmosphere.

The hospital/detox center had two hundred and forty beds, but over the last two decades its occupancy had dropped by more than 50 percent. Patient care was not the reason; not one malpractice suit had been filed in over twenty years. No, it was because the hospital was still recovering from a 1990s scandal involving its chief administrator, Andy's wife at the time, Dr. Jasmine Prudhomme. Andy had been the whistleblower.

"Mr. Shils. Mr. Shils, please, you need to give that to me, sir." Andy opened his hand, wiggled his fingers, awaited the patient's acknowledgment. "It's not a cosmic plutonium electro blaster. It's a plunger. You remember what a plunger does, right?"

The slur was perpetuated by those still on staff who were sympathetic to his deceased ex, the hospital's former CEO. Only a few legacy staffers remained at the facility post–Dr. Prudhomme, but even one hateful person was all it took to make Andy's nursing life difficult.

"Yes, Nurse Ratched," Mr. Shils said. "I mean no, Nurse Ratched. Sorry, Nurse Ratched. Here, Nurse Ratched, take it, but be careful..."

In late 1993, Andy brought his wife, Jasmine, up on charges of sexual misconduct with hospital patients. He had witnessed it himself on more than one occasion—unruly teenagers given a large dose of meds who Jasmine then seduced during their evaluations—so Andy blew the whistle. The charges filed were, unfortunately, deemed too much he-said, she-said, and with no one else corroborating the offense, the Scranton DA decided not to indict.

"Ratched." Jasmine's name for Andy behind his back prior to the incident, their marriage already in the shitter. After the allegations she'd say it to his face, often in front of the hospital staff. When the charges against his wife were dropped, Andy was fired from his nursing position for insubordination, a trumped-up offense, and blackballed at other local hospitals. His wife sued him for divorce. The proceedings turned into an assault on his integrity and that of his family. His surgeon mother had been vocal in her support; it nearly cost Charlie her career. But the vendetta caused a greater heartbreak: it took Aunt Kitty's life. On an alcoholic bender, and in desperation one wicked-weather night, Kitty had requested asylum from her alcoholism at the inpatient's detox unit and was turned away.

"Thank you, Mr. Shils," Andy said, accepting the "weapon." "You should be outside on the lawn, a nice day like this. How about it, bud?"

Andy swung open a pair of French doors and escorted Mr. Shils onto a patio. The patient found his way across the light swale of the lawn to a semicircle of Adirondack chairs and dropped himself into one, next to another male patient. Andy lingered on the patio, absorbing the lawn's expanse, its perimeter enclosed by a tall chain-link fence with barbed wire that glistened in the summer sunlight. To his right, on the other side of the fence and open to the public, a park bench glowered at seventy yards. The bench, as always, was a visual magnet for Andy from this vantage point, much as he wished he could ignore it. It was where a hospital orderly found a reclining Aunt Kitty three days after a blinding blizzard and ice storm, frozen to death, a human ice-and-snow sculpture. The Scranton Fire Department had to use spray deicer, hair dryers, and a pry bar to separate her body from the bench's wooden slats.

Andy's vindictive wife, Jasmine. While on her rounds that night, the admissions desk had alerted her that a Kitty Buchinsky, drunk and depressed, was requesting emergency admittance to the detox unit. His wife made a point of coming to the front desk to deliver her smug response personally, Andy had learned: "All our beds are full. Go somewhere else." It had been a lie.

Kitty Buchinsky, dead at sixty-six. No viewing; a closed casket. At the service, Andy spoke a few words to the grievers, shared cheerful anecdotes about his warm, colorful, one-of-a-kind aunt. At graveside, Andy delivered a resolute, fatalistic message to the deceased: *I changed my mind. I'm in.*

Late that same year Andy's ex-wife relocated to Philly's main line to become CEO of a Philly hospital. On an early evening jog on Kelly Drive, someone murdered her. Shot her twice in the face, no sexual assault, also no witnesses. Philly law enforcement came after the ex-husband, hard. Andy's alibi, with multiple witnesses, held. One Rancor police chief, one bowling alley bartender, three Rancor town watch folks, one daughter, all in agreement: "He was bowling." The homicide remained unsolved.

Internal to Rancor, Jasmine Prudhomme's murderer had a name, explained away with a flat mention and a shoulder shrug: had to be Aunt Kitty, the town's guardian angel, right as rain, common as coal.

Andy's shift ended; he intended to grab a fast food lunch before going home. He put on a sweater, picked up a Red Bull from a cart in the lobby, and headed out the hospital entrance. Cool, comfortable summer air, a crisp breeze with a trace of Pocono pine. He arrived at the bench where Kitty had frozen to death nearly two decades earlier and sat, communing with her, as best he could. Calming moments for him, always.

Andy wasn't "all healed," like he'd told his mother this morning. On the inside this would never be the case. And since his divorce and the difficult years before it, there'd never been anyone close. Sure, there were a few relationships afterward, some physical. Hospital acquaintances, professionals from nearby boroughs, even an affair with a married woman. Hookups he broke off before they could turn serious and complicate things, for him or for them.

The baggage—it would always be the baggage; the rumors. Their gravity guaranteed that, inside, he would always be alone. Alone in spirit, alone in his heart. Physical intimacy, he'd had. Enduring, soul-bearing emotional company would remain forever elusive. His role—his secret, violent deeds—kept his core emotions private, unapproachable. A love-hate relationship that had become a heavy burden. At times they were gratifying, even exhilarating. Other times they were overwhelming, the violence more than his conscience had been able to accept.

For the longest time his only confidante had been his mother, the secret easy to manage, Rancor being a sleepy little burg that rarely hurt itself. But when a street thug in Scranton widowed Dody Frink, Andy went to Dody and spilled. Dody became a plus-one, to the secret and the avocation both. After that, their clandestine congregation grew.

The one bit of fallout he hadn't anticipated: the loss of his adult daughter. Not to death, but to the outside world. Fourteen years ago when Teddy, short for Theodora, turned eighteen, she came to her father.

"I want to enter law enforcement, Dad. I want to become FBI."

Not a stretch, and not a complete surprise, Andy initially thought, all things considered. But there would be... complications. Family history. Aunt Kitty. His ex-wife's murder. "We'll make it work, honey," Andy told her.

But they couldn't make it work. His daughter left Rancor and never looked back.

Painful. Estrangement from her, and his daughter's estrangement from Rancor. His daughter's choice. Regardless, Andy suffered under its weight.

Yesterday, nearby to Rancor, someone committed a horrendous sexual assault and murder. Hearing about its victim, a young girl, had resonated. The monster remained unidentified, walking free among Scranton's population, or among some other town's population.

"I miss your pep talks, Aunt Kitty," he said aloud from Aunt Kitty's bench.

Had Kitty responded, it would have been to tell him to saddle up, doll, because the shit-storm created by the *People* article had arrived. She'd also have words for whoever killed the little girl in Scranton:

Come to Rancor. I beg you. A tacit goad, not an invitation to tea. Kitty was every bit his coal-miner father's sister, worthy of the hero worship, the memory, the legend.

Andy's phone rang. There'd been a robbery and an assault at a local pharmacy.

Lunch would have to wait.

21

Randall dropped sixty-five bucks and his room key on the motel lobby counter. "Where can I get a good steak?"

The stubble-faced motel clerk with a drinker's nose winced at the question, severely hung over. He slurped from his blue-and-gold Greek motif cardboard coffee cup and answered Randall like a tortured prisoner in exile.

"New York." *York* sounded like *tawk*, *squawk*, and *cawfee*. If Randall had asked about good pizza, cheesecake, bagels, or blow jobs, the answer would have been the same.

"Anywhere closer?" Randall managed, adding a play-along smile, except now he had a strong urge to crush this alcoholic's head with the large steel Bunn commercial "cawfee" maker at the end of the counter.

Another sip of coffee, another pained response from the clerk. "Karl Von Kugen's, downtown Scranton, is decent. It has family ties to Peter Kugen's steakhouse in Brooklyn."

Randall smiled and nodded his head in touristy agreement. "Really? *The* Peter Kugen Steakhouse? In Brooklyn, New York?"

"That's the one."

"Wow," Randall said, humoring this pretentious fuck, then his expression turned serious. "Never heard of it."

* * *

Randall parked on the street in metered parking, across from Karl Von Kugen's steakhouse.

Inside the vestibule were a short line and a slender table with menus, wine lists, and dinner mints for on the way out, plus one oddity: a yellow coal miner's helmet with its safety lamp, scuffed and bruised from real-world use, and not fitting in with the vestibule décor. Affixed to the wall above it, an oversize card written in elegant calligraphy explained its affiliation with a charity. Randall stuffed a ten-dollar bill into a large slot in the helmet, making a display of it for the hostess's benefit.

He was woefully underdressed in cargo shorts, sandals, and an untucked, white short-sleeved shirt with a flyaway collar. The hostess sat him at a table with a view of the street. Businessmen and women on all sides drank and ate their power-lunches. He received a few glances from them on and off, no worse than what a clueless uncle got when he wore stripes and plaids together at a family picnic.

The parking space in front of Randall's Buick emptied, was filled quickly by a red, custom-painted Honda Civic with a flaming orange-red rear spoiler. Two men exited the Civic. One dropped coins into the meter, the other opened the car trunk then tinkered with the rear license plate. They jaywalked across the one-way street when traffic cleared. When they entered the restaurant, they got a few stares from the patrons and servers and some additional buzz when they were seated next to Randall. One of these homeboys was Latino, Randall surmised, the other white, the latter with a gauze pad covering his ear to handle what looked like a piercing gone bad. Both ghetto wannabes appeared giddy-nervous. Not a scared, we're-out-of-place nervousness. More like a we're-wired-and-so-fucked-up-we-can't-sit-still kind of nervous.

They were holding, Randall figured, and whatever it was they were holding, he wanted some. When he finished his meal, he'd look to connect.

His steak arrived along with separate dishes of garlic mashed potatoes and creamed spinach. His server spooned each of the sides onto his entrée plate, but she was a little off her game, distracted by the bling on the boys next to him. Her wrist was decorated with artwork that for sure ran up her arm, her long-sleeved waiter's smock covering it, with more of it visible on the nape of her neck. Her phone rang, startling her. She fumbled for it before turning it off. One creamed spinach spoonful dropped dead center onto his beautifully presented, juicy, sixty-two-dollar, fourteen-ounce filet. She apologized.

"So sorry, sir. Would you like me to take it back?"

The bartender witnessed the infraction, was all over her like a plantation overseer. "Phones *off*, Audrey!" he barked. "And you know better than to ask. Just put in another order."

The bartending prick was here as much to rat on the servers as he was to mix drinks, Randall decided. "All goes to the same place, right, miss?" Randall said, smiling at her. "I'm fine with this one. Thanks."

Audrey the server smiled her gratitude then glided by the bartender, but not without saying something under her breath to him. He stared daggers at her back as she hustled to the rear of the restaurant. In a dark corner Randall watched her key in a text then exhale a deep breath. She put the phone away and entered the kitchen.

The medium-well filet sliced like butter, didn't have a speck of fat, and was better than any steak he'd had in recent memory. Audrey the server returned to take beverage orders from the two ghetto boys. Randall witnessed her make a production of carding them.

"Jersey City," she said, reading from a driver's license, flirting some. What it was that attracted young women to small-time gangstas, Randall had never been able to figure.

"You're—let me guess, don't tell me—Scranton," the white one with the bandaged ear said, his response clever, or so his snicker to his buddy said. He leered at her neck tats.

Such repartee.

She filled their water glasses. "Nice try. I work in Scranton, but I live in Rancor."

"Rancor? Whoa," the Latino one said, his palms out. "Been there. Got some crazy old folks and female storm troopers and shit. Not going back. Make it two Yuenglings, babe. Bottles."

Their beers arrived. The server chatted them up on the merits of a porter on tap versus bottled as she poured for them, then hung around and flirted a little more. They sucked their beers down, ate their salads and some bread. Audrey brought two more beers. They drained them. It was then they both headed in the direction she'd thumbed them, which was the hallway that led to the men's room in the rear of the restaurant.

Randall waited for Audrey the server to return, him wanting to settle his bill asap, interested in making his acquaintance with the two young men in the men's room, but there she was, texting again in the rear of the restaurant. He raised his hand. "Miss, check please."

* * *

Outside the restaurant in the alley, costumed party-crashers huddled. Their initial decision had been to wait there until the pistol-whipping punk and his accomplice left the restaurant. Better to not make a scene in the Peter Kugen Steakhouse dining room. Then came the next text. The punks were in the restroom doing drugs *right now*.

Change of plans.

They entered the men's room, the three of them, in dark hoodies, sweatpants, and soft-soled shoes. One leaned against the swinging-door entry to the rest room to seal off the access, the other two advanced. Their targets were now bio-break busy in two of the stalls, punk number one sitting down, the second punk two stalls away, on his feet and peeing.

A gripe from the first stall, from the sitting punk: "Ugh. Fucking breakfast burrito."

One of the three new bathroom patrons stepped closer, leaned down close to the floor, confirmed that only two stalls were occupied.

The standing punk finished his business, started to zip up. "That's what you get when you order a burrito from a fuckin' Greek diner, you 'Rican dipshi—"

The door to the standing punk's stall swung open, pushing him forward into a stutter-step. He spun to face his attacker, was greeted by a large handgun with a suppressor, shoved against his forehead. The attacker pulled the trigger without hesitation, splatting his brains against the back wall of the stall. Two stalls away the seated punk fumbled for a handgun inside the pants around his ankles but didn't come up with it. He stood, his pants down, no gun, only to be pushed backward by someone kicking open the stall door.

"Dude. No. Wait—!"

He flailed at the attacker's hoodie, caught the zipper, which unfastened the hoodie partway. A raised handgun pushed into his forehead, the punk continuing to flail. The silenced headshot was a little off. Blood from the punk's scalp sprayed the white tile of the back wall and preceded by a beat the banger's upper torso slamming into it. Wedged into the corner behind the toilet, the punk was still alive. He gagged, blinked hard at the bleached white uniform top exposed by the unzipped hoodie.

"What the fuck! A nurse?"

The attacker again raised the handgun chest-high.

"Please, no," the punk begged. "Please..."

A moment's hesitation, the time it took a guilty conscience to second-guess a previously steel-nerved, depraved indifference. The weak moment ended. The next shot to his head finished it. The attacker zipped the hoodie back up and left.

* * *

Randall left his table ready to deal. He stopped short inside the hallway when the door to the men's room swung open. Three men emerged in hoodies with dark glasses, their faces covered in charcoal, or maybe soot, only one tall enough to be one of the two gangbanger wannabes, but none of them were. They hustled down the hallway and out the restaurant's rear exit.

Randall entered the restroom. Pills of all colors and sizes littered the tile floor and crunched underfoot inside the stall area. The bodies of the white one and his sidekick rested uncomfortably on blood-spattered cream tile inside the two stalls, one of the stall doors still swinging.

He'd heard nothing, no loud *pop-pop-pop* from a gun, no arguments, no struggle. A decent, properly horrified citizen would at this point have called 911. Randall, of course, was no such person. He helped himself to some pill bottles and left the restaurant through the same rear exit the gunmen used. He surveyed the back alley. No sign of the executioners.

Three gunmen. The thought stayed with him as he strode up the side street to his car out front of the restaurant. Black hoodies, sunglasses, and faces blackened by burnt cork, or camouflage makeup, or shoe polish. Or, considering the region, what could have passed for coal dust mixed with sweat, glistening like it would on miners at the end of their shift, if he wanted to get melodramatic about it. If he wanted to get more melodramatic about it, this was an ambush, the two homeboys fingered by someone inside the restaurant.

Wait. Not gun*men,* his subconscious told him. The hoodie sweatshirts they wore were bulky, but not bulky enough. Two of them had tits.

22

I was done with cruising the police station turned bingo hall. I needed some lunch. I pulled in line at an Arby's drive-thru. Still thinking about St. Possenti's.

Concrete blocks for walls, and iron bars fronting thick, murky-glass windows made it as attractive as a hillside WWII bunker. For fifteen minutes I'd watched as men and women entered and exited the hall, nearly all of them seniors. Five or so in, a different five or so out, their baggage in both directions the same: large, heavy purses, knapsacks, and hefty bingo supply bags. On the surface, it all looked legit. Still, seniors flocking to play bingo in so dismal and uninviting a space seemed... off. A Tourette's riff queued up.

"—flocking fuckers, saint possenti, placenta bingo. Gabriel gringo ringo bojangles, Gunny saint dot-com dot-mom got milk—

"—tits—"

Then again, who cared what went on in there. All consenting adults. I wasn't here for them. I was in Rancor to take a depraved fugitive bastard off the streets.

Tits and guns and guns and tits and gun-tits and bingo. My van moved another spot closer to the Arby's drive-thru window.

Occasionally I missed taking my meds. One-tenth of a milligram of clonidine, twice a day. Missing them was my subconscious telling me I shouldn't need them, that it wanted me to be normal, that my brain had no right misbehaving like it did. Maybe it also wanted me to test how long I could go without meds and not have an episode. Experience showed this to be the better part of a day. A missed-dose indicator: when my dogs and fuzzy keychain were with me but I still verbally wailed on someone I had no real interest in. Strangers, for example. On the street, me like a derelict, or at the mall, or at the local gun shop—hell yeah, twice; I was still able to buy the gun I wanted—or at fast food drive-thrus. I kept my meds handy the same way a heart patient did her nitro pills, in a thumb-size prescription bottle in my jeans pocket.

The word of the day, courtesy of my disease, was apparently "tits."

A moment ago I downed the med dose I should have taken this morning, but this wasn't until after I placed my lunch order then rendered some obscene declarations into the drive-thru squawk box. I now waited for the Arby's order taker to bring me my roast beef sandwich, curly fries, and an additional four or more side orders of tits. And during the episode I, of course, had told her why I wanted these tits, screaming my reasons at her.

"—tit-fuck, tit-suck, someone bite my nipples /

"—tub-o-tits wonder bits super chicks booger zits..."

I apologized on the heels of the order, the apology not as loud as the tirade itself, so the patrons inside the restaurant probably only got to hear the rant.

I arrived at the window. The manager was standing in for the teenager I'd screamed at. A robust woman, blonde, stone-faced. She waited me out, decided my apology was sincere, took my money, and handed me my lunch. I thanked her, apologized some more.

I pulled the van forward to a parking space, Tess my Bull Terrier deputy on the passenger seat, her nose sampling the air. She'd get a fry or two, as would Fungo in the back. Not good for them, but I could never help myself.

A tap on my driver's side window.

No shit. Andy. He had a bagged Arby's lunch in his hand.

"I was at the counter," he said. "You were a hit inside. Mind if I join you for lunch?"

* * *

The Arby's manager had worried more that someone on her young staff might have wanted to take me up on my rant. This was according to Andy, who acknowledged that restaurant patrons had soda-nose chuckle-fits when they'd heard it, and the counter help all wanted a peek at the crazy lady when she picked up her lunch at the drive-thru.

He grinned telling me this, added a great, husky laugh that pulled me into a laugh as well. I felt something for him, here, now. The laugh, his sense of humor, his acceptance—we were having a moment.

Calm down, sister.

I moved on to a different topic and shared this morning's pharmacy episode, mentioned the young woman whose purse was snatched. Also mentioned the woman's grandmother.

"Ursula, her granddaughter and great-grandson," Andy volunteered. "Don't look at me funny, Counsel. We're a small town. Word travels fast."

I went with that. "Ursula. Right. I give her credit. Whatever pictures she took, the sheriff must be happy with them. He hasn't bothered me yet. And I might have expected the State Police to want to have a talk with me. The car had Jersey plates."

"Less red tape for you the better, right?" Andy said.

"Yes. Red tape sucks."

His smile said he already knew this about me. "What you did today was appreciated, Counsel. Ursula was impressed, and she's one of the most cynical seniors in Rancor."

Great. I pulled a gun on someone, wanted desperately to separate him from his junk, and my dog took a chunk out of his buddy's ear, all because of a stolen purse. And yet I had managed to BS an old lady into thinking I was a good person. Purses and money vs. lives. Good to know I was still able to fool people, looking good and righteous on the outside, with some occasional good deeds to show for myself. But on the inside...

On the inside I was wired for mayhem. For most of my life, on the inside mayhem was all I'd ever felt.

Character. It was defined by deeds. *All* a person's deeds, especially the ones no one knew about. The ones that weren't flattering. I'd committed some of these. Some that were on the extremely violent side of not flattering.

Hell, sometimes I just needed to be gracious about accepting compliments, even ones that were off the mark. "Ursula seems like a nice lady. Maybe a bit misguided, but nice." I ate my last fry, thought aloud, volunteered I wasn't sure where to look next for my bounty.

"How about this," Andy said. "According to Dody, the dead man in the car they pulled out of the pothole owned a used car lot in Dickson City. I know his name."

He offered it up. *Excellent.* I would head there next, after I checked in with Vonetta. And after I did this, because of the smug smile he gave me knowing he'd done good. I reached for him, leaned in, and gently kissed him on the lips; he didn't resist. His eyes, when they opened, weren't filled with the wanton savagery I might have thought would be there, were instead filled with wonder and apprehension. I wasn't sure what he saw in mine but in truth, I soon realized, wanton savagery would have been a disappointment. In truth, the sincerity I felt was a bit more than I'd bargained for.

He picked up my hand and breathed a kiss onto my fingers. His eyes indicated the kiss was a placeholder. "I gotta go," he said by way of apology.

Tess poked into my Arby's lunch bag, munched a forgotten curly fry, and watched Andy exit the car, as did I, feeling a little better now.

* * *

I evaluated the stolen kiss, sorting it out while I drained my diet Coke in the Arby's parking lot. Some spark there, for me at least. An admission that yes, I partook, and yes, it was good. Except I didn't know if I could clear out enough of the hurt to make room for the good again.

Feeling maudlin now, self-indulgent, and fucked by fate.

I was twenty-eight, my future husband twenty-nine when we met. He was also a state trooper, also part of the K9 unit. Not much of a stretch to see why we might connect, me a hardcore state trooper and working-dogs handler assigned to peripheral protection for a US vice presidential visit, him assigned to the same detail. Al Gore, President Clinton's VP, was at a chain pharmacy in South Philly to stump for the federal government's new healthcare plan, early April 1994. I liked Al Gore. He served in Nam when he could have gotten a fancy deferment because his old man had been a US senator. Except this wasn't about Al Gore or me. It was about my future husband, Mitch Fungo.

Word ricocheted around the two K9 details during our separate pre-arrival briefings: canines Lucy and Desi were on the job. My new partner was a black Lab named Lucy, and Mitch's veteran partner was a Belgian Malinois named Desi. Cute coincidence. The twain, our respective supervisors decided, should meet.

The detail disbanded soon after the VP visit ended. We, as in the four of us, posed for pictures in our gear. After a few snapshots, my matchmaking photo historian had us close ranks to just the two of us, the dogs off camera. Our leashed partners, however, had a different idea. They snuck into the photo frame in the back. Desi mounted Lucy like a razorback auditioning for king boar. My photographer captured some enthusiastic doggie porn in rapid-fire shutter clicks, managed to stay straight-faced while he posed us, directing our eyes forward, our partners quietly humping in the background until their quiet became raucous, with Lucy taking a chunk out of Desi's ear. Frustration on Lucy's part, I posited to Mitch after we separated them. Au contraire, Mitch countered, the photos clearly showed Lucy's pent-up passion. We agreed to disagree for more than a year, over coffee, dinner, long phone calls, a holiday spent together, and one Caribbean vacation where Mitch popped the question.

I tearfully accepted. He tearfully volunteered that the passion he'd seen in Lucy's eyes that day had been a prospective projection of his own. Love and mutual lust at first sight. It begot a state trooper wedding, with all four of us in uniform.

The start of a wonderful life together.

Mitch was no slouch in the physical attributes department. Six-one, a buff one-ninety-five. A tough guy who worked his K9 partner hard, and who was also tough enough to housebreak me. When Desi was euthanized, he held his face in his hands and made sure his smile, his love, was the last thing his partner would experience in this life. When I got down on myself, he became my angel of mercy, my confessor, my strongest cheerleader. The warmest, most adjusted, most accepting human being I had ever known. Over time, I convinced myself I didn't deserve him, and that's what ruined our marriage. Mental cruelty on my part, pushing him and his compassion away. It was also his compassion that took him away, forever. Compassion for a sibling, his older, mentally unstable brother.

I don't blame his brother; I never could. Schizophrenia takes no prisoners. A teenage diagnosis for him, kept in check as an adult but with lapses, same as my Tourette's.

Their lives ended with a panicky, sky-is-falling distress call, one of many from Mitch's brother to him on Mitch's day off. Flash-forward to Mitch, at his brother's apartment, seeing his brother's self-inflicted stomach knife wounds. Mitch's high-speed rush with him to the hospital. His flashing rooftop magnetic police light and siren to clear their way. Their instant obliteration in a crash-and-burn broadside by a semi as they raced through an intersection.

Two charred bodies, both in closed caskets. If I blamed Mitch's sick brother, I would need to blame my sick self. On the one hand, nobody at fault. On the other, at fault, me. Or Fate. Or God, for creating less than perfect people. I didn't know; I just didn't fucking know.

Fuck you, Fate, you dream-crushing motherfucker. You left me for dead when you took away the only person I'd ever had to share my dreams with.

The van door opened. Andy climbed back into the passenger seat, pulled the door shut.

"I suddenly realized," he said, "that the other place I needed to be could wait."

* * *

There were five guest rooms in the Willow Swamp Farm B&B.

"Let's go to your place," Andy said with mischief in his voice, "to start."

It was the middle of the afternoon. The stairs creaked as we ascended them. Rooms three, four, and my room, five, the Maurice Prudhomme, were on the second floor.

The door latched shut behind us. Just inside, he cupped my face in his hands, admired it and the dash of a beauty mark that I had just below my cheek. I cradled the nape of his neck, guided him closer for a read inside those dark, exotic eyes. He leaned in, blinked softly for a beat, the hesitation, I felt, for assurances, his and mine both. A soft kiss, our lips barely touching, then it was a passionate, moist kiss with our eyes open then closed then open again as we drank each other in. A momentary pause. He reached for the scrapbook on the white antique bureau next to us, connected with it, and snapped it shut.

"My dad doesn't need to see this," he said.

I pulled him into me for a full-body embrace, my back against the door, our toned forms each with parts supple and spongy and firm and full, mixed with cherry blossom and musk and scented lavender, each of us offering the other beckoning and cooing reassurances. He helped me lose my camouflage tee and unbuttoned my jeans then waited until I found space on the bureau for my holstered Glock.

"*—my flustered smock*

"*—a crowded jock—*"

Oh no—nonono, I needed to choke it all back, not say any more—

"*—rhymes with, sounds like...*

"*—rock-sock-block-knock...*"

I held the waist of my jeans, didn't let them fall, desperate for the attached keychain, my teeth clenched, gritted, worried my mouth would betray more of me.

"It's okay, Counsel, it's okay," he said, his breath warm in my ear. He covered my hand with his. "If ever there were a time for you to talk dirty..."

It was never a good time to hear my head rattles verbalized, but my mind did calm, Andy's touch keeping me from giving in to the crazy. We let my jeans drop. I helped him lose his nurse's uniform, and we helped ourselves to each other's writhing, dampened passion and tenderness and apprehension and trust, the sensitivity all so breathtakingly good for this bruised and battered and verbally nonsensical ex-cop. A wondrous relief, for the remainder of this afternoon and hopefully longer, if it still seemed right. Also my hope that this heaving, giving creature in my arms was seeing and feeling this the same way.

In bed, with the tender tempest ended, Andy whispered to me. "Three o'clock tea on the porch." His lovely head of brown-gray hair was on my chest. A frilly bed pillow cradled my dark pixie cut, the two of us settled into a much-needed time out. "But my other guests, sad to say, will have to miss their host this afternoon. Unless they catch a glimpse of him in the upstairs hall, moving from room to room with a woman in a camo shirt and panties." He unwound from my embrace, climbed out from under the covers, and stepped into his nurse uniform pants. He extended his hand.

"Care to join me in the next guest room, Miss Fungo?"

* * *

Room four, the Aunt Kitty, was also now in need of a second housekeeping visit today. We relaxed in steamy tub water. The empty Theodora and the Loretta Lynn B&B rooms—had this been Andy at eighteen they might have been a consideration—at his current age, he fessed up, were safe.

I leaned into Andy's lazy embrace, the two of us fitting nicely into the slipper tub's contour, my head against his shoulder. Our legs were entwined, the bubbled bathwater luxurious. His eyes were half-lid sexy.

"About my scars," he said.

"About your scars," I said.

The physical wounds from the childhood trauma that took his father were small purple craters on his dark shoulder, indents that pressed against his collarbone. He intertwined his fingers with mine, lifted my hand and placed it there, had me touch the wounded areas with my fingertips. I did this gently, for fear they somehow still hurt.

"Only on the inside," he said, reading my mind.

We lay there in silence, watching the bubbles dissolve, a comfort, an oasis to each other, whatever troubling times percolating on the outside be damned.

"Why are you here, Counsel?" he asked, breaking the mood.

"In this tub? Because you seduced me," I said, going for cute. "There I was, minding my own business ordering up some female body parts with my fast food lunch, and you showed up as part of my takeout, no extra charge. An incredible vision in your nurse tighty-whities—"

"Seriously, hot stuff, if you find your bounty, what do you get? Is the amount worth the danger?"

I gauged the question. It wasn't gold digging. He was interested in understanding if there was any emotion attached to this business for me.

I went for cocky. "*When,* not *if,* I find and deliver him, Vonetta my bondsman will part with a thousand bucks in bounty money, and maybe pony up a nice dinner out with me and her family in celebration. A king's ransom, the payout is not." I swallowed, surprised at myself by the nerve the question hit. "The money means little when it comes to a sexual predator who's into kids."

"I see," he said, and I believed he did.

Downshifting to a lower emotional gear, the names of three of the B&B rooms, the Charlotte, the Loretta Lynn and the Maurice Prudhomme, I said I understood. I asked about the Aunt Kitty and the Theodora.

"My Aunt Kitty was a little wild," Andy said. "A principled free-thinker who took my mother and me under her wing. She married later in life, and often." A pleasant sigh revealed these memories were precious to him. "Buried a few husbands, drank too much, and stayed wild into her sixties. We lost her soon after her sixty-sixth birthday."

His cheeks flushed; he was missing his aunt right now. I squeezed his shoulder.

"Mom and I owe much of our closure over Dad's death to Kitty. She was a force, was there for us, larger than life in so many ways. It's only fitting she have a room here in tribute."

"And the other room?"

"The Theodora is named after my adult daughter. She... I..." Andy caught himself. "Teddy and I are on different pages."

"Is she an only child?"

"Yes. I married young, was divorced young. Teddy and I were the only good things to survive the marriage."

Andy's daughter was gone, something he was less than thrilled about, and a second tragic story about an estranged family member. Because I'm in the people-tracking business, I asked, "If there's anything I can do—"

"Nothing. My daughter's alive and well, and I know where she is. My ex isn't. A victim of an unsolved murder in Philly. Nursing career wise, I'm picking up the pieces. Father-daughter-wise, Teddy is living her life now and it doesn't include me. I keep the room for her in case she ever wants to come back. Thanks for the offer, but no thanks."

"How about your ex? I can look into her homicide—"

"Counsel, please, no. My ex is where she should be. If she were still alive, and if you knew her, had she skipped town after her charging, she's a bounty you would have taken down for free."

23

"Fill it up," Randall told the kid tending the gas pump.

Randall was feeling well fed. The meal cost him almost a hundred bucks, but the Karl Von Kugen filet had been worth it, misplaced creamed spinach notwithstanding. Plus he got to see the aftermath of an execution, coal-region style. Impressive. Similar to a mob hit in precision, but more like a gang hit considering the victims. Except for the hit men, two of them women. It sounded off, "women hit men," these words together. Mob hits were all too frequently about hormones, except estrogen wasn't typically one of them. "Good stuff," he said to himself, an admission that he was having a blast.

He waited patiently for the pump to finish. The kid handling the gas jockey duties here at Jim's Rancor Gas 'n' Go reappeared in his rearview mirror. Short and chubby and in a tan uniform, he was a Boy Scout or a junior park ranger or some such shit, which made him extra cute, Randall decided. Sixteen at most, and he was by himself. Stores in quiet towns off the beaten path like this got away with teenagers managing them. The kid be-bopped his fat head to music Randall couldn't hear, topped off the tank, and showed up next to the Buick window in the throes of a one-handed text messaging frenzy, waiting to be paid.

Randall felt the need. It might have been death-wish stupid on his part, but he didn't give a shit, considering.

He held the two twenties chest-high inside the window, there for the distracted kid to retrieve. With the twenties out of the way, young Johnny-Boy here got a full view of Randall's open-trousered lap and enormous, liberated hard-on. To Randall it was humorous and thrilling, and on impulse it ended abruptly with a hand around the kid's chunky neck and one heavy-handed knockout punch to the kid's face. With some effort Randall dragged his unconscious body into the passenger's seat and tossed the kid's phone back out. Time to find another cheap motel.

24

A clatter of crashing bowling pins in the background.

"Dody!" Andy called into the phone, too loud, a reflex because of the noise on the other end. He took his voice down a notch. "Dody. Hey." The pin noise helped steer the call. Andy went for cavalier and upbeat. "Practice games? Really?"

Andy was on his B&B landline and doing busywork at his secretary desk, trying hard not to think about earlier today at the Scranton steakhouse, dwelling instead on his time with Counsel. On his mind in a distant third place was his team vs. Dody's for the summer mixed senior bowling championship tonight.

"Yeah, well, rumor has it," said Dody, "that tonight's opponents are pretty goddamn good, and they're gunning for us."

Poor choice of words on Dody's part, they both realized.

"Let me try that again," she said. "My sixteen-year-old nephew's pumping gas until late. Which means he left his babysitting aunt home to eat by herself. I decided on a few warm-up games and dinner at the alley instead." More bowling pin racket blasted Andy's ear. Dody continued. "You have your way of releasing tension, and I have mine."

"Meaning?"

"You didn't answer your cell earlier, so I called the B&B. Your housekeeper blabbed. Good for you, Andy. Not too shabby a lay."

There were very few secrets in this town, Andy reminded himself. But was that all it was, a tension release? A lay? He asked, "And you called me why again?"

"Our sortie into Scranton today. Penny said you seemed... less than excited once we got there. Like you should have been guarding the door instead of, you know, what you and I did."

The sortie had been Dody's idea. So much of all this was her idea lately. Her show.

"It's been a while, Dody. You did this for a living. The rest of us are still making it up as we go along."

"All for the best of causes, my dear, I might remind you."

Andy wasn't in the mood to hear the end justified the means speech today, especially when he wasn't the one delivering it. He could still see the punk's terrified face before his handgun tore half of it off.

"Andy? Still there?"

In their car, speeding away down a back alley after the hit, the contented, quiet happy places Dody and Penny had retreated to were much different than where Andy's mind had gone. His place was for sure quiet, but there was no happy, and no contentment.

Their retribution: Did it fit the crime?

"Andy? Hello?"

One of the two thugs had pistol-whipped the female pharmacist, a senior. This put her in a coma with significant head injuries and possible brain damage. Yes, the retribution did fit the crime. Why the remorse then?

Because the punk had begged him.

The sexual release with Counsel, the instant gratification... it was out of character for him. Maybe a mistake. A weak cry for intimacy, to be held, soothed by someone, after so unsettling an act today.

Initially, this was true. The attraction was there. Their kiss at the Arby's was soft, gentle, wonderful, and after the surprise of it, he selfishly dived in. He knew how to love a woman, physically, yes, but there needed to be more. Could he be an all-in kind of guy again, able to go deep inside himself, turn himself inside out emotionally for a partner, and do it long-term? Could she? Because that's what he needed. He needed help canceling out all this outstanding immoral debt and restore the capital he'd continued to plunder from morality's coffers, or at least figure out a way to help him live the rest of his life in its wake.

Which brought up his own mortality. He wasn't getting any younger. Would he live the next fifteen years like he'd lived the past—lonely? He didn't want to die alone. And what about Counsel's needs? One thing he knew for sure her needs wouldn't include: the world of hurt she'd be in if she were attached to this violent avocation. If discovered, its repercussions would be life changing for her as well as him, if she were anywhere around him.

He already had feelings for her. But for her sake, he'd need to walk away.

The screen door to the B&B opened revealing Dody, still talking to him into her phone, being silly, the bowling alley that close by. "What, I talk, you ignore me?" Andy heard her say in stereo, in his ear and in person. "Besides, hugs are better in person. You need a hug, baby?"

They hugged, and Dody took the edge off the embrace by fessing up that she just bowled a 224. But she did have a serious pitch for her close friend.

"Sit the next one out, Andy. Might be tomorrow, might not be for another five years, but you need some distance. You're burned out. Someone else will handle it."

Andy's extemporized version of the Aunt Kitty retribution model, where one person wasn't a lone wolf, included clandestine, selective recruitment and multiple participants, all plug-and-play prepared. But there was still this: no matter the spin, they were killing people. It left a mark, on both sides of the gun.

Dody. A good friend. Sincere, but also a pragmatist. Indecision at a moment of truth like what almost happened with him today could have made a big difference in who got killed. Andy decided yes, he'd take that rest, so he wouldn't be a liability to them the next time something like this needed to be done.

Dody left, to head back to the bowling alley for the food she'd ordered from the grill. Andy declined eating with her. He'd eat with Counsel, so he could make things right.

25

I opted for trading in the van and my puppy dogs for my Suzuki bike and a backpack. If I were a murdering sexual predator scumbag who stole cars, stuffed bodies into their trunks and drove them into ice-age potholes, where would I be now? I had no other particular leads, which was why I was following Andy's suggestion to check out the small used car dealership of one "Nap" Napoli, recently deceased.

My time with Andy today had been a surprise. Daring and ballsy on his part. On my part, it had the freshness and intensity of a schoolgirl crush on the hot high school boy, the one you knew you never had a chance with. Except I had gotten the chance, and it was glorious and memorable. Forget the sex, although I wouldn't. What made it a keeper was our shared afterglow. The communion. The intimacy.

Hadn't used that term in a while: *keeper.* That moment. Him. It. Both.

I parked my bike outside the auto dealer's office. At one time it was a Dairy Queen, a massive soft serve ice cream cone still taking up most of the flat, slanted roof. On the other side of the small building sat a parked Crown Vic cruiser in your basic black. The feds were here, talking with what looked like the dealership's grease monkey. Young guy. Probably the only grease monkey, considering the size of Nap's operation. I texted with Vonetta while waiting for the feds to finish with the mechanic.

Chevy with the body in the trunk is history netta. Bounty still out there

Where to next sarge?

Dead guy dealership. There now. Feds are here too

I decided to share. Not that Vonetta needed to hear any of it, but I was feeling good at the moment.

I met someone

Course you did counsel. You always do

Not what you think netta. Different

Then carry on, trooper. At ease and carry on, my friend ☺

I trailed the mechanic into the shop's only repair bay and introduced myself. The kid was distraught but receptive.

"Nap gave me my first job right out of tech school two years ago," Zach said, his name stitched above his pocket. "I do everything mechanical here, plus body work. I'm his only employee. Or was."

Zach's face twisted, his upper lip curling. He was still in shock. "Nap was like a father to me, ma'am. I lost my dad when I was ten..."

I listened, but I needed to stay away from the father doldrums angle, something I couldn't stomach.

I mourned the father I never had. I loathed the father I did.

When he took a breath I showed him a picture of Mr. Linkletter. No recognition on his part. I asked a follow-up. "Any cars sold yesterday? Or stolen, or missing?"

He took me inside to Nap's desk, showed me a picture of a white Buick Electra sedan, then pointed out the front and center empty space where it had been on the lot.

Same white car that was "out of gas" on Rancor Road last night, damn it.

A major fail on my part here, but not a total loss. I was surer now that Mr. Linkletter's scent was on both plastic bottles of water.

Confirmed, here and now, for me and apparently the feds both: Mr. Linkletter saw the Electra on the lot, acquired it, and ditched the Chevy. But why an old Buick? Another text to Vonetta.

Answer: *Must be partial to them sarge. He left one just like it behind in Mrs. Spezak's driveway in Allentown*

Mr. Linkletter wasn't doing much to hide himself. Not typical of a child molester. This bothered me.

* * *

I sent some good karma Zach's way as I pulled away from Nap's car lot. He'd lost his father, had found a surrogate in Nap, would grieve a second time in his young life for the similar loss. He wasn't in a good place at the moment, and yet, narcissist that I was, I was envious, because what Zach had had twice, I hadn't had once.

I was back on the bike cruising Rancor Boulevard, smoothing out the corners, stretching the curves, glad for the preoccupation they provided. The straightaways, I wasn't so glad about. Thinking pleasant thoughts, like about my time with Andy today, but the longer the stretch, the more my mind wandered. Not enough distractions; no defense from the childhood memories.

My father's lack of compassion. His shame about Judge, my older brother, and eventually me. His crooked politics. His grandiosity. His temper.

Contemplating all of this was whipping me into a frenzy, making me seethe.

His infidelities. His dirty secrets. Uncle Ernest's sexual abuse of Judge. My PTSD from witnessing it at a young age.

All of this, my private hell.

The media knew nothing about my uncle or his despicable habits until my father was no longer a politician. They learned what Uncle Ernest did to other kids when the authorities found him lying in a pile of blood-spattered child porn in his bedroom, his throat ripped out from an animal attack. His nasty Doberman had turned on him, the authorities decided.

Looked legit, I said when the local cops interviewed me and my brother, both K9 handlers, and them looking for an expert. That had to be what had happened. *Sure.*

My brother's working dog partner at the time, Rufus, was also a Doberman.

Payback could be a bitch.

No compromising pictures of my brother in Ernest's pile of child porn, or in his computer. My mom, brother, and I made sure of it. And no remorse from any of us. Dad, complicit by his silence and savaged by the media for it, eventually committed suicide.

I slowed the bike down as I neared the entrance to the celebrated pothole, back here for a second look, this time in the daylight. The two tall, black entrance gates abutted and were padlocked. The park was closed to tourists today. Emergency maintenance, the sign said, understating the truth. I got off my bike, left it on the shoulder near the entrance, strapped on my backpack, and hoofed it the rest of the way. A lot less freaky in midafternoon than it had been in the dark last night, where one misstep could have turned into a 150-foot drop and some serious hurt. In the daylight the park came across as a living, breathing wonderland with a picnicky, fresh, early-summer feel. Pavilions, barbecue pits, hiking trails. A tall forest that surrounded acres of green grass and ball fields. The park's geologically correct name was lame. "Glacier Pothole State Park" highlighted the park's main attraction, but it ignored everything else about it. And at the moment, a quarter mile of yellow crime scene tape conspicuously decorated it.

A four-by-four SUV, the lettering *SHERIFF* painted across its door panels, centered the space in front of the chain-link fence that had been cut away, protecting where a few skeletal pipe rails had been uprooted. The fencing had been wired back together, something far from permanent. The vehicle had one occupant, in there with the windows up, the engine running. If he was here on watch he was doing a shit job of it, too interested in his phone. I startled him when I tapped on the window. The door opened; I gave him room. He stepped out, all aristocratic, an older dude who filled out his khaki uni really well. A former cop or cop wannabe; a bruiser. No gun.

We faced each other, his nose and cheeks with cavernous pores, him a hundred pounds bigger, five inches taller or more. He looked me up and down, then looked past me to see no vehicle in my wake. "Park's closed, miss," he said, showing eye contact with attitude. "You're trespassing. Turn around and leave the way you came, right now."

It was so close to the pothole here, a nicer cop might have added, "Have a nice day and be sure to watch your step." He instead stayed with his gonna-fuck-you-up death stare. I raised my hands palms-up to signal I came in peace, gave him my name and my occupation, then pleaded my case.

"I was first on the scene here last night. Trevor the Park Ranger Cadet, or I should say his aunt Dody, can vouch for me." I offered my hand. He eyed it, left me hanging bad as if he'd just seen me pick my nose with it.

"You're the broad who went after the two gangster types at the pharmacy. You stiffed me. I came by looking for a statement about them, had to get the skinny from Ursula instead. Stay put."

He went for his phone and walked off some distance between us. A few grunts later, his face still hard as a hand grenade, the call ended. He wandered back. "You check out. Al Pemberton." We shook hands. "I'll suffix that with 'the law in these parts,' but I'm thinking you know that now. Dody says hi. You're free to look around. Anything I can help you with?"

I told him no. I wasn't up for explaining myself at the moment.

"Suit yourself." Then, over his shoulder on his way back to the SUV: "I got stuff to do in the truck. Watch your ass, Miss Fungo. First wrong step's a bitch. Don't ruin my day."

A C-minus for customer service, but we were good for now, him and me. I dropped my backpack, retrieved my binoculars and stayed outside the yellow tape while I circled the pothole looking for anything else Mr. Linkletter might have left behind. The perimeter was spotless, with grass, dirt and gravel all mixed underfoot and absent any litter, and odorless go-green compacting trash receptacles instead of bee-rimmed trash barrels that smelled like landfill. I checked out the glacial hole from all angles, occasionally leaned over the crime scene tape for a better look, the sunlight sparkling off shiny flecks strafing the rock strata like tiny stars. Some TS whispering crept over me.

"—sunlight sparkles sinful sinkholes shitty heinies shiny pecs, the schwartz be with you, strafing stogies starry starry night you bite the big one, wrong step is death—"

Halfway around the hole I trained the binoculars on Al's SUV. He was napping.

Something glinted just below the section of the pothole his SUV protected. It was metallic but more substantial than the flecks in the rock strata. I trekked back over there for a closer look.

Al's head was on his shoulder, his eyes closed, his mouth open and drooling like a liquid-center chocolate cherry. I found a cut in the fencing then stepped between his SUV and the pothole rim and leaned over it. I now made out what glittered there: coins, on a narrow ledge not too far from the top. More glances around the rest of the pothole and it finally sunk in: coins were everywhere. This looked like the largest wishing well in the world.

Except the coins on the ledge below me didn't look like real money, like the others did. Too big and too brassy, probably with some aluminum in them. More like large tokens for a bus or the subway.

Head down, I adjusted the binoculars for the short distance, ten feet or so. I looked straight down into this beast of a hole, managing the vertigo and focusing the lenses, one more twist, there, yes, clearer now, not tokens, casino coins, yes, a gambler, he's a gambler, yep, *Sands Casino* it said on the coins, maybe if I got closer—

—no no awFUCK NO, oh shit I'm sliding, the abyss the dirt the grass my feet—

—grab something, anything—

—fuck fuck fuck—

Full stop, abrupt, dirt under my shirt, in my bra, in my mouth. My heart... it was so far up my throat I could have chewed on it.

One foot on a ledge, the other foot dangling, I pressed my face cheek against the jagged rock, was glued to it, my arms and body angled forward and pressing the hole's uneven wall like it was bumpy Velcro, but I was totally fucked because it wasn't. A strained glance above me told me I was about ten feet from the top.

"Al! A little help here. Dude. Al! Wake up..." A Tourette's release didn't help matters.

"—RANGER DANGER DINGLEBERRIES!"

Don't look down—

But I did. Holy fucking mother of God. My foot wasn't on the ledge, it was next to it, on something that got spongy and bowed with my weight shift, something with give to it. Wrong. Something with grab to it. It was wrapped around my heel, pushing it, inching it, and me, up.

Al's voice from above. "Don't—move—a muscle."

I looked up, saw Al's scrunched face peering over the rim at my sorry ass. He disappeared, was gone five seconds, ten, stretching to twenty, the longest twenty seconds of my life...

"*—shit-fuck shit-fuck shit-fuck—*"

My mouth convulsed itself, cursing unrestrained until I was out of breath, gasping, my upper body sweating, shivering, swaying, I was losing my balance, but holy baloney shit-shit-*shit* the rock—the fucking rock I was standing on—it shifted to rebalance me.

"*—what the fuck, what the fuckity fuck-fuck—*"

"Grab this," Al shouted from above, "and hold on. Both hands."

A rope ladder slapped the pothole wall next to me, down as far as my shoulders.

"It's tied to the truck bumper. Don't climb, just hold tight, hands, arms, whatever. The truck will pull you out."

I reached for the rope ladder, wrapped a hand around one rung, eased it in close under my face then snaked the other hand and arm through two more rungs. A cautious breath. I left my perch, Al watching. All of me was on the rope now, no support below.

Al: "Ready?"

Me: "Go."

The second longest twenty seconds in my life passed while Al started the truck and backed up, the rope ladder slowly dragging me up the side of the hole, scraping my knuckles and elbows and chest against the wall's rough surface, up, up, and finally out. I lay prone on the grass. No pee in my pants, far as I knew, but there should have been.

Al: "You can let go of the ladder now, miss."

I got to my feet, reached out and hugged the big motherfucker, and the big motherfucker hugged me back.

* * *

I needed to see what had kept me from the 150-foot drop after Al stopped verbally kicking my ass. I wrapped my arm around the rope ladder a second time, this time was practically sewn to it, the ladder still attached to the SUV. After a slug of courage from Al's flask, I leaned back over the edge, located the rock that held me, a small thing that jutted from the wall, cupped at the end like a large soap dish, and no bigger than one. Christ, how incredibly, unbelievably lucky.

Fully upright again and leaning against the truck with Al, I shared more of his Jack. His hard-ass demeanor had softened; he knew he did good. We talked warrior to warrior, marine to army K9 ground-pounder, both of us in Iraq One, Desert Storm. The war talk petered out. Next topic, my Tourette's. Next topic after that, the hamlet of Rancor.

"I have to tell you, Al, this place stymies me."

"How's that?"

"No reported violent crime for fifty years? That crosses generations. C'mon, there had to be a felony in there somewhere. Hell, I witnessed a drugstore robbery and an assault just today."

"Yeah," Al said. "That got the town's attention. Punks."

I picked up on some short-stroke action going on inside his clasped hands, a subconscious knuckles-to-palm piston pumping to go along with his distant, vengeful look. "No one around here has any interest in any no-crime record," he said, his eyes narrowing. "That's a bullshit media thing. The only thing going on here is our town watch has been a major deterrent. A bank robbery put the town on notice. I'm here as sheriff for window dressing, although I do get my share of busting up fights at the local watering holes on occasion."

"Major deterrents," I repeated to him, "apparently included avenging his death by killing the bank robbers."

"A long time ago," he said, "so I can't really comment. Who knows for sure. I was maybe ten years old. I can tell you that no one in Rancor was upset about what happened to those bastards. Then, or now."

Al talked about other close-knit communities similar to Rancor. Places like South Philly, South Boston, New York City's Little Italy. Places where residents knew who belonged and who didn't.

"Know why I'm the only cop now? Low crime, upstanding citizenry, that all helped make the decision easy. Our population is declining. Which meant that when our police chief Dody Heck wasn't chasing petty crimes like underage drinking and shoplifting, she was stuck sitting on her ass. When she retired, the rest of the police force was disbanded. The town elected a sheriff instead. Me.

"Enough about Rancor. What the hell was so important in this pothole that a pretty woman like you had to try a stunt like you just did? Some of the landscape around here is fragile. Plenty of holes, man-made and otherwise. Lots of soft soil."

"Something big and shiny," I told him. "I had to have it." My near-death experience yielded one souvenir. I handed him a Sands Casino coin. "It was on the ledge."

Not a plastic chip, mind you, but a minted metallic coin the size of a silver dollar, its center a shiny aluminum. Just like my binoculars had advertised.

"The car that took the header into the pothole," I said, "there aren't that many cherry sixties Impala convertibles out there. It was just like the one belonging to a missing Allentown woman. Sands Casino is close to her house. Ergo, the coin is from the car. The guy last driving it is the bounty I'm after. A bail-jumping attempted rapist. My guess is he's still around here somewhere." I fished out a flyer for him.

"A 'guess'?" Al said, studying Linkletter's mug shot, some side-eye at me, "and not an 'ergo'?"

Al was funning me. Fine, it was all good.

"Yeah, not an ergo," I said. *Ergo* was a good word. It was okay if he thought I was deep.

"Ergo me this then, Batman. Are you fucking kidding me? A near-death experience for *that*?" The corner of Al's mouth lifted like it had been tugged by a fishhook. He found this entertaining. "Here. Got something for you. Happy gaming, grunt."

Two large coins dropped into my palm. Sands Casino coins, same as the one I came out of the hole with.

"They were on the grass ten or so yards back, in the path the car took. Other scattered change too. Keep 'em. I'm not planning to be in Bethlehem any time soon. All you had to do was ask."

* * *

I now saw better what went on with the Impala. A straight path down the incline toward the pothole, clear of trees but far from flat; uneven as hell. The car started its run, shook and rattled as it sped over large bumps that abruptly lifted and dropped it down hard on its shocks, the coins going airborne, scattering in its grassy wake. A repeat occurrence as the car bumped its way over the edge into the pothole abyss.

What I learned from this: one, Mr. Linkletter liked to gamble, or had been to a casino, or someone he was with had been to a casino, and two, I had not just cheated death this time around. I was one off-the-chart lucky bastard recipient of some skunky juju that curb-stomped the Grim Reaper on my behalf. The rock that wasn't a rock had gripped my heel like a hand, held it, cupped it, shifted and rebalanced me. Had I lost my balance, it wouldn't have let go. Swear to God, what was now a rock was a human hand before.

I had trouble processing this, felt queasy. I needed my fuzzy keychain.

"—tits, titties, titty-tits

"—ergo—ergo, pergo, leggo my eggo..."

26

The fat kid hadn't been easy. He woke up a mile down the road, threw a tantrum, then blew chunks all over himself and Randall. Now the car was a mess and reeked of semi-digested Doritos, Pop-Tarts, stomach acid, and energy drink. Randall's interest in him decelerated from extreme boner to dead-dick flaccid in the time it took the boy's projectile vomiting to travel from his mouth to Randall's crotch. The kid was unconscious again, slack-jawed from multiple fist pummels to his head when Randall couldn't get him to shut up, although one of the kid's outbursts had been entertaining.

"... they will find you..."

He for sure had balls, but Randall decided it wasn't worth the effort to clean him up and keep him alive and quiet for the afternoon snack he'd planned for himself, so seeing those young balls in action wasn't going to happen. His gag reflex told him to cut his losses and get the kid out of the car, now.

He found a small stretch of road momentarily empty of travelers in both directions, heavily forested save for an abandoned farmhouse. A faded coal mining mural on weathered gray sideboards adorned an adjacent barn. Randall pulled the car onto the shoulder then onto grass and stopped under the mural, a rendering of a pair of palms-out open hands cupping black coal nuggets. The kid groaned as Randall yanked him out the car door with a handful of khaki shirt. He dragged his chubby body around the back of the barn, a heavy copse of evergreens stretching up a hill that surrounded them on three sides. He dropped the kid onto a patch of grass, the soft landing unintentional, considering Randall intended to kill him. Next to the kid, a neglected coal pile, and lying next to the coal, a rusty shovel, its blade exposed, but most of its handle was under a layer of dirt and leaves and overgrown by weeds.

A shovel. Perfect. Gruesome, but with less noise.

The kid groaned again, louder this time.

Randall needed to close this aborted interlude out. He pulled at the shovel's buried handle. The dirt gave a little, the handle loosening. He tugged harder, breaking a sweat. It loosened more but then wouldn't budge.

Behind him, the kid moaned.

Randall brushed away the leaves and uprooted the weeds to get a better look at what was making the shovel's extraction so difficult. He tugged at it again. The handle rose another inch but no more.

"Goddamn it..." He planted both feet, put his body into it. In a minute he would give up and simply strangle the noisy fucker or get one of his guns.

What—the fuck—is the problem here?

He struggled, and the handle lifted a few more inches, exposing... something. Randall strained, pulled, and blinked hard at what now broke the surface.

... a tug of war—with a—with a—

... holy FUCK—

Wrapped around the wooden shovel stock was a fist, or what used to be a fist but was now five boney fingers with hanging flesh black from desiccation, its grip on the shovel like a vice. The fist would not let go.

Behind him the groggy kid staggered to his feet. He stumble-rushed Randall, surprised him with a massive squirt of pepper spray to his face and head. Randall released the shovel, covered up and cursed, reaching wildly for his attacker. The fat little bastard staggered around the side of the barn and was gone. Randall doubled over in stinging agony and dropped heavily onto his butt, where his tailbone greeted the hard, jarring edge of the exposed shovel blade.

* * *

Randall needed to move. The kid was gone, either into the woods on foot, or maybe a passing motorist picked him up. Twice before, this had happened, where someone he'd had plans for had gotten away. First was a prostitute, his word against hers; he pulled up stakes before anything came of it. The second survivor said she was a practicing witch, but she never filed charges. Her witch curse of a painful genital dismemberment still haunted him. Eyes swollen from the pepper spray, he needed to get back into the car and onto the road right now.

Squinting through the pain and having trouble staying between the lines, he guided the car to wherever this road was taking him, as long as there was a motel on the way. Mother*fucker* did the pepper spray still sting, a thousand hot pinpricks to his eyes and face. He'd wash out what he could, planning to hole up for a few hours.

The kid could ID him, so Randall would need a new look, would lose the beard, dye his hair, and get another car; regain the upper hand. And yet, even with this setback, he was still having way too much fun. Except for what he'd seen in the dirt behind the barn. That shovel, restrained by, at closer examination, a tangled tree root, something that his wild shoe-scuffing and blind hand-grope of the layered dirt eventually confirmed.

Except it for sure first looked like a dead person's hand, the boney thing holding on long enough for the kid to clear his head then surprise him with the pepper spray from behind. Not fucking possible, but it sure as hell had looked like it.

* * *

Fucking pepper spray.

At the Red Roof Inn in Clarks Summit, the sting was gone from his face and hands, and his hair color was now a light strawberry blond with white at the temples. No more beard, only a trim white mustache, the rest of the gray-white stubble washed down the sink of the motel room.

A longer look at himself in the bathroom mirror.

The surgeon had been an all-star. A new cheek structure, a reconstructed jaw, both necessary after the buckshot to the face and upper torso that had almost killed him. His chin also acquired a dimple, covering in part a scar; facial markers that the beard hid. A change of clothes, into tan Dockers, a belt, and boat shoes, and he was back in business, this time as a clean-cut, middle-aged man.

Randall left his room, walked the motel parking lot on recon. He needed another car.

And he would have one. A newer, silver Caddy sedan with the keys still in it, right here in the parking lot, late afternoon delight going on inside one of the rooms. No, the noise level in the room had just increased, tunes a-blasting. Sounded more like the start of a par-*tay,* with a few other cars there apparently for the same reason. They wouldn't miss the Caddy for a while.

He pulled his newly acquired vehicle around to his room in a rear building, quickly packed up his things, and tossed the Buick's keys into a dumpster.

Some funny cigarettes and other drugs—in large quantities—were in the Cadillac's glove compartment. Funnier yet considering the bookend rear bumper stickers, a red-and-black *D.A.R.E.* on the left, a *Just Say No* on the right. Out on the road he lit up, sucked in the weed, mellowed out. With the stash he'd found, there was no chance the car would be reported stolen. Then again, a stash like this meant the owners would be extra interested in getting it back. He'd deal with it, or with them, if he had to. Right then, he was feeling lucky. Also hungry and horny.

A check of his watch. Still time for the early bird specials at the Greek diner, but only if he hustled. He'd press the honeypot blonde waitress about his former girlfriend. He'd gotten "never seen her before" answers to his photo reveal, but if cocaine entered the discussion it might loosen some lips.

27

"Ma. Mom. *Charlie.*"

"Yes, Andy. No need to shout. I hear you, dear."

Andy entered his mother's bedroom in her assisted-living apartment, part of a retirement community its developers labeled as five-star living in Clarks Summit, ten minutes from the B&B. A comfortable one-bedroom accommodation. Charlotte, seated, lifted her arms in front of her face, her hands unwavering as they gripped a quilt like she was exhibiting a piece of juried artwork. The steadiest of hands, Andy reminded himself; a necessity for a surgeon. Considering his mother's mental challenges of late, her hands occasionally shook when she didn't concentrate. Not this time.

"How do you like it, Andy?"

Another themed quilt. Crazy quilting at its finest, this one more so than others, and even more deserving of the quilting genre's name. "What am I looking at?"

"I call it 'Three Hundred Game.' Isn't she a beauty?"

Twelve fabric panel jumbles spread out haphazardly across the quilt's landscape, all odd cuts that depicted the twelve strikes needed to earn a perfect score in bowling. Twelve balls striking twelve ten-pin sets of glacier white pins with red collars, the twelfth ball a flaming crimson. The representations of the pins in different crisscross patterns were detailed enough that Andy could almost hear the clatter of wood against wood as they scattered from the impact.

"Very nice, Ma. So you remember what tonight is."

"Indeed I do."

Bowling and surgery, the two topics where his mother was at her sharpest. "I'll be by after dinner to pick you up. Promise me no X-rated talk tonight, otherwise your cheerleading will end early."

Charlotte lowered her hands, looked offended, but that wasn't what this was; her mind had already made a sharp turn. The quilt became an unruly mountain of folds bunched up in her lap, her forgetting she was holding it. She raised her finger, shook it at Andy. The quilt tumbled off her lap.

"No hanging around with your aunt Kitty tonight, Andy. She's a bad influence. You hear me, young man?"

An age digression, out of the blue. Lately, her sideways comments had become more common. Andy wasted no time getting right to the point. "Aunt Kitty's dead, Ma."

"Oh." A few hard blinks, then Charlotte was back in the present. Almost. "Yes. Right. Because of your hedonistic wife. I hate her for what she did. Somebody should—"

"Somebody did, Ma. She's dead too."

Andy moved to his mom's closet, preoccupying himself by shoving aside hanging blouses to find her red satin bowling shirt with black stitching. He pulled it out; it needed pressing. He moved to an open ironing board, put the iron's temperature setting to low, let it warm up. "I'll be back sometime before eight," he said then started in with the ironing. "Can you get ready by yourself after dinner and be waiting for me downstairs?"

"Of course I can, dear."

Charlotte straightened her back, cleared her throat like she was about to continue, then restrained herself. Andy felt his mother's stare just outside his peripheral vision; he continued pressing the shirt. Silence meant Mom was loading up. Andy admonished himself that he needed to remain gentle, not be short with her.

"Andy."

"Yes, Mom."

"I want the gun."

Andy stopped pressing the shirt but didn't lift the iron. Steam rose from underneath. "What?"

"Aunt Kitty's gun. The old Colt. I want it. With bullets."

"Why?"

"You and I know what this disease is doing, Andy. It's only fitting that I use that one. When the time comes."

Over breakfast, at restaurants for occasional brunches, when out to dinner, during his mom's infrequent nightmares, Charlotte often brought this topic up, espousing that there was only one surefire way to address her dementia, but before now, she'd never been so direct.

"You're doing fine, Ma. No need to be talking that way. I love the time I spend with you. All of it, under all conditions." More steam from the iron. "They'll be no more talk of any 'when the time comes' bullshit today, okay?"

"No more talk," Charlotte parroted. Then, "But when you find someone you want to grow old with, and I hope so much that you do"—she was fully lucid now, pausing for effect—"that will be the when."

The bowling shirt burned. "Damn it," Andy said, parking the iron upright. He held the shirt up in both hands. Ruined. Not to worry. He was pretty sure Ma had a backup in the closet. Andy flipped through the hanging blouses and found the spare. He started ironing again, his gaze at his mother warm, reassuring. This woman, his mother, was the closest friend Andy had, inclusive of any age and either gender. Friends this close deserved to be heard, and accommodated.

"If the time ever comes, Ma, there will be no gun. I'll take care of things. I promise."

His mother's puzzled face told Andy the lucidity window had already closed. "Things?" Charlotte said. "What kinds of things, dear?"

Patience, Andy told himself. Another example of why it was a virtue. With his mother, nowadays the subject matter changed without warning.

Besides, her wandering mind missed one important point that rendered her need for Aunt Kitty's gun moot: Charlotte already had a gun. It was in the quilting supplies bag sitting in her lap. No bullets, but she had a gun.

Still, his mom was right on one point. An elderly woman in possession of an old gun was a morbid, yet perfect, association.

28

I was preoccupied with swinging-door glimpses of the diner's kitchen. A guy in street clothes sat casually at a butcher-block counter, sampling a dessert. Within his reach next to his bowl, a large handgun loomed. He spooned pudding into his mouth, dripped some on the gun, fumed in Greek about the mess he'd made.

I blinked hard, second-guessing about this armed, barking restaurant boss. Where the hell was I? A saloon in Tombstone?

Andy faced me in the booth. He'd asked to meet for dinner, here, local, no big production. I was here to eat first then talk, then after that maybe we'd see where things took us. He was here to talk first then maybe eat, but there wouldn't be any of that after-that stuff for the two of us together, me forgetting his mixed seniors league bowling finals at Thunder Wonderland tonight. I stopped midchew when I caught that first glimpse of that dark smudge of a weapon so out of place against a backdrop of stainless steel and soapsuds, all of it showcased by the shiny white-light glare of a gleaming kitchen. Andy read my mind.

"That's Mr. Stavros," Andy said. "Gun enthusiast. And a perfectionist about his diner's rice pudding. The gun is here for show, Counsel. He's probably never shot anything worse than a groundhog. Relax."

I grunted. Whatever sexual chemistry there was between us went to the back burner. We would break bread, acknowledge our incredible afternoon together, and talk more about what else had gone down today. I worked on my meat loaf platter. Andy sipped his unsweetened iced tea. He'd barely touched his Cobb salad. Tess and Fungo awaited me in the van, parked beneath our diner window, the van windows open enough for someone to reach a hand inside, but that would have been ill advised.

"Shooting groundhogs," I said, playing it back to him. I helped myself to a forkful of gravy-soaked ground round, chewed and swallowed, offered a smile. "I thought Groundhog Day made shooting groundhogs in Pennsylvania a-number-one illegal."

"Punxsutawney's on the other side of the state," he said, enlightening me. "Morally questionable, there and elsewhere, to shoot them, but not illegal. They can be real pests. Personal property damage, family safety, people looking to protect themselves and their possessions—when people feel threatened, they respond."

My comment was meant to be light and silly. His feedback was as serious as a body bag.

"Counsel," he said, averting his eyes; heavier feedback was forthcoming. "You seem like a great person—"

Aww, fuck. He was about to discuss our afternoon. A thanks-but-no-thanks, I-changed-my-mind, I'm-just-not-into-you was on its way. I had a mouthful of green beans that I needed to not choke on when he said it. Seeing this, he waited for me to finish chewing and swallowing.

"Today was a wonderful... gesture, on both our parts," he said. "Incredible, actually, but... there's just too much baggage here. Mine more than yours." He rethought his comment. "Mine way more than yours."

His eyes were an intriguing, milky indigo. They searched mine for understanding. I was pretty sure my face reflected his revelation as nothing short of a kick in the nuts, so to speak. I powered through the pending low blow. "There's a *but*, I gather," I said.

"Look, I'm sorry, Counsel." A doleful glance at his salad, then he was back for another serious-as-all-hell look at me. "Once you take care of your business, maybe you should do yourself a favor and head home."

Maybe. He was closing the door, but I didn't hear the lock turn.

Too much baggage. For once the hey-it's-not-you-it's-me wasn't coming from my own lips.

Do yourself a favor. He'd convinced himself it really was about him. Fine. I went with the ambiguity. Gratuitous, self-serving ambiguity, but in this case I knew the truth. He had underestimated my baggage, saw only the Tourette's, and might have even thought I'd been too easy. I liked him already, lots. Maybe too much for my own good, or his. I wanted to show more of my cards, let him know I felt a connection. But whatever I would offer, a similar response from him wasn't likely. So what came out of my mouth instead was an arms-length, Teflon-dipped reflex.

"Too much baggage. Sure. Me too. Enough to fill a circus train." I let that settle in for the both of us, for this moment at least, then, even though I might cry some of it out later, I forced myself to move on. "What's up with that waitress over there?"

My chin gestured at the far corner of the dining room, near the restaurant's rear exit. Andy took a peek at the chatty, sweet-faced forty-ish waitress lingering at a booth. Bottled honey-blonde; cute. She was interested in the booth's male customer, was way too obvious about it. He tucked money —a single bill—under the tall sugar container. Her eyes lit up; it had to be at least a twenty. The smile she gave him was take-me-home-with-you-size.

We were back to an equilibrium, the both of us focused on someone else's issues.

"Be nice, Counsel. Rosie's led a tough life. Married twice, some boyfriends before, during and after. Likes to party. She's too much like her younger sister, the other waitress. Eternal flirts."

Rosie left her customer, whispered to the other waitress, who then pulled her into a hallway. I now saw the resemblance. Gesturing arms and elbows and pointing fingers, and the back of the younger sister's black-haired head, bobbing and weaving and thrusting, made for a spirited argument. She was dressing down her older sister and doing a good job of it. Rosie's gentleman customer paid his bill at the register, winked at the elderly cashier, then stuffed a few bucks into a Maurice Fund helmet at the exit, this one a baby blue. Outside, he stepped between a Cadillac and my van. He admired Tess a moment, asleep in the van's passenger seat. He backed the Caddy out; it disappeared around the rear of the diner. Tess's head popped up. Her nose snaked out the window opening and sniffed, her animation too late to do anything about her sleep disturbance. She settled back down into her nap.

Rosie removed her server's apron, said she thought it was the flu, shoved the apron into her sister's chest, and disappeared through the kitchen's swinging doors. Mr. Stavros scolded her in Greek when she stormed past him and the big black gun-phallus, now in his lap.

"New topic," I said, except I was nervous, the baggage thing and all. He didn't need to think I was nuts, but he might. "Something odd."

"Uh-huh." He lifted a forkful of lettuce heart, ate.

"Today I experienced an... unexplainable event."

I got into it. The pothole in the park. My slip off the ledge, down the slope. The rock that wasn't a rock that had saved my life. Al Pemberton, the Iraq One sheriff, also a lifesaver. Andy heard it all, smiled, wasn't creeped out, stayed quiet.

"A hand," I repeated, giving him another chance to comment, on my sanity, potential drug use, senility, something, anything. "It felt like it gripped my heel. A *hand,* protruding from a dirt-and-stone *wall.*"

Andy's lips pursed. "It could have been Maurice."

"Maurice." I looked at him deadpan. "Maurice-Fund Maurice?"

"Yeah. My dad. It could have been him."

Andy laid it out for me, was totally serious. Spooky shit. Rancor had been a hot bed for it over the years. Dead coal miners. Mining accidents. Widow suicides. A bowling alley poltergeist or three. And predating the one murder committed during a bank robbery that had been so very personal to him, were a few murders with lingering paranormal after-effects.

"That's my story and I'm sticking to it," he said. "Unless you tell me you were coked up, overmedicated, and drunk."

Funny guy. Liking him even more.

"Otherwise, if it was a paranormal event, it could have been Maurice or some other guardian-angel type. Maybe a miner coming back to finish the job, as local folks like to say." More Cobb salad. "Part of the charm of this town. All pretty benign stuff, but charming nevertheless, the tourists tell us."

"Far from benign," I said. "More like benevolent. Nothing benign about saving my life."

"There's that too," he said, his smile warm, uncomplicated.

Whatever other complications he thought might exist for us, I wanted to un-complicate them.

29

Time for a quick party. Randall and the waitress left the diner's rear parking lot in the Caddy together.

"I'm Rosie. We'll go to my place," she suggested, her giggle not befitting her age. She looked extra comfortable in the front seat, her hands caressing the plush leather, her mood playful. She opened the glove box without asking. Out came a large plastic bag. "This is a lot of coke," she said.

"Yeah," Randall says. "Crystal meth in there too."

"You are full of surprises, Mr. Isaacs. I want some of this. Right. Now." She gave him an expectant look.

"Call me Howard. Go for it."

She fumbled around for something in her purse. Randall pulled the Caddy up to an intersection, next to a late model metallic blue Dodge Challenger with a wide white racing stripe, the traffic light red, the Challenger in the left turn lane. Cars on the cross street with the green light whizzed by the intersection in front of them. The Challenger's driver was a guy in *Risky Business* sunglasses super interested in the mobile device in his hand. Randall watched closely as Mr. Challenger absentmindedly revved the throaty engine, nourishing it with big gulps of clean, Pocono Mountains air. The driver sneaked a look at their long red light then zoned back into thumbing more letters of text into his phone.

Rosie didn't find her straw, instead found the fifty Randall had left for her tip. It rolled back up easily for her. She unzipped the plastic bag. The traffic light was still red.

"Wait," Randall told her, eyeing Mr. Challenger, who was still texting.

"Huh? It's right turn on red, Howard. You can turn now."

Randall ignored her, glanced at the red light, smiled big time at it and Mr. Challenger and the streaming cross traffic. Randall released the brake, punched the gas. The Cadillac lurched a few feet forward before he jammed the brake pedal again.

The Challenger reacted, jackrabbiting into the intersection. An RV crossing left to right in a hurry to beat a yellow light clipped the Challenger's front end, twisting it sideways. Its bumper tore free at impact, skittered ahead of the RV and was crushed by both sets of the RV's tires. Both vehicles screeched to a halt.

Randall's stoplight finally turned green. The Caddy signaled its turn, made a right, threaded itself around the accident and cruised slowly away.

Rosie leaned back over the seat for a look at what was left in their wake. "You are sooo bad," she said, her mock-scold preceding a teasing poke at his arm. She returned her attention to the coke.

She would do fine, Randall told himself.

The Caddy settled into an even speed on the straightaway. She did a quick bump off the small mirror she kept in her purse just for this purpose. Her head raised, her eyes closed, she absorbed the rush. "Mm-mm-*mm*. Loving that. Up ahead a mile you'll turn right, lover, then two miles to my house on the left."

"Husband or boyfriend?"

"Single. At the moment," she said, laughing at herself. Another scoop of the coke. She shuddered, her top-heavy chest heaving with additional air intake. "Oh my. Wow-*eee* is that good, Howard. If we bring this shit inside, I am so gonna fuck your brains out."

Yes, you are, Randall thought. Then there would be a question-and-answer session.

Wow-eee indeed.

* * *

It was over. Front, back, up, down, over, under, every orifice utilized, Randall's as well as hers. The coke and some Viagra helped. An hour of wired and depraved sex, in Rosie's bedroom, on the living room sectional, the kitchen center island under recessed lighting, the plush carpet that gave her rug burns. Drugs, food, and condoms, the condoms at her insistence, at least at first. Then the coke and meth took over and she didn't give a shit. She had a nice place, and they had messed it up pretty good.

Exhausted, she lounged in a T-shirt on the sectional, eating an apple and marveling at his penis from across the room, limp below his paunch, but still ever so magnificent in length and girth.

"You've got a python there, Howard. Been in any movies?"

"Maybe."

"Well, it's awesome. And this was so much fun. Now I need to freshen up so I can go back and finish my shift. I had a great time, sweetie. Stop by the diner when you're next in town. We'll do this again."

"I don't think so," Randall said, his face long, sweat-soaked. He raised his naked girth from the chair.

"What? You didn't have fun? You sure looked like you were having fun..."

She'd insisted she didn't know a Regina Briscoe or a Juicy Luster, but there'd been a slight tell, a hesitancy. He'd beat it out of her if he had to. "The woman I'm looking for"—he arrived alongside her—"I think you know her."

"I told you. I don't know no Regina Briscoe or no Juicy nobody. Case closed. Sorry." Rosie slid away from him, across the sofa, making him suddenly aware of her interest in a messy end table, or what was in it.

Her place was about to get a lot messier.

He reached across the sectional, took a firm grip of her arm. "We'll do it again, right now."

"Howard, baby, sweetie, I can't. I'm tired and sore and I need to take a shower. The next time you're in Rancor—"

"No next time. Now."

"Howard. No..."

He pinned her beneath him, his python stirring yet again, this time while he wrapped her bra around her neck. She squirmed, one hand in his face, the other desperately reaching for a drawer in the end table, connecting with the knob. He grabbed the hand doing the reaching, started folding it backward—

"You know Regina! Where is she? *Where?*"

She screamed, her fingers now folded the wrong way, close to the top of her forearm.

"WHERE—THE FUCK—IS SHE?"

Bones crunched then her wrist snapped. She screamed in agony, her arm and wrist dangling. He tied the bra off and pressed his face hard against hers, her breath starting to leave her—

"*Bowling... bowling alley!* Please, Howard, no—"

He needed a few final, euphoric thrusts to finish, him cursing her and her genitals, her one fist pounding him, her hot, apple-juicy, beseeching, terrified last breaths wafting into his nostrils, the last of the last giving him a rush better than all the coke and sex of the past hour combined.

He suddenly felt like eating some fruit. Then he'd take a shower.

A lead. Finally.

30

Andy's fondness for his mother, tonight's bowling league finals, idle chitchat, coffee, rice pudding—it was all good. Except for Mr. Stavros and his large handgun. I did however see his point about dessert quality control. Best rice pudding I'd ever tasted. I was on my second dish.

Andy, still sharing: "If you take Mom to a bowling alley or hand her a scalpel, you'd never guess she sometimes has trouble dressing herself."

The proof, as he laid it out for me, was Andy's bowling team, started decades ago by Charlotte, the team's anchor at the time. "The Fighting Cadavers. Nurses and doctors, past and present. Mom's now our head cheerleader and coach, and a major trash-talker."

Andy went maudlin for a moment, traveled to a far-off place, left the diner behind, present company included. He rallied, pulled himself back to the here and now. "So. Arterial red bowling shirts, and our team name scribbled in longhand across the back, in a black stitch that oozes like zombie blood. You can't miss us. Our match starts at eight tonight. If you're not busy, stop by."

Yes, sure, hope to get there, I told him. We slid out of the booth, hugged like we were cousins, but at this point I couldn't help myself. I held his shoulders and gently pulled him closer. He ignored the intimacy, kissed me cordially on my cheek. His lips then moved to my ear and lingered there long enough to whisper, “Please, Counsel, no, it’s too… complicated.” The sensuality and the warmth of his gentle delivery of the words did not make up for the message. He cupped my chin then left the diner to pick up his mother. Bummed, I sat back down to nurse my coffee.

A black Crown Vic pulled into the space Andy’s Jeep vacated. Two guys in charcoal gray suits climbed out. Had to be feds. They wandered over to my van, pressed their faces against different windows, passenger side and rear. Tess’s head popped up. She sniffed, gave Fed Number One an inquisitive head tilt, stayed calm. The van’s rear end suddenly bounced as Fungo left his crate, reacting to Fed Number Two, a big ugly dude too close to the back window for Fungo’s comfort. The second fed backed off. Both turned their heads up, now interested in me, the woman staring back at them from her booth inside the diner, drinking coffee.

I left the booth, paid the bill at the cashier. They were waiting for me at the bottom of the cement steps, their badges blazing.

Fed One: “Agent Van Impe. FBI. This is Agent McQuarters. Is this your van?”

“Yes,” I answered with my best smiley face. “Is there a problem?”

“We have a few questions. Can I see some identification?”

I knew the drill. I told them my name, also told them immediately that I was carrying a concealed weapon, and I showed them my empty hands. I let the second agent take the Glock from my holster in back, under my shirt. These pleasantries delivered, I opened my wallet. My driver’s license, my Fugitive Recovery Agent’s license, my old PA state trooper ID, my permit to carry, all were lined up opposite my credit cards.

“Former state trooper,” Agent Van Impe said, impressed. Agent McQuarters examined my gun.

“Retired,” I said.

“The dogs?”

“On the job with me.” I told him Tess was a former working dog, then I went for some levity. “The larger one’s a shepherd rescue turned trained assassin.”

Neither agent smiled. Assembly line cookie-cutter goons in suits. J. Edgar would have been proud. Fuck ’em if they couldn’t take a joke.

Agent Van Impe: “You say you’re on the job. Tracking whom?”

Whom. Even his grammar was good. J. Edgar, you rock. "A bail jumper from Allentown by the name of Stephen Linkletter. Wanted for attempted rape of a minor."

Agent Van Impe's face gave nothing up, as in no recognition that we were on the same case, until: "So tell me, Miss Fungo, what's your next move?"

"What?"

"Your next move. A simple question. Where will you look for him next?"

He was fishing. Ha. They had shit on my bounty. Emphasis on *shit,* not *had.*

Fuck this. I saw no reason to share tonight's bowling alley plans.

"After I billet my canine deputies for the night, I'll find a bar, maybe try to get lucky. Tomorrow I'll do more canvassing."

I told them where I was staying, asked, "Why the interrogation?"

Agent Van Impe again. "Your van keeps turning up. The touristy pothole park, the car dealer... We felt it was time for a chat."

"So I guess we're after the same guy. No big deal. A healthy competition never hurt anyone. Let me have your business card. When I catch him, I'll be sure to give you guys a call."

Oops. Too smug on my part. My comment apparently roused Agent Van Impe's partner, the sleepwalking giant.

"This ain't no fucking competition, Miss Fungo," Agent McQuarters growled, a neck vein popping.

He was around six-five. His suit was too small. His tie was loose, his shirt collar unbuttoned. Dark circles under his eyes, pockmarks on his cheek. And his grammar was poor. Sorry, J. Edgar, a miss with this one.

My left hand twitched. I needed fur. And things had been going so well.

"Look, I do need to deliver him to someone if I catch him, is all I'm saying." My hand felt for my belt loop. *Nice fuzzy doggie. Soft fuzzy doggie. Happy fuzzy doggie.* "And since you guys are here visiting Rancor, the collar's yours if you want it."

Sleepy fuzzy doggie...

Both agents saw the twitch. They watched my fingers and thumb gently caress my talisman. Agent Van Impe's eyes shifted between my face and my waist; he was processing this. He was close to getting it, that this was only a harmless tic that needed controlling. Fuckface McQuarters, not so much.

"What the hell is that? A dog dick? You jerking off a dead dog?"

The disease gripped my subconscious with no spoiler alert for my interrogators, was about to get me into trouble, again. Fuck this fucking thing—

Some choice words for him entered my head: *Ram this up your ass, McQuarters. That's right. My fist. Your ass. Right the fuck up there, with a big twist.* Except I wasn't just thinking them, I'd said them. Or some of them, because the Tourette's wouldn't let me get past the key words.

"—fist fuck—your ass—ram it ram it ram it—

"—fist fuck—your ass..."

My gesturing left hand didn't help. An uppercutting middle finger nearly connected with McQuarters's chin. Agent Van Impe pinned my arms to my body from behind and attempted a takedown.

I was wrong. McQuarters was six-eight if he was an inch 'cause he was in my face now, looking down, about to tear off my nose with his gritting teeth. I was still on my feet, the smaller agent wrestling me but not able to get the right leverage. I didn't pull back, my face and McQuarters's face inches apart, him for sure smelling my meat-loaf breath, his breath smelling like unwashed penis and semen. I told him this, loudly, in a major Tourette's outburst, and it was true as all fuck because I knew that smell from my travels.

That sealed it. Down I went, the two of them on me, my hands forced behind my back. They cuffed and stuffed me into the perp seat in the Crown Vic. Tess and Fungo almost devoured themselves trying to get out the passenger side window of my van.

I was going to be late for tonight's bowling match.

31

Randall had marked his territory in here but good. Satiated, he showered and dressed, was now noshing on microwaved leftover pizza at Rosie's kitchen table, but he was also feeling sorry for himself. He wandered through her bungalow looking for cash and valuables, a force of habit. What he found: two engagement rings, four hundred bucks in a bedroom dresser, and in her purse, the rolled-up fifty he'd left her as a tip. He'd held each of these things in his hands, didn't want them, wouldn't need them. Which made him uncomfortable about being in here now.

Back in the living room he eyed the body again, the twisted, broken wrist dangling inches away from the end table next to the couch. The end table drawer, of major interest to her during their struggle, was partly open. He slid it open all the way.

"Wow."

He lifted out the biggest, heaviest handgun he'd ever seen in the possession of a woman. *Rhino .357 Magnum*, it said under the four-inch barrel. Black and ugly, and distinctive because the barrel was aligned with the cylinder's bottom bullet chamber, not the top. And it was loaded. This, he decided, he would take.

Her body in here with him wasn't what was causing his discomfort; this actually excited him. He'd thought about doing the unspeakable, the body half-naked and defenseless and sprawled on the sectional sofa like a drugged college coed at a frat party. But he'd been there, done that already, many times, considering how many victims he'd stayed with, stayed inside, sometimes needing to still work it, work it, work it so he could climax even after he'd already snuffed out their pilot lights, after the muscles—muscles that only moments before had been molded around and grinding his throbbing hammer—had all suddenly relaxed at the same time, turning everything to dead meat. He knew not to kill them before climaxing but occasionally he wasn't able to control himself. It was the fight that he liked. The life that wanted to go on living that he extinguished with extreme prejudice. Life expiring in front of his eyes. Quite the rush.

He had no reasonable explanation for why he'd killed so many people, other than maybe he was a death junkie. When caught, they'd label him sick. Sociopathic, maybe psychotic. He planned on living through it all. He'd enjoy the hype, the fame, would take the media and medical and psychiatric professions for all they were worth, intended to feed them, nurture them, tell them what they wanted to know about his depressing upbringing and his depraved life. The death penalty? It would cure his disease, but he'd just as soon avoid it if possible, thank you. Prison was the preferred alternative. Prison would be fun, given how physically gifted he was. They'd love him and revere him in prison, maybe help him beat this disease.

But only after he found Regina and her kid. *His* kid.

This town was the end of the line for him. His final destination as a free man.

She already stank, bodily fluids and multiple sphincter releases and all that. The smell sealed it. He needed to leave.

It was almost eight p.m. He'd head to the bowling alley. Slot machines, a bar, undersexed grannies, and maybe, somewhere in the mix, Regina.

Things he knew now: Regina was nearby, and short of a threat of death, the people of Rancor wouldn't give her up.

No more photos or missing person questions asking about her whereabouts. No more telegraphing his intentions. New approach: lead with information that she had money coming to her.

32

About the unwashed dick comment: I now knew more about Agent McQuarters than I cared to, including the science experiment going on inside his piehole, the kind of bad breath that came from poor dental hygiene.

Agent Van Impe had accepted my apology for the Tourette's episode, told me I "checked out" wherever it was that FBI agents went to confirm that a person wasn't on any watch list or criminal database. I knew this was bullshit. I was on a list somewhere; multiple lists were more like it. Someone didn't flip off a college recruiter, get manhandled by the cops for doing it, get 302'd, then not end up with at least one file somewhere. Chances were it was out there and working to my advantage, validating my Tourette's, my State Police service and—gag—my pedigree as daughter of a former senator from Pennsylvania.

Agent Van Impe took off my cuffs but hadn't let me leave the perp seat of their car, maybe more for my sake than theirs, considering McQuarters was still seething. I had just outted him as liking guys. He knew I outted him, and he knew I knew that he knew. His FBI agent partner knew now, too, if he hadn't known already.

Live and let live, as long as it was between consenting adults. I held no bias. Still, having my disease was like coexisting with a child inside the same skin, an extremely brash, uncontrollable, questioning child. Kids. They said the darnedest things.

It was eight o'clock give or take. Andy's bowling match was getting underway, and I expected to be fashionably later than I had anticipated. The door to my seat in the rear of the Crown Vic opened.

"Get the fuck out," McQuarters growled. He eyed my keychain still attached to my belt loop, suffixed his grunted order with "How's George, Lenny?" and a mocking smile, finishing with "You fucking retard."

A funny guy, McQuarters was. Fucking hilarious. Hidden behind the bluster and bone-headed-ness was at least one positive J. Edgar attribute, for which I commended him: "Wow. *Of Mice and Men*. You can read. The classics, even. I'm impressed."

He maintained his distance while I climbed out. I didn't blame him for not willing to chance another Tourette's outburst that getting up close might have prompted. Plus I noticed some slight action going on inside his mouth. Chewing gum; a decent breath-freshener. I resisted the urge to comment, but I knew I was smiling. And McQuarters was resisting the urge to decapitate me.

I was free to go, but chances were that the van was now bugged. If it was, it had to be on the outside, considering Fungo and Tess were on the inside. Agent Van Impe returned my gun, handcuffs, keys and phone. McQuarters stayed out of the way, preoccupied with a call that sounded urgent from his side of the conversation.

"The Kugen steak house in Scranton," he said into the phone. "Yeah, I heard. We'll be there."

I climbed back into my van. My waiting deputies jumped me, kissed me up big time, as much from affection as it was from their need to reassure themselves that I was okay. We drove back to my room at the B&B. I needed to assess the damages to my person, take a shower, and rub some ointment on muscles starting to ache now that the adrenaline was gone.

* * *

Out of the shower. My shoulder muscles were tight, my upper arms throbbing like I'd just left the gym. No punches were thrown back at the diner, so there was no damage to my face. I rubbed muscle ointment on my shoulders and back. Greaseless and odorless, my ass; smelled worse than original Bengay. Tess and Fungo stayed on the other side of my room, keeping their distance. They knew not to look for any pats from me whenever I slathered myself up like this. I pulled on another camouflage tee and some clean jeans, then a red blouse over the tee. My eyes wandered to the scrapbook on the dresser. The one with Andy's father's picture in it.

Maurice Prudhomme.

Let's get a closer look at you, Maurice.

Thirty-two years old when you died. Prominent crow's feet. A forehead so wrinkled and dirty from the mines, you could have passed for a mentally ill senior living on the streets. A taut body, arms like suspension bridge cables, much like Andy's. Big, square shoulders. Shoulders, your blank face was saying, that accepted the weight placed on them, that of nurturing a struggling young family's dreams of bettering itself. You weren't a complainer; you were a doer. A protector. You were the type of father a kid looked up to, aspired to, emulated. Well honed, physically and mentally, for your lot in life.

In this picture we could see all this in you, Maurice, and validated twice over in the person of your wife and your son. And I wanted badly to fist bump you for whatever it was that you or a coal-miner buddy of yours did for me today inside that pothole, but a verbal equivalent directed at your one-dimensional likeness was all we had to go with.

"Thank you, Maurice."

I affixed my Glock, handcuffs, keys, phone, and wallet to various body parts, patted my fuzzy keychain. My untucked blouse hid whatever didn't go into a pocket.

I planned to visit a bowling alley full of seniors tonight, women mostly, to be correct. Not quite a reason to expect Mr. Linkletter to show there but hey, the place would be busy and the guy liked to gamble. At one time or another, if he were still in the area, he would stop in. Tonight could be as good a time as ever.

I added an ankle gun, plus I'd add a taser and some pepper spray when I got out to the van. Best not to be underdressed. The Suzuki needed to remain sidelined. My two deputies though, they were entirely welcome.

"Ready, team?"

Tess whimpered, my shepherd Fungo farted, neither moved in the direction of my beckoning fingers. Their way of saying *wash that ointment off your hands first, Momma.* Which I did as best as I could, then I lassoed them with their leashes and we headed out.

* * *

I pulled out of the B&B parking lot. My phone signaled I had a text, so I stopped on the shoulder.

Vonetta.

Feds talked with me sarge. Sup with that?

They don't like me netta. I'm in their way

No surprise there. Got some news. They found Loretta Spezak's body. PA turnpike exit

Too bad

Was maybe raped

I processed this. Linkletter liked kids. Adult women too?

It still fit. It was all about the control.

Sarge? You there?

Yes. Sorry. That's terrible

Yeah. I confirmed for them you're working for me. Feds told me you check out. You should be good now

They bugged my van netta

Aha. Where are you now?

At the b&b for an amorous encounter

Figures

Not what you think

Splain

I found the bug and put it on another b&b guest car. New guests are screwing themselves silly in the room next to mine. Newlyweds. Feds will think it's me

☺ *Honeymooners,* she texted back. *They won't come up for air for days.*

Older couple. Old as you netta, you zombie bitch

Stfu sarge. Go find my bail jumper. You're costing me money

Fuck you netta

Fuck you fungo

We were done here, me and Vonetta, with our sexting, but before I put the phone away, I checked my voicemail for messages. The sheriff and I were squared away about the pharmacy mugging, but still no contact from the State Police. I supposed I should have been happy about this, but it surprised me.

Another text from Vonetta. *Be careful honey*

Will do netta

33

Randall had trouble finding parking at the bowling alley. Even the handicapped spaces were taken, all fifteen of them. Of course, it was Seniors League night.

He looped the lot again. A forest of Pocono evergreens bordered the single-story building on three sides, the trees old and tall and full, with white halos circling their tops from a descending mountain fog. On one side the trees stretched out below the alley, down and away and well beyond what his eyes could see in the evening's declining light. Dense and uninviting, the swells were thick as Christmas tree farms, but also with dips and a few small, craggy trenches—sinkhole craters—where trees were sparse or conspicuously missing. Randall navigated the parking lot a third time.

Still no empty spaces. He retreated to just outside the lot's entrance, drove a short stretch to where an overflow of cars lined the highway. Too visible on the main road, the stolen Caddy would be an issue, but there was nowhere else to park. Four hours had passed since he'd helped himself to it, a beautiful late model CTS coupe. Drugs in mass quantities in the glove compartment. The motel partyers he'd ripped off were for sure dealing, and apparently cavalier about it, considering that people who tried to rip off drug dealers tended toward stunted lifespans. An implied deterrent, yet deterrents didn't mean shit to Randall anymore. He grabbed the next open spot on the shoulder. The parking lot should thin out as the night progressed, the senior patrons' earlier bedtimes a factor. Then he'd come back out and find a less conspicuous parking space closer in.

Two guns went into his sport coat, one of them the ugly *Flash Gordon*–looking Rhino magnum. They took up the two vest pockets, his jacket now evenly ballasted. A pair of light-colored slacks, a white button-down shirt, and boat shoes gave him a clean look. Classy. Older women, bowlers or otherwise, liked classy. Squirty mouth spray for his breath. He was dressed for a night at the casino or the yacht or the lake house. There would be some laughing, some chatting, some charming, maybe even some cheering at strikes and spares if he could get himself into it. And reconnaissance. On the lookout for a mid- to late thirties female bowler; his Regina. And, of course, a sexual liaison or two, at gunpoint if necessary.

He checked himself in the sun-visor mirror. A distinguished older gentleman with strawberry-blond hair, cheerful eyes and a white mustache. His persona oozed a taste for the finer things in life. These lonely small-town senior bitches didn't stand a chance.

What happens in Rancor...

... had no chance of staying in Rancor. Not after tonight. Tonight would make headlines.

* * *

The bowling alley was noisier than what Randall had anticipated. A far cry from the reverence he remembered during TV bowling tournaments in the seventies, coverage he'd turn past on the dial on Saturdays so he could find cartoons or *Three Stooges* shorts while his barfly foster mom banged someone in the next room. The only quiet came before each rolled ball while the bowler set herself up, the silence broken by pin concussions then minor cheering on solid pocket strikes, major cheering on executing difficult spares, and grimaces from pins left standing. Rancor's Summer Mixed Senior League Championship had center stage on lanes twenty and twenty-one out of forty. The five lanes east and west of the championship match were dark, showcasing the lanes the two teams occupied. Left and right of the darkened lanes was the bowling public, where business as usual provided the white noise of rolling balls, thundering hits, gear-driven pin-setting machines, and ball returns.

"What did you do with my sister?" she said.

The black-haired waitress from the diner had materialized next to Randall at the bar. No intro but they knew each other from the casino room, where he'd first noticed her noticing him while he pumped tokens into the slots. Now that he could see her closer up, the resemblance to her sister was obvious. Exposed shoulder ink and face piercings said she was younger, or wanted to look younger, than the impression she'd left on him at the diner. Her skin-tight, short, club-hopping sequined outfit with a tube top showed she was gifted above the waist like her sister, but was more substantial in the booty department. Or perhaps it was just how it spread itself on the barstool.

She stared at him expectantly, tapping her manicured nails on the bar.

"I'm sorry," Randall said. "You are?"

"Pissed at my sister is what I am. She picks up a high roller, bolts from her shift at the restaurant, leaves us short-staffed while she goes off and parties with a sugar daddy. So, what did you do? Have some fun then chop her into little pieces?"

Screw them, kill them, sometimes twist their bodies to fit into places where they shouldn't, but he'd never chopped any of them up. That was just too barbaric. He maintained his smile.

"So you're from that diner," he said, staying with his clueless and refined older gentleman routine. "I'm sorry, but yes, she was extremely flattering to me over dinner. Made me feel like a million bucks. I don't usually take chances, but—"

"Can it, tiger. She told me about the fifty-dollar tip and the coke. And your bragging about your pecker."

"Look, Miss—?"

"Stella."

Now for his busted-but-fun-loving, innocent-party-guy routine. "I'm Howard. Yes, we were naughty in my car. Afterward she made some calls then had me drop her off at a motel in Dickson City. She said her friends would bring her back to the diner."

"Yeah, well, she never came back. She'll be out all night, bingeing," she said, pouting, "without me."

More nail tapping on the bar, with Stella stewing while she was thinking. She dished. "We were supposed to go clubbing in Manhattan after Mom's bowling final tonight."

"Huh. Bummer. Which one is your mom?"

She pointed at lane twenty-one. "The tiny one with the red hair and the nice tan," she said, gesturing with her drink. "She wears too much make-up for her age. She's part of Clooney's Concubines, the team in pink. They used to call themselves Lethal Women. Then Mr. Mel fucking dickhead Gibson torpedoed his acting career. Before that they were Newman's Own until, you know, he died. Guess her average, Howard."

"Her what?"

"Her bowling average. Guess it." Stella already seemed to be past missing her sister, was partly drunk, and was now flirting.

"Okay." He focused on the skinny, tiny mother. "I'll go with one-ten."

"You're definitely not from around here, are you, Howard? Christ, with an average like that you might as well not even show up. She carries a one-seventy-four bowling average. She's seventy-two years old and weighs a hundred pounds, but she's still a player. Order me another gin and tonic, Howard."

Randall heard about the diner, about how her mother raised two precocious girls and two older boys who all worked in the family business. He heard about the diner's famous rice pudding and how its preparation, when it was her mother's turn, kept Mom's upper torso in shape. "A lot of stirring," she volunteered. "The woman's biceps and shoulders are scary."

Randall nodded politely, listened for any leads, glanced some at her tits, endured more bowling bullshit from her, and started thinking this was going nowhere until Stella blurted, "I've got it. How about *you* take me to the City instead?"

* * *

Randall was in the driver's seat of Stella's VW Beetle, in the far reaches of the bowling alley parking lot, her head in his lap, a slight chill in the mountain air, the motor running. At this distance the alley's rooftop marquis had lost its battle with the fog, its lighting so fuzzy it looked like a hovering aircraft in a grainy UFO photo. His eyes were on the car's digital clock; 8:45. Still plenty of night ahead, although he had no plans to spend any of it in New York City. He patted the top of Stella's bobbing head hovering over his crotch. She was good at this, he'd give her that, but she had a lot to work with. Randall closed his eyes, still feeling the rush from the line of coke he did with her. She made cooing noises while she worked on him. His eyes reopened, returning him to the foggy night dreamscape that surrounded them. So thick, someone could, yes, commit a murder in the car right next to them without discovery.

She came up for air. "Uno momento, big boy," she said, wrapping her fingers around where her mouth just was. "Home stretch in just a sec, right after I get another taste." She was adept at setting up another line while working him with her hand.

It was time, Randall knew, soon as she was back on him. He reminded himself not to strangle her while her mouth was occupied.

She went back to work, got schoolgirl giddy, and finished him off. She disengaged, and at that moment he wrapped his large hands around her throat. He fended off her thrashing and punching, squeezing her neck until she, too, was every bit of finished off.

He was in a small car with a dead woman in it. He'd rather be in a larger car without a dead woman in it. Randall reclined the seat next to him and rearranged the body, belting his sleepy passenger in. He drove the Beetle out to the road so he could swap it for the Caddy. He tapped the brake at the exit then waited, needing to make sure an approaching car did what its signal advertised, which was to turn into the bowling alley lot.

The car executed its turn. Not a car, a van. Randall checked out the driver as the van glided by. A woman with dark, short hair, and the van a custom black-and-gold paint job. Randall remembered it from the diner earlier tonight. It had a cute dog in the passenger's seat.

34

He admitted it to himself. Now that it was after eight p.m. and the match had started, Andy was keenly interested in each person who entered the bowling alley, hoping one of them would be Counsel. His woe-is-me bluster about keeping his distance from prospective suitors... at fifty-six, it was equal part altruism and equal part that he found most eligible women under forty lacking substance. Few had what he needed: a compassionate disposition; a hard shell, but with a soft and gentle inside; the patience and understanding that came from great personal loss and one's own need for healing; and, his sheepish admission, a slam-bam-thank-you-ma'am boner-worthy physical presence. For him it wasn't practical to let women get too emotionally close. Still, when dealing with the prospect of being partner-less ad infinitum, his idealism sometimes lost out.

"You're up, Andy," his mother said. She sat in the scorekeeper's chair for lane twenty, near the ball return chute. For the most part, Charlie was behaving herself.

"Thanks, Ma."

Andy blew on his fingers, grabbed a small towel and wiped off his silver ball, all part of the delivery ritual.

Charlie called to him. "She'll be here, honey, she likes you. Now go fuck up all those pins."

35

Almost an hour late. Goddamn feds. Fucking fog. And now a crush of cars in the bowling alley's parking lot. No, wait. A space, far right corner, rear. "Here we are, deputies."

An excited Tess sat upright in the passenger seat, readying herself for her leash.

"No, Tess, sweetie, not now. You guys need to sit here quietly while I go inside. Think you can do that?"

Tess's head lowered, awaiting a pat or an ear scratch. I gave her both, plus a smooch on her mouth after I cupped her face. Yes, I kissed this Tasmanian Devil in the same place she utilized to rip and shred different members of the rodent family, plus smell Fungo's ass. It's a dog-owner thing.

I opened all the van's windows a few inches for air. My mental check-down: guns, cuffs, taser, pepper spray, phone, ID. Fuzzy keychain. Medication. I took another look at the Stephen Linkletter mug shot. Long, gray-white hair, a chubby face, a white beard, brown eyes. Height, six-one. Weight, anyone's guess, but at six-one and bearded like the Jolly Old Elf, he was probably two-forty. Age, forty-five, but the hair and beard made him look older. Nice-guy older, the crow's feet next to his eyes suggesting he liked to smile a lot. Could definitely play Santa. So dangerous when they looked like this.

Fungo left his crate and wandered forward, poked at my shoulder and snorted. His body language—his butt shaking back and forth, a counterbalance to his wagging tail, him all nudge, snort, shake and wag—meant only one thing. A grunt through his pursed dog lips suffixed by an overpowering stench validated it.

"Fine, you guys need to go. Tess, let's saddle up." I grabbed and leashed her. Fungo, forever dressed for the occasion in his lead, waited alongside her.

A small patch behind a row of evergreens did the trick for them, but it was a nasty mess from Fungo. Ugh. Late at night, some out-of-the-way weeds... Damn, son, this one needed to stay where it was. At the rear of the van, I waited for the parking space next to us to empty as an older couple backed out and pulled away.

I locked my buddies back up. Time to see how Andy and his team were doing in their quest to earn a tacky bowling trophy.

36

Randall exited the alley's parking lot entrance lane with dead Stella in the passenger seat, turned right onto the highway to retrieve the Caddy, which had acquired some interest. Two guys shielded their eyes as they looked through the tinted windows at the interior. A third guy eyed the rear bumper with its bookend anti-drug stickers.

The car's owners.

Randall drove past them, put some distance between him and the bowling alley before he doubled back. Only one guy left at the Caddy now, leaning back against the driver's door enjoying a cigarette, uninterested in the passing Beetle as it cruised by on its return trip. The other two partyers hoofed it alongside the road in full guido stride toward the entrance to the alley parking lot. North Jersey reality-TV-show types, over-the-top in the gold-chain bling department.

Farther down, another U-turn brought Randall back around again. This time he pulled Stella's car onto the shoulder, eight cars or so back from the Caddy. The bling on the two guys approaching on foot reflected the Bug's headlights.

Ignition off, Randall took his time exiting the car, wanting them to pass him before he finished locking up. He nodded as they walked by, flashed a big, happy, gentlemanly smile. Hot-shit punks that they were, he got nothing in return.

Randall liked the Caddy, would not give it up unless he had to. The two punks on foot left the highway shoulder, turned left onto the lane that would take them to the rear of the parking lot, for sure looking to settle a score with whoever stole their car. Randall followed, gravel crunching underfoot as they neared the paved lot. He glanced over his shoulder, sized up the surroundings: dark highway cloaked in a heavy fog that included the smoker at the Cadillac. Randall quickly closed the distance on his prey on light, tiptoey footsteps; he drew both handguns. One loser he dropped with a shot to the back of the head, and a split second later blew apart the surprised face of the second when he turned, his gun dropping harmlessly in the brush. *Bang, bang,* that quick, execution style, except for the subdued echos of the gunshots, and what to do with the two dead bodies.

The third guido back at the Caddy had to be smiling now, expecting his buddies were on the delivering end of the shots. Randall dragged each body behind a row of evergreens lining the entrance lane. He doubled over, caught his breath, coughed and wheezed, his disease staking some of its territory.

Now to retrieve the Cadillac.

37

Bang, then *bang*.

Sequential strikes on lanes one and two, nearest the front door. Why I heard these two in particular I had no idea, but they pulled my attention away from Andy's all-business release of his silver bowling ball on lane twenty. At the bar I ordered up a Yuengling Porter and planned to nurse it while I looked the part of interested coal-country bowling groupie checking out the bar area and the lanes. I had no intention of getting juiced, but for the rest of the busy bar-leaners, old and young alike, it was a different story. A lot of people here. Bowlers, drinkers, gamblers. I hoped my bounty was one of them.

Back to Andy. I heard, didn't see, his ball's impact. Ka-*pow*. A strike, then fist bumps from his teammates. Some serious old-school bowling was going on here, and considering the age of some of them, I was surprised at how good they were. A page out of the seventies and the eighties. No. Farther back, I'm thinking now.

Road House, a late 1940s movie, entered my head. Richard Widmark, Ida Lupino. Celeste Holm, Cornel Wilde. Black-and-white noir. One of my mother's favorites, the setting a nightclub with a bowling alley attached. The Thunder Wonderland bar had the same feel and charm, with cozy, softly lit nightclub lamps on café tables, and a piano with cigarette burns on its glossy black finish.

Background music from overhead, far from the seductive, torchy stuff Ms. Lupino delivered in the noir movie. Ozzy Osbourne's "Crazy Train." The selection made sense, considering that heavy-metal Helen, the fry cook, was tending bar. Above her, along the back of the bar, the hanging TVs showed baseball games on two of them, streaming music videos on a third, and the local news on the fourth, all with closed captioning. My beer arrived.

"Counsel, right?" Helen said, a pleasant smile from her to go with her careful, almost reverent placement of my Yuengling and an order of onion rings on the bar, food I didn't order. A bit different from our previous encounter yesterday, when her attitude had me hoping there wasn't too much spit in the lunch she'd made for me.

"Yes. And you're Helen. These rings aren't mine."

She nodded. "Floyd heard what you did today. He says you eat and drink free tonight, lady. Just don't get sloppy. Sorry, I can't stay and chat, I'm needed in the kitchen."

A person could get used to this small-town familiarity. I raised the pint glass in thanks, lamenting my need to limit tonight's intake, took a sip. *Ahhh.* The girl could pour too. Moving in behind Ozzy was Fogerty's "Fortunate Son." Where the hell had that come from?

My eyes sifted through the crowd at the bar, trying to stay on task while I powered through the song's psycho triggers, doing my best not to pound down the entire pint in one gulp.

One bit of comfort: Andy. He allotted me some eye action and whispered to his mother when he realized I was here. That gave me a little flutter in one place and a tingle of pleasure in another.

38

Randall climbed back into dead Stella's VW. The third guido might be expecting his drug-dealing thug buddies to return, like, maybe right now, otherwise he'd soon realize he was wrong about which end of the gunshots they were on. Randall started the car, the headlights on but useless in this fog. The mist relented for a moment. There. Guido thug number three. Tall, dark from a spray tan, porkpie black hat, fidgety. Still smoking, but no longer leaning against the Caddy. The guy tossed his cigarette and started walking, coming Randall's way.

Randall checked the foggy road in both directions. No traffic he could see.

He decided how to play this. Yanking dead Stella's tube top down bared her chest, she looking completely alive, just spaced, in the reclined passenger seat.

Randall pulled onto the road then braked the car a few lengths up, waited for the thug to arrive alongside. He leaned over the body to manually roll down the passenger window then turned on the car's interior light. Burying his hand between her legs would sell it better.

"Hey. Buddy. My young friend here is partied out but will perk back up if I can find her some powder. You holding any?"

He had the punk's attention. The punk slowed and smiled at the wasted chick and where Randall had his hand. He leaned in. "Sorry, man, maybe when I get ba—"

The hesitation was all Randall needed. He extracted his naughty hand and the Rhino magnum from between her legs. The shot took off the front of Mr. Jersey Shore's head, dropping him like a sack of Purina next to the car.

A powerful gun. Randall liked the Rhino a lot.

39

I felt better with every step I took away from the bar and the Fogerty song. Threading my way with my beer through the standing-room-only jumble of onlookers, I moved closer to the lanes that showcased tonight's main bowling attraction. The three rows of stadium-style spectator seats were all occupied.

Andy's team, the Fighting Cadavers, versus Dody Heck's team, Clooney's Concubines.

Five bowlers each, three women, two men, silky custom bowling shirts on all ten of them. The shirts were distinctive, Andy's with an elaborate willow tree in brown and green on their red shirt backs, the B&B's name above the tree in the dripping black blood embroidery he told me about. One lane over was crowded in Pinky Tuscadero pink, with first names stitched in a midnight blue longhand above a breast pocket, their sponsor Aristotle's Diner. An airbrushed Parthenon looked small on their backs. Plenty of room left over width-wise for additional billboard content for all the Concubines except the skinny elderly redhead I recognized as the diner's cashier. The other men and women including Dody looked like they ate at the diner a lot.

A mistake: *six* Fighting Cadaver red shirts after I noticed Charlie, Andy's mother. The overhead scoring said it was early in the second game of the match, the Cadavers up one game to none. Charlie sat nearest the ball return in a plastic chair and tray combination, one of two chair-tray combinations side by side, one for each team. These were the scorekeepers' seats in earlier days, before electronic scoring; the best two seats in the house for the match. I was able to hear Charlie. She was putting her seat to good use.

"That's a shame, Dody, a real shame," she said, talking trash. Dody's first ball left her the most difficult spare to convert in bowling, a seven-ten split. "Anyone know how many times the pro bowlers convert a bedpost split?" Charlie asked.

"Less than one percent, Charlie," Dody and each of her teammates droned together.

"Damn straight, ladies. Point-five percent. And that's the pros. I made one, as in once in all my sixty-two years of bowling. No chance, Dody. You've got no chance."

"Then watch this, Charlie, and be amazed," Dody said. She picked up her ball from the ball return and wiped it with a soft cloth.

I held up my phone like every other person around me and pressed record. You just never knew.

Dody, a hefty lefty, set up behind the floor dot farthest right, lining up in front of the ten pin. Hers was a three-step approach with an exaggerated pendulum motion and a powerful release. The ball went cross-alley with pure speed and only a slight curve. It caught the left side of the seven pin. The pin exploded against the back wall, dropped into the pit underneath, then, rising from the dead, it skittered back up and out to take out the ten, converting the split. The crowd erupted with frenzied hoots and hollers.

I sent the video to Vonetta, followed it up with a text.

These bitches be serious here netta

Cmon sarge really? A murdering molester out there and you're recording u-tube shit?

She made a 7-10 split you asshole. Less than one percent conversion rate

Wtf is happening to you fungo? You gonna start mining coal too?

I'm working dude. Not like you, you loan shark

Fuck you sarge

Fuck you netta

The crowd stayed mesmerized by Dody's circus shot, Dody included.

Andy was up next. He picked up his ball; the crowd noise leveled off. He lined up for his approach as everyone quieted. Charlie spoke, her voice weak and elderly-woman cranky. She mumbled something I didn't hear but she was clearly upset. Dody wandered over, put her arm around her. Charlie whimpered through her words as tears flowed, Dody listening.

"Sure, Charlie, sure," Dody said, smiling through tears of her own. "I like it. I like it a lot."

Andy lowered his ball, was about to walk back to help. "Ma? You okay?"

Dody waved him off. "We're good here, Andy. Charlie's just, ah, she just coined a new bowling term." Her voice shook a bit then recovered. "For the spare I just made. The way that pin came back, she wants to call it the 'Maurice Split.' I told her I was good with that."

Andy's eyes misted up. He got back to business and fired another strike.

40

Randall pulled the punk's body between two SUVs parked on the shoulder, had to drop it there when a car on the highway approached, the car inching along because of the fog. He crouched below hood level, close to the body while the car crept by. The victim was a blood-spattered cranial mess. The bullet sent chunks of scalp and gray matter skittering off a parked pickup's windshield, also sent the dude's silly porkpie hat spinning to the asphalt. Randall helped himself to the Marlboro pack in the dead man's shirt pocket then frisbeed the hat into the woods.

Another car passed. He lifted the dead guy by the armpits again, dragged his body off the shoulder and into the weeds. Here, with vehicles still parked between the weeds and the road, the body would be out of view of the highway and people getting onto their cars.

Bon appetite, forest critters.

Randall found space for the Beetle farther up the shoulder, past the Cadillac. He turned off the ignition. Right about now a cigarette sounded good, but not in here with her.

He left the VW in favor of the Caddy, climbed inside, lit up one of the Marlboros, relaxed a bit. Four more dead in the span of thirty minutes. When the news-watching public heard about all the carnage in crime-free, small-town Rancor, they would be horrified. Aghast. Outraged. Maybe he would surrender, or maybe he would be caught, maybe even in the act. Yes, in the act would certainly work. Gratifying. Orgasmic. Surrender to whom, caught by whom, he didn't know. Here in wholesome, defenseless Rancor, getting caught by a decrepit old woman bowler wasn't likely, and staying caught by her afterward was less likely yet. The FBI had to be out there by now, on his trail somewhere. Or the State Police. Either would have been fine.

When word got out, the media would be all over the town. All over his background, all over his story. All over him. Yes. Splendid. It would be all about him.

And his ex, and his kid, as long as he could find them first. Or maybe after all this hubbub, they'd find him.

This busy a night at the bowling alley, he could feel it. Could feel that this foggy, dangerous night, and this rocking bowling alley, would surrender them both.

* * *

One parking lot space was open. Not the one the Beetle originally occupied, but the one next to it. Randall pulled in next to the black-and-gold custom van, the last vehicle to enter the lot. He cut the engine, found himself face to face with a dog sitting upright in the van's passenger seat, two windows and five feet of empty space separating them. He pushed open his car door, releasing cigarette smoke into the Pocono night air, the smoke lost in the mist. He climbed out, brushed himself off.

"Nice doggie," he said to the cute brindle-colored thing with penetrating brown eyes. Same dog he'd seen asleep in this van earlier today, at the diner. The dog raised its nose to the window's edge, the window open slightly for air. Randall was close enough to see the dog's nostrils constrict, its pores wet and glistening. The dog slid its nose along the opening, sampling all there was to know about Randall, who was interested in making the dog's acquaintance. Randall lifted his hand so the nice doggie could get a whiff of his fingers.

The springs on the van squeaked as it tilted toward him, its interior erupting into a barking apocalypse with teeth gnashing and paws clawing at the window. Two mouths and noses jammed into the window opening, interested less in his smell and more in the meat on his fingers, the second dog a large black-headed German Shepherd. Randall recoiled then stood his ground. The display amused him, especially after he realized he'd drawn a gun in response, which incensed the dogs even more. He put the gun away.

He liked dogs, but not these two nasty, furry fucks. Still, he'd never done a dog. It would pain him if he ever had to.

He reentered the bowling alley, found room at the bar again, eyed the bowling match in progress. The middle of the second game. Six clueless female bowlers on the two lanes when you included the women of both teams. No one under forty, maybe no one under sixty, far as he could tell, which meant no Regina.

41

Ten minutes into my first beer, the bar a distant landscape of shoulders away, it had become standing room only between here and there, people crammed their tightest closer in to the bartenders. Fry cook/bartender Helen patrolled her stretch of it, her head piercings and rave-blue hair shining and glinting, her cute face showcased by under-bar neon. Trip-hammer arms and hands slapped glasses and bottles onto the polished hardwood top. Helen was one of three bartenders working the trough, Floyd the bowling-shoe guy another. I lucked out, got Helen's distant attention when I raised my nearly empty pint glass. She nodded and got busy drawing another.

Middle of Andy's second game, and the electronic scoring showed his team trailed by a bunch, the seven-ten "Maurice Split" the catalyst for the other team, a shot that stoked up the bowlers on both sides.

"A turkey, Andy," Charlie called to her son. "Three strikes is always a charm..."

Andy assumed his coiled spring stance, unwound, slid his feet smoothly up to the foul line, and buried the ball in the one-three pocket. The pins crisscrossed, scattering in all directions; turkey executed. A "splasher," Charlie called the hit. For every hit, every pin combination, there was a name, each of them part of Charlie's vocabulary.

Next bowler up was a Concubine, her ball in hand. Charlie continued her bench work on the opposition. "You look tired, Myra. We keeping you up, toots? Ball too heavy?"

Myra was on the small side and overly made up beneath a short red wig. She released the ball, a lazy roller that hooked extra wide before it came back in and entered the pocket from the wrong side. She left four pins, none of them next to each other.

"A Jersey hit," Charlie said. "A shame, honey, a real shame. All those lonely pins. Looks as bad as your grandmother's teeth. Trade in that pink thing you call a ball, Myra. I've seen better hits from a six-pound house ball..."

Helen waved me back to the bar, set up my new Yuengling Porter at the corner. I took out a five, looking to stuff it into her tip jar. She thumbed me in the direction of the Maurice helmet. I did as I was told.

I was crammed in with younger folks, them sucking down their drafts and drinks and shots like it was a competition, all dressed to impress. A lot of exposed body ink, including on a guy who'd planted himself in front of me, young and tall, with a genuinely gifted, buff upper torso, plus a headful of blond-brown dreads. And apparently interested in me.

"Hi. I'm Eli."

Eli sipped, stared at my pixie hair, then face, then his eyes lingered on my chest. He seemed on the sweet, coy side. I needed to do my best to not be rude, so things wouldn't get out of hand Tourette's-wise.

"Hi, Eli."

"Nice head," he said. I guessed that was a new bar thing, lines like that, about a woman's haircut. I went with it.

"Thank you. It pays to have a good hair guy."

He gave the rest of me the once-over. "No, I meant mine. I've got a nice big head, ma'am, the one you can't see. And I like older chicks with great tits giving it some attention. Interested?"

I got this from guys sometimes. Hilarious. Supposed to impress me with his big-balls approach and his sexy smile, maybe even get me hot. Not tonight.

"Eli, sweetie, you and that landscape of Strawberry Shortcake ink on your arms and your neck are in my way. I'm watching my friends bowl. Move your entitled ass."

Tats. Tits. Tits and tats. A quick rub of my furry luck charm on my belt loop and Eli escaped otherwise unharmed, free to work out his sexy mommy issues elsewhere.

Only a few of the drinkers were seniors closer in to the bar, mingling with the twenty- to forty-somethings. I took quick stock of them. Curvy black woman, shiny gray ringlets. My mother would have labeled her 'demure'; a black Ida Lupino. She slowly stirred her drink, seemed bored with it or herself or with life in general, or bored at least with her interested other party, a dapper reddish-haired guy, his age debatable. A second older woman, a lumpy, rinsed blonde in her forties, her dress too tight, her roots black but not stylishly so, took a sloppy sip from her martini, seemed a bit drunk. The man next to her was overweight and white-haired, with a full white-gray beard. I took a good, hard look at him.

Looked like my guy.

I felt the pressure, stroked the fuzz, and resisted drawing my gun, hoped it wasn't needed. My facial muscles tightened around gritting teeth. I waded in.

The buzz around the bar suddenly elevated, heads turning quickly, mine included, to focus on one of the TVs. The other three TVs switched stations to join the fourth, all tuned to the same local news event. The bartender turned up the volume and the patrons went church quiet. A quick glance at my maybe-bounty; he was still there. A voiceover accompanied a video taken during daylight hours, recorded outside a restaurant in downtown Scranton.

"Two dead in the popular steakhouse's restroom earlier today... pills... Executions or drug deal gone wrong, or gang slayings, it's unknown at this time. Local Scranton investigators were on the scene. And now, so is the FBI..."

Soon as I heard FBI, I concentrated. All four TV screens showed footage of EMTs carrying two body bags out of the restaurant earlier in the day. A cut to live footage on the street showed evening patrons entering the steakhouse, some J. Edgars visible in the backdrop. And there they were: Agent

Van Impe plus two other FBI types plus Agent McQuarters, an ogre in a too-short, shitty suit. What interested them was a car parked across the street. A custom-painted Honda Civic. No shit. It was the car I had the pleasure of confronting earlier today at the strip mall drug store. I was now liking this news story a lot.

So too was everyone else in the bar area. Around me I saw a few low-key fist bumps and arms drape more freely over shoulders, the crowd getting chummier with each comment the reporter delivered while they looped the video. The restaurant storefront, the dining room, the bathroom, the bloody toilets. Shell casings littered the brown tile floor, with glimpses of the reflective crime scene chalk that outlined them. Next to me, an unsteady bar leaner raised his hand, looked to me for a high five.

"Ha! Look at all them bingo chips, Walt. That'll learn ya, ya bastards." He squinted. His rosy-cheeked, alcohol-fueled smile disintegrated when I left his high five hanging. "You ain't Walt. The hell you do with Walt?" He high-fived another bar patron instead.

The bowling alley background noise subsided. Rolling balls and pin-breaks dropped off, became sporadic like the last few kernels of microwave popcorn. The TVs became center stage, the alley's patrons riveted.

"... precise, quiet, deadly. Upscale lunchtime dining marred by two murders that looked like executions. Tune in at eleven for more details. WSWB reporting live from Scranton..."

The news became the weather, the other TVs stuttering back to their baseball games and music videos, my white-haired person of interest still charming his lady friend. The quieted viewers re-engaged each other, returning to the business of drinking and small talk and pickup lines and noisy strikes and spares.

What the hell just happened? Before I moved on my person of interest I made another visual sweep of the alley patrons, out on a Wednesday night to bowl and drink and share some grins, but all of it had stopped for a basic, garden-variety local shooting. *We interrupt your late night hookup for this breaking news...*

To a one, young and old, they'd watched it, and only after they'd reveled in it did they go back to the business of brag and bling. Except I'd heard it.

Heard the pride buried within their reveling, and I was expected to share it by way of the high five meant for someone's good buddy Walt. Heard the drunk talk that went with it too. *Bingo chips.* Apparently slang in these parts for shell casings. I filed that one away, but not for long because my subconscious had heard it too.

"—bingo bongo boob-o, bibbidi-bobbidi-boo, Babalu! BABALUUUU!"

I gritted my teeth to minimize the drivel until I found the fuzz. No one noticed my lapse because of the surrounding noise level.

The blonde martini lady chatting up my prospective bounty pointed her manicured finger at the TV then at Helen, busy as hell bartending. Martini Lady had apparently been at the Scranton steakhouse, or lived near it, or Helen had been there, or something else about that news story was important to her the way she was gesturing. Martini Lady grabbed her wrist before she could leave, pulled her close, then patted Helen's shoulder like a proud, drunk aunt, jabbing at her own bicep then at Helen's, making a point. Helen shushed her and took the new martini away.

The woman pouted then pleaded to her prospective lay for the evening. He gave up his drink for her and she gulped it down, rubbed his upper thigh in appreciation. It was then that he and I made our visual acquaintance. I broke it off, else I'd have spooked him at this distance. He re-engaged his female target.

Before I could move, Helen was at my end of the bar deep-sixing the lady's martini at the sink, cursing under her breath. She released a few "fucking idiot" sentiments that filled the unexpectedly quiet, dead air around us. She rubbed her left bicep where Martini Lady had jabbed her, her sleeveless top exposing major artwork, shoulder to wrist. The jab—it couldn't have hurt her, but her mindless massaging of it, and her narrowed eyes, said it had taken a toll, that somewhere beneath the artwork it had hit a nerve.

Same as it did with me right then, me staring at her upper arm, awestruck.

There, camouflaged, other tattoos surrounding it like a collage, with interlocking dragons and unicorns and trolls, one particular tattoo in the middle of the mix shocked me. A puppet head. Kangaroo ears, smiling platypus face, red nose. A fucking bunyip. *The* fucking Bunyip.

Bunyip's property. Here, in the Poconos, tending bar, not turning tricks in Philly. An old cold case. I called her over, said two words to her when she asked what she could help me with, me staring her down.

"Bunyip Deveraux."

She stood statue still, maintained a poker face with no eyelid flutter, her jaw muscles tightening. Her hands... they were going for something under the bar—

Shit. I'd left the wrong impression.

"Helen—no—wait—the dude's an unsolved missing person in Philly—"

I raised my hands palms up, I come in peace, no mas, don't tase me bro, etc., etc. Her hands stayed where I couldn't see them.

I explained. "Sorry. I'm an idiot. I've got no interest in the Bunyip or anyone associated with him. Your tattoo—it surprised me."

She eyed me closely, stayed deadpan as long as she could. Her hands reappeared atop the bar, empty.

"Some teenagers make really poor choices. He can't hurt anyone now." Her jaw still tight she spoke again, calling to someone farther down the bar, her eyes still locked on mine. "Audrey! Over here." Helen's fingers beckoned her friend to join us. "You need to meet someone, Counsel, so you get a better understanding of things."

Her friend excused herself from a conversation and unwound her lower half from the stool. The shorthaired brunette with an oval face had made-up eyes that she'd done a professional job with. Her lacey yellow top was tucked into stylish jeans, the blouse with short sleeves. A few thousand dollars' worth of exposed ink ran from wrist to neck, the tattoo sleeve broken by the dash of yellow that covered her upper arm and shoulder.

"Helen, honey," Audrey said, me getting some side-eye. "You good here, sweetie?" Her opinion of me was no doubt still formulating, pending Helen's answer.

"This lady here, she needs to see it." Helen nodded her head in my direction then in Audrey's, giving Audrey permission.

"'It'?"

"Yes, 'it.' Please."

Audrey hesitated, a pronounced eyelid flutter greeting Helen's stare at her. "You sure, honey?"

"Yes, I'm sure. This is Counsel. She's a friend."

Audrey got up close and incredibly personal with me. Her dark eyes stayed on mine, making me wait a few beats. Then, "Look closely at my arm."

So I did. A sleeve full of *A Midsummer Night's Dream* tats, faeries and horned nymphs and cupids all scampering north from her wrist, a dizzying array of green and red and peach flowers sprouting everywhere. I followed the artwork up her forearm to her bicep. She lifted up the short yellow sleeve, exposing more blossoming flowers. One bore the face of the Bunyip.

"See Big Drew over there?" Helen said to me, accompanied by a chin point. I looked, saw a heavier woman, anywhere from twenties to forties, slow-dancing near the bathroom with a date, her exposed arm a rather meaty mirage of tattoos. "She's with her husband. The lighting's low, but if you look close enough you'll see she likes Thomas the Tank Engine, because her toddler is a big Thomas fan, although Thomas's face looks a bit bunyip-y."

Helen had to draw a beer for an impatient customer. She reached over Audrey's head to deliver it. "One last thing, Counsel. No one survives a hit like the one they put on Deveraux. They should have found a body with only half a face behind that bar in Bristol, but it never turned up. No body meant that people had to take precautions."

"There are procedures that can remove your ink, Helen," I said. "They can be painful, but why not have it removed?"

"Maybe a person never wants to forget how bad things can get. Maybe a person wants, needs that reminder. Maybe it's something that keeps her sober. Or so I've heard."

I was impressed. Safety in numbers. Some misdirection. Overkill. My next question to Helen: "What's under the bar?"

She gave me a hard face, her eyes now cold as a gunslinger's. "What you're thinking is under the bar, is under the bar. Loaded."

Lovely. Helen left to get someone else a drink. I gulped down my beer and started toward the other end of the bar where Martini Lady and her suitor were swallowing each other's tongues.

"A Woolworth!" Charlie hollered from the hardwoods. All the heads at the bar turned toward the lanes, including mine.

"Stop into the five and dime, Andy! Hairbrush the five and put some lipstick on the ten. An easy split..."

I recovered from the distraction, had a difficult time pushing my way through the other bar leaners, jostling many of them, pissing off the women, getting leers from the men. The crowd cheered the spare. I reached the end of the bar, and fucking shit bastard son of a motherfucking bitch, both Martini Lady and her suitor were gone. I scanned the crowd, then the perimeter. The door to the building's entrance was swinging shut.

Outside. I needed to hustle my ass outside.

In the parking lot, a few smokers and gropers were tucked in against the building, another couple in an embrace had settled against the hood of a Hummer in a handicapped space. The flashing overhead marquis meant there was no privacy anywhere, but this didn't matter when you were drunk. Except there was no older drunk blonde and no potential Stephen Linkletter out here among them.

One minute into my walk through the lot, the fog became prohibitive, but it didn't mask the pockets of sweet-smelling weed I passed through. A blow job was in progress in a white Beemer sedan. Not my guy; too young. I reached the last row of cars and ended the search at my van. It was noisy inside, Tess growling at my approach. When I opened the driver's door she sat up, her eyes on me, her growl low key, her wiggling butt on my seat but resting there only lightly. In her mouth was the Linkletter plastic bottle, shredded in spots, crushed and chewed flat elsewhere, the green of the Poland Spring label only partly intact. She hopped out without permission and sprinted around the back of the van, on a mission. I followed, circled the van, found her growling, hopping and springing at the window of the car next to us. A Cadillac sedan. Nice. Empty. She didn't stop with the hopping, the driver's door getting scratched in the process, but right about then I didn't really give a shit, because right about then was when I realized whose car this was. I wrestled what was left of the shredded bottle out of her mouth and tucked it into my pocket. I opened the back of my van.

I went for the body armor. I suited the three of us up.

"Fungo—dude—sit. You're staying back here for now. Tess, let's go. No squirrel hunting inside, capice?" I shook a finger in her face. "Or no bedtime treat later. You understand, sweetie?"

She lowered her head and whined. She knew what I meant.

42

Randall might well have been a misogynist but he'd never considered himself a bigot. Meat was meat; color never mattered. Except he wasn't breaking through to this sexy older black woman at the bar, which was making him frustrated. She was like, *ho-hum, you tell me you got a big dick and some drugs, so what? You got anything else, white boy*, her perceived disinterest implied.

Yes, was his mental response. Yes, he did have something else.

"Guns. I have guns. You ever shoot a gun?"

Her eyes, dreamy slits a moment ago, opened a bit. The question had registered. They stayed lazily interested in her daiquiri, but this sleek-looking woman with fuzzy gray ringlets, flawless black skin, wondrous pink lips, and nice round booty was for sure intrigued. She paused, didn't take the sip she'd intended to take. "Your name again?"

"Howard," Randall, aka Howard, said. "I'm a lawyer."

"Howard. Huh." Another pause. "Yes, I've shot a gun before."

She stirred her drink, then sipped. She again settled into searching for the answers to life's mysteries in her rum and lime juice. One more try, Randall decided, this time with a different angle. He leaned heavily on the bar with both elbows, faced forward, spoke some into the long mirror that ran partway behind the bar's length, some into his drink, but what he said was meant only for her.

"I kill people. For fun," he said.

Some contemplative blinking accompanied a turn of her head, as in, had she heard him right?

After a few beats, "That's a joke," he said. "Your name is?"

Her frosty lip-sticked pink lips went back to the straw in her drink. They sucked the daiquiri glass dry, slowly and sensually. This time when she spoke, she faced him. "Order me another drink, Howard who jokes about killing people for fun. I'm Iota Jean."

There it was. He could waste time overthinking her ridiculous first name but he didn't, because he was in. He motioned for the bartender at this end.

"By the way, Howard," she said, eyeing two rude young adult men leaning over and pushing past seniors waiting their turn at the bar. "I kill people too, when I'm in the mood. Like those two. The entitlement generation. When they act that rude, they deserve it."

Randall analyzed the two fools she'd just outted, then reanalyzed her. She didn't flinch, staying deadpan. His smile emerged. "Ha. That was really good. Wow. You had me there."

"I did, didn't I?"

The young, alcohol-soaked, invincible nightclub population was where he'd start too, he said, hypothetically speaking, because the smug bastards were at an age where they thought they couldn't die. His fantasy included binges of sex and drugs before, you know, strangling them, keywords fantasy and strangling.

This storytelling was new, thrilling territory for him, because this time he was all but telegraphing his intentions.

"I get the part about the sex," she said. "The part about the strangling," her eyebrows tented, "I'm not so sure."

He'd pegged her as a bored older housewife, deep and nonjudgmental, someone who, rather than running away from him as fast as he could say *Natural Born Killers,* was maybe willing to ride the wild side if she could get some cheap thrills out of it.

"I figure the ultimate orgasm," he said, "would come by killing younger people after sex, because they're at an age where they think they'll never die. Still hypothetically speaking, of course."

"The sex I can get anytime," she said. "My fantasy would be in killing people who do bad things to other people. Hypothetically speaking, of course."

"Of course."

A segue coming up, right... now.

"So there was this young woman in Philly," Randall said. "A teenager who said she was from Rancor. She was, I guess you could say, exciting. Different."

The pivot was smooth, seamless, no need for him to produce photos, which would have called attention to themselves, maybe make this talk too serious. "She made some big mistakes in an unforgiving environment, did risky things that could severely limit her life expectancy, except, hell, she was young, right? And invincible. She started abusing her body, at first because it was fun and she could, but then it was to keep from having to admit that her naiveté about getting into the movies had put her in a very bad way—the family way to be specific, and with a drug monkey on her back."

"From Rancor," Iota Jean said. "Interesting. She have a name?"

"Regina Briscoe. Also went by Juicy Luster. Twenty, twenty-one? A sugar daddy kept her from making additional bad decisions, and the truth was, she finally got it. Figured out soon enough that life was a marathon, not a coked-up sprint. Except she bit the hand that fed her and bolted, leaving behind some heavy damage. Funny thing was, it was just before she was about to cash in and become the sugar daddy's queen and the mother of his child. The love-struck older guy wanted to leave her his money, all of it. Wanted to do right by her even though he'd scared her away. A fool thing on his part, right?"

"Explain what you mean by 'bit the hand that fed her.'"

"A real tragedy. A shotgun, to the neck and face, at a range close enough that he should have died, but he didn't. So where the hell is that drink you ordered?"

Randall rose, searched the south end of the bar, was about to get rude with the female bartender at the north end if he could get her attention. Iota Jean's hand firmly gripped his chin, redirecting his attention away from that end of the bar—"Howard; *Howard.* Over here..."—to where she greeted his surprised look with another demure pout. "Relax, honey, please. Let me handle this. Floyd? Doll face? A little help here please with my drink order—*Floyd!*—yes, over here—Excellent. Thank you, Floyd."

Her drink arrived tout-suite, and they clinked glasses, Iota Jean staying intensely interested in their face-to-face discussion. The bowling crowd buzz increased. Randall's interest was momentarily sidetracked, moving away from this hot black woman to the alley's center lanes, the end of the bowling match's second game in best out of three. Lining up her shot was the team's anchor, the tiny old redhead who dead Stella had pointed out as her mother. She was about to strike her way through the final frame of the current game.

Her ball hooked extra wide, was a heavy hit in the one-three pocket. A late slider bounded across the lane to take out the ten pin and complete the strike. Fist bumps accompanied low fives from her teammates, with a crescendo of applause from an appreciative crowd.

Randall scanned the faces of the two bowling teams. Six additional women to choose from, if Iota Jean didn't work out. He'd set them up with drinks after the third and last game, treat them extra nice, and talk about how much he liked this town, and how he might decide to move here permanently. He'd foster their feeling of safety in numbers and close down the bar with them if necessary, try to work in more info about Regina, about a child, to see if anyone bit.

More small talk with Iota Jean, until a put-together woman in leather—the one he'd seen leave the building a few minutes earlier—reentered the bowling alley, this time with a brindle-colored dog on a tight leash. A service dog of some kind with a harness, or maybe it was a black sweater.

Wrong. It was the dog from the van, and it was wearing a Kevlar vest. Ditto for his handler.

Randall suddenly needed to be somewhere where the dog owner and her K9 partner weren't. The side exit was farther, a rest room respite would have to do. "Excuse me, Iota Jean, I need a bio break."

"Aren't you forgetting something, Howard?"

"What's that?"

"Swapping phone numbers?"

43

Two side rooms. I should have checked them first before I ran outside. Slot machines in one, video games and kewpie dolls and other sideshow gaming apparatus in the other.

"Tess—in here."

I pulled hard on her leash for the right turn I wanted her to make. She was intent on going forward, toward the bar. "Yeah, sweetie, I know, he was over there before, but we're going here first."

I was bigger than her so I won. We needed to do a room-by-room search for my bounty and the drunk blonde, starting right here, in the room with the slots.

Twenty or so one-armed bandits lined ninety percent of the four walls of the room's perimeter. Video poker machines took up the floor space in the center. Every machine was occupied. No one was giving me any crap for bringing a dog into the bowling alley. To the contrary; we got a wide berth. I scanned the large room. No bounty, no drunk blonde.

Wait. The right corner, too dark to see it; I needed a closer look. And there she was, her back to me, straddling an armless chair, her one hand outstretched trying not to spill her drink. In progress was a spirited lip lock and what might have passed for a lap dance. Tess pulled up quickly alongside her, or rather, them. Underneath the blonde was my white-haired, bearded person of interest.

My threatening scowl manifested itself. "I'm a fugitive recovery agent. Stephen Linkletter, you're under citizen's arrest."

"What? Who...?" The couple disengaged, the woman unsteady yet keeping her drink level.

"You jumped bail in Allentown. I'm making a citizen's arrest. Let's go."

"But that's not my name. You're making a mistake. Here, I have ID..."

Tess was sidetracked, should have been all over this guy, was instead sniffing at the woman, or rather sniffing between her legs for the squirrel at third base. The blonde didn't seem to mind. "Aw, nice poochie, just look at you, such a sweet face..." She patted Tess's head. Tess burrowed farther into the woman's crotch. "Nice poochie-pooch..."

I raised my finger at my dog. Her ears lay down and she pulled out, wounded by my look.

"Mr. Linkletter, stand up—*now*. No need for me to embarrass you in front of your lady friend."

"But I am standing up—"

And so he was, damn it. The guy was no bigger than five-five. According to the police flyer, my bounty was six-one.

My apology went to a Mr. David Jarret of Three Bridges, Pennsylvania, per the driver's license he offered, but the apology was cut short. Tess pulled out from under the blonde's cupped hand, turned me around and nearly separated my arm from its socket. She strained, nose to the floor, wanted desperately to leave the room. The two of us reentered the bar area. When Tess barked, the crowd separated. My verbal disclaimer startled any and all patrons too slow or too drunk to get out of the way: "Service dog—yes, I have issues. Service dog—yes, I have issues..."

We reached the bar. Tess sniffed the pleather seat of an empty barstool. This amused a gray-headed woman of color in the chair next to it. My attention went to her. "The guy who was sitting in this chair before. Where is he?"

"Been a number of guys in that chair tonight, sugar. I have no idea."

"Older white guy. Over six feet. White hair. Santa beard."

She laughed. "And none of them with that description. Sorry. You're what? A cop? FBI?"

Tess's doggie butt and tail stub wiggled, telegraphing her disposition. She sniffed some at the woman's hand lowered to greet her, and some at her crossed legs. Tess got back to business, went low to the floor again, searching for more of the scent.

"Neither," I answered. "Bounty hunter."

"Ah. Of course. You're staying at Andy Prudhomme's B and B. I'm Iota Jean."

Right about now this small town shit was getting in the way. "Counsel Fungo. Sorry, ma'am, I gotta run."

Tess and I left the bar area, cruised the nearest bowling lanes, Tess twisting the two of us through the crowd. "Excuse me, service dog. Excuse me, service dog—"

The sea of people parted when they noticed Tess and I were in flak jackets. She pulled me, hard, to lane twenty, Andy's lane, stretching her leash taut as a high wire, the two of us skipping down the few vinyl-clad steps that put us on the hardwood floor at lane level, Tess still straining. She reached Andy and his team members, some seated, some standing, all unaware of our approach, with Tess interested in Charlie. Tess sat next to her, put a paw onto Charlie's lap before pulling herself onto it. She could spot the friendlies a mile away. She was here, paying a social visit. Sometimes this happened.

"Fungo!" Charlie said, her face animated, reaching for my deputy's wet nose. "You're here. Wonderful."

"That's Tess, Charlie," I said, correcting her. I went for Tess's collar and tugged her off Charlie's lap.

Charlie's friendly face turned mock stern. "Don't confuse me now," she said. "You're Counsel Fungo, and you're named after your dog. You know how I can get confused..."

"Sorry, ma'am, you're right about me, but this is a different dog. Good to see you, ma'am..."

Andy and I exchanged glances. He was subdued, but a smirk gave away that he was happy I showed. It dissipated when he got the full impact.

Seeing body armor on a woman and her dog deputy could do this to a person.

"He's here?" Andy mouthed. I nodded.

Tess needed to refocus. I retrieved the chewed piece of water bottle from my pocket and shoved it under her nose. After a few nasal constrictions her nose lowered to floor level again, sweeping the hardwoods. She moved over to the vinyl steps, climbed them, padded onto the street-level carpeting.

Before Tess's nose discovered him, I did, on the periphery of the crowd, him exiting the men's room.

I remembered him. Making time with the waitress at the diner. Him getting into his car, a silver Cadillac, next to my van then like it was now. Him acknowledging Tess, his hair white and shorter than in the mug shot, but not the strawberry blond it was now. His Santa beard was gone, a tidy gray-white mustache left behind. Easy adjustments. And he was tall enough. But no beard meant an exposed face with visible scars above the jawline and below it, onto the neck. Trauma of some sort, maybe with reconstructive surgery the outcome.

He was dressed casually in a sport coat, the pockets heavy; could be hardware. We'd need to convince him that it was in his best interest not to resist.

Our eye contact was distant but pronounced. Dog on a leash, parting crowd, body armor; he couldn't misunderstand my intentions. He pushed through an out-of-the-way emergency exit near the men's room, a shaft of exterior floodlighting illuminating the carpet for the short time it took for the thick metal door to seal shut.

Tess now had his full scent. No clear path to the exit, but I had no shame.

"Move, rabid dog, move, rabid dog..."

We arrived, Tess jumping at the closed door. I cracked it open a sliver. An exterior floodlight shined in my face, looked like it bathed the entire rear of the building. I wouldn't see him, but he'd see us. Walking out this exit would be suicide.

Just a little wider...

The opening gave him up. He was entering the wooded perimeter twenty-plus yards away. Still, if he decided to stop now, stay hidden in the evergreens, and pull out some firepower, Tess and I wouldn't make it more than a few feet from the exit.

Plan B: go out the front door, hustle around back, enter the woods from the side.

Plan B on steroids: add my shepherd Fungo to the lineup.

* * *

"Fungo. Looking good, boy. Ready to rumble?"

Fungo sat on his haunches at the rear of the van, had stilled himself except for his butt-wiggle thing, grunting once then growling when I tightened up his harness, waiting for my command to deploy. I reached inside the van, grabbed my Smith and Wesson mini flashlight that fit under some vest Velcro, plus a warm headband. The diamond studs in my ears needed to come out. The studs gone, I pulled the headband on. My flip-down night vision goggles slid over the ear cover. Now to get a look inside Mr. Linkletter's vehicle, next to my van.

Locked; a temporary condition.

Tess assumed the position behind me. I hammered the butt end of my handgun against the driver's window once, twice, with the third time —*crash, tinkle-tinkle*—a charm. The driver's side window rained mini glass prisms onto the blacktop.

Empty front and rear seats. A luxury car, but nothing else was special about it except for the drugs in the glove box. I popped the trunk. Clothes, shaving kit, shoes, a handgun, ammo for the handgun. I could either wait for him to return to the car or take the dogs around back after him, into the woods.

No real choice. He'd made me in the bowling alley, knew the van, knew he was parked next to me. He just hadn't known I was after him. Now he did. But just in case I was wrong—

Pfutt.

Pfutt, pfutt, and *pfutt.* A pocketknife to all four of the Caddy's sidewalls. I grabbed his handgun and ammo from the Caddy and threw it in my van.

Back to a squirming Fungo, waiting for the command.

"Fungo. Fetch."

He jumped down next to Tess. The three of us entered a controlled full trot, heading toward the side of the building. Before we turned the corner a black sedan careened into the parking lot, didn't notice us on foot as it slowed and passed my van, a flashlight shining from the sedan's passenger seat, scoping the van out. It accelerated to the bowling alley's entrance and parked in an empty handicapped spot.

Agent McQuarters exited the driver's door, *FBI* in stamped white block letters showing front and back against the black of his protective vest. He marched into the building. Agent Van Impe, dressed likewise, trailed him. My two deputies and I trotted around to the rear of the bowling alley.

44

Randall waited out of breath just inside the protection of the evergreens, one handgun drawn. If the tracker and her mutt exited the bowling alley, fuck their Kevlar. A barrage of shots from a semiautomatic aimed at their heads at this close a distance would take them out.

No markings on the woman's vest. No *POLICE* or *FBI* or *ATF*. Not government-issue body armor, just commercial Kevlar. A private contractor, probably a bounty hunter.

Discounting the dog, and he knew there were two, there was a good chance she was working alone. She and the dogs were here for him, and they looked prepared for a takedown inside the bowling alley or out, regardless of the elements. But where the hell were they now? Aside from his comfy boat shoes, Randall's head-to-toe Dockers-and-sport-jacket attire wouldn't help much if he trekked into the woods in the dark and the fog. He re-laced his shoes, never fully taking his eyes off the building's rear exits. He waited.

Dog-lady wasn't accommodating him, and he decided why: she was probably out front of the building, waiting for Randall to come back to his car, considering no sane person went into a chilly forest unprepared this time of night. Which was why he had to do it.

They would come after him; he would take them out. He'd play it this way, otherwise there'd be no chance of heading back to the alley to continue his search plus maybe re-engage the locals for the raucous night he'd planned.

His prepaid cell shook once against his side; a text. Who the fuck was this?

You coming back lover? Or are you out there killing more people? ☺

A nice surprise; the hot black chick from the bar. Big tits, big ass. Getting hard just thinking about her. Maybe she changed her mind, could dish about Regina.

A quick text back to her. After he did the deeds, he'd clean himself up and take her up on her offer.

He entered the wall of dark pine trees behind him.

45

Counsel didn't come back. Her gear, her body language, putting her dog in play had confirmed it: her target had surfaced, either here or somewhere close by. Andy let this sink in. This was real. The bowling match was still in progress, but Andy was now preoccupied. He traded glances with Dody.

"What?" Dody said, puzzled. "Spinach in my teeth?"

"The guy Counsel is after," Andy said, "there's been a sighting."

"I got that much when the dog was down here drooling all over Charlie. Good for Miss Fungo. Bounty hunter gets her man. Happy for her. Now bowl. No excuses for you choking during this last frame."

Dody. So cavalier. Another day in the life of a retired cop. Right now, what Dody wanted was the championship trophy. Andy's priorities... He wasn't so sure what they were, but he thought Counsel Fungo might fit in there somewhere.

Dody, seeing his conflict: "Andy—sport—the guy jumped bail in Allentown. Attempted rape. A horrible thing, but it happens. Let's finish this thing then we'll deal with it. Bowl."

Andy's blood pressure was elevated, could smell that his deodorant was falling down on the job. Tenth frame, final game of the match. One strike from him would seal it, a come-from-behind victory for the championship. At the ball return carousel, he wiped down his silver ball, the wiping more to still his nerves than to improve the ball's performance. His mother beamed at him from her seat.

"Thank you, honey," Charlotte said to him. "Or did I thank you already?"

An unprompted sentiment not lost on Andy. This was about Aunt Kitty's Colt .45. Andy had made the swap before they came to tonight's game, per Charlotte's request: the antique six-shooter Kitty bequeathed to Andy in exchange for him taking her small snub-nose revolver. "Yes, you did thank me already. No worries. Love you, Ma."

No harm in letting his mother have the sentimental peacekeeper, with no bullets, of course. Except for one unanticipated outcome.

Charlotte, from her seat near the ball return, now had her hand raised in admiration. "What a beautiful gun this is."

"No. Ma. Wait. Put it away..."

Dody got to her first, relieved her of the pistol, and checked the chambers to confirm it wasn't loaded. "Better off if it stays in your purse, right, Charlie?" Dody zipped the purse closed with the gun in it, placing it on the floor next to Andy's bowling bag, ten feet from Charlie.

"Why of course, Dody, dear. But it's beautiful, isn't it?"

"Certainly is, Charlie."

Andy put his game face on, eyed the floor arrows, and started his approach. Step, step, release and slide. The ball left his right hand with a small *pop!* as his thumb liberated itself. A silent, rolling silver bomb spun into its wide hook, picking up speed on its way to the one-three pocket. The pins scattered. A black *X* registered on the overhead scoreboard. The strike tied the pin count between the teams, earning him two more balls. He needed only one pin in two tosses to win the match.

The second ball exploded into the pins for a crushing second strike. Hoots and hollers from his teammates and clapping by an appreciative audience. He awaited the return of his ball, entitled to one additional toss, but it wouldn't matter. The Cadavers were league champs.

At the front entrance, two men in *FBI*-emblazoned Kevlar vests pushed through the doors and entered the noisy crowd, one of the men a giant.

"Christ," Dody said, keen to the new patrons. "Must've been a fucking sale on body armor today."

The agents scanned the crowd then approached the bar first, to talk with the bartenders. After that, a trip to the rear exit door for them to take a peek outside at the brightly lit rear of the building. Back inside, they stepped down onto the hardwoods at lane level. They worked their way toward the two bowling teams from the building's far end, crossing each lane, issuing no apologies while forcing a few bowlers to stop in their tracks; an effective attention-getter, with a flair for the dramatic. Andy rechecked the location of his mother's purse. Still a safe distance from her, which would hopefully avoid any misunderstanding.

Dody stepped in front of the other bowlers and stood her ground on the lanes as the agents approached them.

"FBI," the smaller agent of the two announced.

"Yeah," Dody said, her tone serious, "we pretty much got that. I'm Dody Heck, retired police chief. You see the sign? No street shoes on the hardwood."

"Agent Van Impe, ma'am," the agent said by way of introduction, ignoring the shoes comment. "Busy night like this, we decided to drop in here again." He extended a hand with paper fliers in it. "Seen him before?"

Dody bristled, leaving him hanging, was less than impressed. Andy had seen this inflated posture on his friend before.

"I need some ID," Dody said. Then, for good measure, "And like I said, take your shoes off."

The agent grinned, his smile big and friendly. His partner closed ranks, took a position on the other side of Dody. Agent Van Impe leaned into her face, spoke quietly.

"You really want to bust my balls, Ms. Heck? Flex a little muscle here to impress your friends? Okay. You get to see one ID. Mine. Here. But I'm not taking off my shoes. And believe me, you don't want my partner to take his shoes off either."

Dody relented, examined the agent's credentials, accepted one of the fliers. "Saw it already, more than once today. Everyone has. We haven't seen him anywhere."

The agent pushed. "Fine. Anything else you'd like to volunteer? Seen anything else out of the ordinary?" The agent produced another picture before she answered. "How about this person?"

Dody checked it out, showed the picture to Andy. It was a posed photo of female State Trooper Counsel Fungo in uniform on one knee, a dog sitting on its haunches next to her.

"Yeah, she was here," Dody said, "she and her dog. Both Kevlar'd up, just like you guys," she looked up at his super-size partner, "but not as ugly. They left in a hurry. Feel like telling us what's going on?"

"No." This came from the large agent. His scowl said he didn't care jack shit about cops or state troopers, current or former.

"Sorry about my partner. Long day," Agent Van Impe said. "All you need to know is we're after the same guy. The ex-trooper's not in any trouble, just some noise we wished we weren't stuck dealing with. Thanks for your time, folks, and be careful getting home tonight. It could be dangerous out there."

Andy spoke to Dody as soon as the feds were out of earshot: "What the hell was that? You trying to piss them off on purpose?"

"Jurisdictional bullies. I don't like the feds. And I don't like other outside influences either."

"Meaning what exactly, Dody?"

"You heard them. Your guest Counsel is 'noise.' Noise that I admit is adorable and well intentioned, but noise anyway. We don't need any more noise around here."

Dody's dismissive attitude, some mounting resentment on Andy's part, plus Andy's own conflicted heart. An emotional tug-of-war. Andy wanted to call Counsel, to let her know the feds were right behind her.

Dody, on her cell, was already mobilizing. "Al? Hey. Good evening, Sheriff. It's Dody."

Andy picked up his bowling ball and rocketed a screamer with bad intentions down the alley. It exploded against the pins for a third consecutive strike, closing out the game and the championship match's final frame with an exclamation point and a standing O from the spectators.

Al and his sheriff persona—if Dody got him involved, things would get noisier.

And there was this: Andy watched as Iota Jean pushed through the crowd toward them. Like Andy, Iota Jean was a nurse, but unlike Andy she hated bowling and wouldn't be caught dead on the hardwoods. Her evening visits to Thunder Wonderland were for grins and gambling and, occasionally, younger guys. She arrived, stood diva-like next to the ball return, her trip a special one to get face to face with Andy and Dody.

"We need to talk," Iota Jean said.

* * *

Iota Jean's input: a guy calling himself Howard hit on her at the bar. Hair shorter than the mug shot in Dody's hand, and a different color, but the right age. A mustache, no beard. Some facial scars. "I say that's him," Iota Jean said. "Told me he likes guns. When I didn't bite, he went for shock value," she told them. "He said he's murdered people. For kicks. Swear to God. Then he backed off, said he was joking.

"And he's looking for someone we know. I gave him my phone number."

Dody wasn't impressed. "Now what, we wait until he calls you tomorrow, or next week?"

"The deal was," a sly smile from Iota Jean, "my number for his."

"Sure. A phone number from a guy at a bar. You've got shit, Iota. You'll never hear from him."

"Spare me the sarcasm, Dody. I already did hear from him. He texted me to say he'll be back. Midnight or thereabouts."

Dody checked a clock. "That gives us a coupla hours. All right, I'll go for it. Someone get some drinks over here for us. A round of shots. I'm buying."

Andy checked in with a beaming Charlotte. "You okay, Ma?"

"Look at this trophy, Andy." Height-wise, it reached eye level to the seated Charlotte. "Bert will love it."

Andy sighed. Bert Carbone would have if he weren't already dead. "A beauty, Ma. Great." He patted her on the shoulder, caught Dody's eyes while Dody spoke into her phone.

"Al? No posse for now. We've got this."

46

We trotted to the corner of the building and gave it a wide berth, instead entered the cover of the trees and held there so we could view the spot where Linkletter went into the woods thirty yards away. The leashes were taut, my troops looking for the signal that would let them go all-out full assault. Our bounty had a ten-minute head start. We needed to determine if he'd used it to leave the perimeter. I flipped down the night goggles.

No Linkletter along the edge of the copse. We moved quietly just inside the evergreen periphery, on alert, the trees tall, majestic, their pointed tops not visible in the night fog. The three of us shuffled through layers of pine needles, thick in some spots, thin in others. I tugged at the leashes, held my charges back, and had them sit a moment while I gave them another sniff of Linkletter's water bottle. All fired up again, they pulled me along, closer to where we saw him last.

Fungo growled and barked, pawing at the dirt. I grabbed his snoot and shushed him; no need to broadcast our position. He whined, dropped his nose to the ground again and we were off, winding around trees and negotiating evergreen deadfalls and other forest litter. Hooting owls, crickets, and the flapping of wings from startled birds surrounded us, but so far no ground-level critters close enough to distract my deputies. Fifty or so yards in, we reached a major dip in the forest carpet.

"Whoa." This was both a command and an exclamation.

More than one major dip. In front of us was what looked like a battlefield pocked with amoeba-shaped craters the size of Pocono cabins, thick moss hanging like stadium banners from their uneven edges. The firs inside the craters at one time were ground level. They'd dropped below the surface, into deep pits. Some trees were dead while others thrived a full story or more down. Small sinkholes, or maybe cave-ins. Good to know.

I held the leashes tight while we walked the edge of each hole, letting my charges sniff for signs of Linkletter. The perimeters were clean, and neither dog had any interest in whatever was in the pits. They pulled me back into the trees.

Forty more yards in, Tess twisted me into an about-face. Two flashlights crept into the periphery from behind, on our left flank. Had to be the feds. I gave them credit. Ask enough people questions about fugitives, you got answers that would bring you to bowling alleys and the woods that surrounded them. A tough call, using flashlights. They telegraphed their position, but they'd be working blind otherwise.

A decision I suddenly realized I needed to make: to announce, or not to announce. My team and I were out here at night like jacklighting poachers, negotiating dangerous terrain in unfamiliar territory. Out here with other law enforcement with guns and badges, one of them with a grudge. Accidents could happen, ones that could be written off as collateral damage while in search of a fugitive. McQuarters would tell Van Impe just that, then spend all of ten minutes crafting an apology to his superiors for the oopsie.

Fuck. I wanted this guy, but I made the decision to pull up. Also decided to not announce our position. No sense giving McQuarters any such idea, close buds that he and I were now. We needed to back off, let them get ahead of us, painful as it was to let that happen. We'd be their backup even though they wouldn't know. The guy needed to go down; who the hell cared who did it.

We held fast, me in a crouch, Fungo sitting quietly, Tess's nose pushing into the underbrush like a pig rooting for truffles. The feds' flashlights swept back and forth as they passed us on the far left. After another few minutes, we were safe to go.

Fungo and I stood. I saw now what kept Tess so interested in the forest floor. Animal poop; she was eating it. And to think I kissed those lips.

A hard pull on her leash, another whiff of the plastic, and the three of us were on the trail again.

47

Randall's pursuer and her dogs were out in the dead of night for one reason: him. He'd made it through the first leg of the mess he found himself in, a four-hundred-yard trek through a maze of pine trees and boulders that stretched from behind the bowling alley to a road he knew was out there somewhere. He stopped for a breather, one of many his diseased body dictated he needed, leaned heavily against a small fir losing out to overcrowding. The branches buffeted his shoulder while he sucked in the slightly chilly Pocono air. In front of him were two lanes of blacktop he now realized were the less-traveled kind. Only one car in the few minutes' rest he was allowing himself. On the road's other side, more forest.

Behind him, the picture was off. He'd drawn additional interest: two flashlights not close enough to each other to be the same person.

He could have called this thing off right here. No confrontation, live for another day. He was out here trailblazing, looking specifically for this road to give him this option. Circle around, forget the bowling alley, look elsewhere in the region for Regina. A friendly town like this, a guy in Dockers and a sport jacket should have been able to flag down a passing car or pickup truck easy. That and some cash would get him into the next town.

That's if another car came by. Nothing passed him going on five minutes.

Advancing headlights illuminated the wall of trees lining the road a half-mile or so away. He left the tree cover and waved his arms, but the semi didn't even downshift. An eighteen-wheeled lumber truck rumbled past. The two flashlights in the woods drew nearer.

"Fuck it." Randall rechecked the ammo in both guns, returned them to his vest pockets and hustled across the road.

On its other side he flashed his short penlight beam at a rough-hewn, double post sign with foot-high recessed letters embossed in silver: *Anthracite Acres.* In smaller letters underneath, *Preserved by the Dickson City Coal Heritage Society.*

Dickson City. Too bad. When he killed whoever was following him—and he would, soon as he found a perch where he could rest his tired ass and watch his pursuers' approach from a safe height—the executions wouldn't add to the quaint town of Rancor's murder toll. *Bummer.*

He stepped into the darkened forest that rose up steeply in front of him, the incline too steep to push into the interior. His only choice for flat terrain was to go right. A different environment on this side. Leaf trees, not evergreens. More animal noises, more owls. Colder. The sweat he worked up dried quickly on his back and shoulders, leaving him with a chill. His small penlight blazed the path but its narrow beam sucked, providing late notice of snapped tree limbs and deadfalls. Inland of the road but not by much, he was paralleling it. He'd follow its slight curve for a few hundred yards until he found a decent spot to make his stand.

A massive felled tree lay flat across his path, the circumference the size of tires on an earthmover. No climbing over it, it was too big; he walked its length to get by. A rush of heated air from the tree's underside suddenly dusted his legs like a hot afternoon breeze skimming a steamy blacktop in August. Chilly as it was in these woods, the tepid air blast drew him closer to the tree. The wood was warm to the touch, like it was generating heat. Strange. A gift horse that felt great after toughing out nighttime exposure in the Poconos' naturally refrigerated mountains.

Right here, Randall decided. This would be it, as long as he could figure out how to climb atop the monstrous deadfall in his path. He followed it until he reached its trunk, found the help he needed. Another felled tree leaned against a few low-lying boulders that in turn led to the side of the large tree he intended to make his perch. The boulders were stepping stones, lined up against each other like a child's backyard play set. He walked the incline, hopped from rock to rock, stepped up onto the massive felled hardwood.

Ten feet up, he sat and crossed his ankles. He relaxed here in his oasis, the warmth of the deadfall fending off the night chill. His guns were out, loaded and ready, the smaller handgun beside him sitting on the tree, the larger, definitely nifty Rhino magnum resting in his lap. He was a hovering Cheshire Cat with firepower, waiting for his Alices to materialize so he could blow their fucking heads off. His pursuers, when they crossed the road, would make the right turn and come this way. Too steep a hill to go any other way. When they got close enough he'd use both guns. Point and shoot. Pop, pop. More pops as required. It would be noisy, yes, and this concerned him. Randall saw or heard no indications that the bounty hunter and her two dogs were still out there, yet he was sure they were.

Two flashlights reached the road's shoulder. The lights turned off. No additional movement. They were waiting. For the fog to lift or for Randall to walk up and surrender or maybe for a valet to bring their car around, who the fuck knew, but most likely it was for reinforcements. Minutes passed.

The flashlights clicked on again. They crossed the road, turned right, were coming his way. So much for waiting for back up. Two impatient FBI cowboys. Advantage, Randall.

When they got within fifty yards Randall decided he was too visible from his perch. Plus taking off a person's head with a .357 magnum from a distance... Hell, it'll be more fun if it's face to face. He retraced his steps along the length of the tree and dropped back down onto the forest floor, moving behind a thick trunk. This tree felt the way it should have felt against his shoulder, cold, jagged and harsh, and noticeably chillier than his warmer perch a few minutes earlier.

The darkness was black and impenetrable with the backdrop of a mountain close in, no light showing from any horizon, like midnight inside the coal seams that ran beneath this and other Pocono Mountains, before the mining had hollowed many of them out.

Randall produced the second handgun. He raised both guns against his shoulders, ready to lower them for headshots at the closest range he could manage, at whichever one of the two he could cozy up nearest to first.

48

Headlights moved right to left on a road ahead of us. I heard the rumble of a diesel engine from a road-weary tractor-trailer that downshifted to handle the rising grade. It passed, my deputies and me still deep within the cover of the trees. The truck upshifted after it conquered the hill. When it got far enough into a long curve, the two FBI agents appeared on the road's shoulder, their flashlights a-blazing, then they turned them off. My charges and I sat and waited, weren't going to move until they did.

This short a distance reminded me of the difference in the size between these two men. McQuarters was a freak, a giant compared to his partner. The giant lit up a cigarette, blew some smoke, paced, chewed on it, blew more smoke. The cacophony from cicadas, owls, mountain lions, tigers, bears, Bigfoot, whatever, swelled the air then leveled off to become the ebb and flow of forest din at midnight. Agent Van Impe ended a phone call.

What I made out, Van Impe to McQuarters: "... Escobar... her posse from Philly... here in under an hour."

McQuarters: "She's a grandstander... fuck procedure... fuck her, we're gonna lose him..."

McQuarters made a grand gesture of tossing his cigarette and checking his weapon. He and Van Impe flipped on their flashlights again and crossed the road. My team and I stayed quiet and watched. The huge mountain that rose up quickly just beyond the other shoulder forced them to go right. They paralleled the road inside the forest cover until the woods flattened out and opened up a bit. But there was no missing the two of them with their flashlights.

"Let's go, team," I said, rousing my charges. Tess and Fungo sprang to all fours. We'd stay on this side but get closer to the blacktop, so we could better see what was in front of the agents as they walked, and scope out the direction they were headed. I let my guys pull me another twenty yards then—*holy shit*—

My night goggles picked up someone, a sliver of white, a shirt under a dark jacket, pressed against a tree, both arms raised shoulder high, both hands with guns.

Linkletter. An ambush, going down now.

49

The crunch of twigs underfoot and the tamping of damp, cushiony leaves from an infinity of autumns: Randall heard their approach. He'd broken a sweat again in the crisp night air, his adrenaline coursing, warming him from the inside like brandy from a St. Bernard. He was on fire now, breathing harder, hot, ready, eyes straining to see, waiting for someone to pass on his left. One flashlight beam entered his line of vision close in and right where he wanted it, left and forward of the tree he was behind. The beam pulled its owner ahead; Randall hazarded a peek. Beam number two moved in behind number one, a few feet farther away, both pursuers unaware of Randall's presence behind Anthracite Acres tree number five thousand or so, with no clue how badly this oversight was going to turn out for them.

He stepped out, quickly walked the few paces separating them, came up from behind and raised the Rhino high because the first guy was huge, stuck it in his ear and pulled the trigger.

Boom, one head destroyed, chunks of skull and scalp traveling as far as the owner of the second flashlight forcing him to wipe blood splatter from his eyes with his fingers. Agent Two raised his gun. Too slow; Randall fired the Rhino again.

Boom. The glancing shot disintegrated the agent's ear, dropped him like a cuff from a gorilla, slapping him sideways against a tree. Unconscious, the agent slid down and slumped forward, bleeding onto the shoulder of his Kevlar vest.

Randall checked out the dead guy with his penlight, the man's head cut nearly in half by the single shot that traveled through one ear and missed coming out the other because of its upward trajectory. He reached the other victim, a bloody mess and out for the count, but still breathing.

This was the one. This was who would give Randall the jollies he was looking for. He slapped the agent's face, woke him just enough to have him realize Randall had stuffed the barrel of a big firearm into his mouth. No comment from the bleeder, his mouth a bit too occupied at the moment. *Ohhh baby*, Randall had the feeling, was getting all righteous and pumped and hard, his hand wrapped around the agent's neck, wanting to see this guy's eyes pop out when he pulled the trigger, wanting to watch his life drain right the fuck out of them, right here, right now.

Here we go, loser, here it is, time to meet your maker.

Randall shoved the gun barrel farther down the agent's gagging throat, his finger tightening on the trigger, Randall's delighted, grandfatherly smile the last thing this asshole would see—

Crack-ack-ack, bullets zipped by Randall's head, taking out chunks of the tree behind him. He shoved the writhing agent down face-first into the undergrowth, scuttled behind a tree.

"Fucking cunt bounty hunter! Where—the fuck—are your dogs—"

He heard leaves rustle just before teeth sank into his wrist, short, sharp, savage teeth that grabbed and shook his arm like it was a sock monkey, ripping off the sleeve, pulling the arm down to dirt level, the pressure threatening to separate his hand from his arm and his arm from his shoulder. The rest of Randall went down with it. The Rhino was no longer in his palm, sent elsewhere by the dog's ferocious shaking and a clamped mouth that tightened the pressure. Randall raised the other gun, shoved it between him and the dog, pressed the barrel into the dog's ribs, was gonna blow this demon bulldog bastard away—

The next bite was to his groin, with instantaneous pulses of pain radiating like nerve damage from a dentist's drill. This dog was the bruiser, its mouth large enough to grip his junk and his upper thigh at the same time.

Sharp teeth were about to puncture his scrotum; any further movement and he'd lose some important body parts. The second gun dropped from his hand.

"Sit—the fuck—up, Linkletter," a woman's voice said, "nice and straight, but don't try to stand. And try not to rile up my dogs any more than they already are. They'll stay attached to you until I tell 'em to back off. You are now officially our bounty. I'm dialing 911 for an ambulance."

Randall grimaced, the pain of the impacts to his wrist, arm, shoulder and groin debilitating. No parts of his offended body were detached, broken or separated, but the pressure of two nasty sets of canine teeth to his arm and groin remained a warning of what would happen if he didn't pay attention.

He wheezed, gasped for air, but as batshit crazy as this was, he was still able to detach, able to look on the bright side. One dead FBI agent, another one maimed bad enough that he was a short-timer. Randall was bruised, yet he'd survived. And all his pursuers were now present and accounted for. An okay outcome, he decided, under the circumstances, for the moment at least.

And the take down was by a woman. That meant he still had a chance.

50

My forty-five was drawn. I repositioned a dropped flashlight with my foot so it showed the top half of my prone bounty. Two ambulances were on their way. I did my best to give the dispatcher our location, in woods close to some quiet road behind some other woods behind the bowling alley. *Good luck with that*, the dispatcher's sigh indicated. She wanted me to stay on the line. I told her I was a bit busy and dropped off.

FBI agent McQuarters was dead. Agent Van Impe was incapacitated and drifting in and out, bleeding badly from a head wound. Linkletter's status was whatever I wanted it to be, and the reason I hadn't put the phone away. I wanted to text Vonetta, but I was still deciding what to say.

Bounty neutralized was correct.

Bounty dead sounded so much better.

I was seriously thinking of terminating this asshole right here, after seeing what he'd done. And he was being coy about it.

I tucked the phone in a pocket, would text Vonetta later, instead caressed some keychain fuzz in passing, my fingers in the general vicinity.

A lie. I needed the fur. This wolf in sheep's clothing made me nervous.

"The name is Isaacs, miss," he said, laying on his side and gasping. Fungo's mouthful of his balls had significantly reduced his air intake.

"Howard—Isaacs. I'm not, *unnhhh,* whoever you think I am. I have ID, a license to carry, just let me get it..."

Bullshit. It was always a case of mistaken identity in this business. Although saying he had a gun permit was a little different.

Still not buying it, what with these two FBI agents shot to shit and all.

His free hand twitched. Fungo growled, repositioned his bad dog self on his groin to reemphasize the importance of keeping still.

"Right about now," I said, glancing at the mess that had been Agent McQuarters, "I have no reason to give a shit what your name is. And my dogs are here to remind you that you have every reason to shut the fuck—shut the fuck—shut the fuck..."

Shit—deep breath—grab the fur—

"*—shut the fuck, suck-a-dick, dick-suck, dick-suck—*"

The word torrent blasted through my lips, twisted my tongue, wouldn't stop, the poorest of timing...

"*—dick-suck, sick dick, suck a ducky, duck duck GOOSE—*"

I gripped the fuzz on my belt loop. I squeezed the keychain tight, determined to keep myself together. Nice doggie... cute doggie...

"... that you have every reason—to keep—your fucking mouth—*shut,*" I said, finishing.

Linkletter calmed himself, was sizing me up, staring at the death grip I had on the keychain. I shoved my hand into my pocket. It didn't want to stay there, my upper-cutting fist jamming against the denim from the inside, tenting my jeans. But still in evidence big-time was my drawn forty-five.

My bounty's anxious breathing slowed, his look turning smug. He was about to address my lapse, which would be a big mistake. How big, I was eager to find out.

"You've got—Tourette's—tics—I take it? Verbal, physical, and—"

Fungo growled, breathed hard through his nose, growled louder.

"—incurable, *unnhhh,* last I heard."

It was mostly a question. My answer was a cold stare, still sizing him up, his exposed wrist and arm bleeding, was he still a threat...?

This emboldened him. More smugness.

"Yes," he said. "Must be tough, a disease like that, being a woman.

Assuming that's what you are. Whatever's tenting your pants isn't helping your cause."

Wrong reaction, asshole. We were done here.

I moved in close, pulled him to his feet with the dogs still attached, positioned the barrel of my forty-five under his chin, right about now extra glad I hadn't called or texted Vonetta, because Mr. Linkletter's status was about to change. Fungo and Tess growled through their clamped teeth, sensing my disgust, my anger, my new endgame...

"You're a sick, sick fuck, Linkletter. No reason to prolong this. I earn my bounty either way. You're outta here, you prick..."

Tess squirmed, whined; something distracted her. Same with Fungo, which made him disengage—

The ground beneath me rumbled like a subterranean jackhammer attacking the soles of my boots. My gun discharged as the forest floor tilted, separated, a crevice opening and snaking outward. The crevice widened, me straddling it, my hands groping as I lost my footing and slid down into it, my gun AWOL, no fur, no grip, my fingers ripping the bounty's shirt open like it was a bodice, then slipping past his belt, his pants leg, his shoes. The crevice broke off, and a black pit opened, swallowing me and everything around me, the floor rippling out like a shaken blanket while it skidded below the surface and folded in on itself, dragging nearby trees, earth and rocks along with it. I didn't lose consciousness, was instead aware of my surroundings and what was happening on my way down, and keenly aware when I bottomed out, buried up to my armpits in loose, hot dirt and rocks, and composting leaves layered with wild animal piss and feces. And whatever was happening wasn't done. More dirt and rocks cascaded until another section of hardwoods tilted and separated from the shelf that was the forest floor above me. It rumbled downward, dropping farther into the abyss than where I was. The second slide settled, mist and dust trailing its descent, the dust rising until it dissipated. Left behind was a cleaved wall of earth with one large section darker than its surroundings. In the darker section was an exposed cave.

I was in a sinkhole big as a schoolyard. It dropped off into a second sinkhole like the deep end of a huge swimming pool. And it was warm down here. I bent each knee, moved each leg in loose dirt that had too much give to it, with no leverage to push against to extricate myself. Below the waist felt fine, felt good to go, ready for me to climb my ass out of here. I freed my right arm, checked out what I could see of it, some cuts on my hand but nothing major. My luck ran out with my left. The slightest movement sent a jolt of pain up to my elbow, reminded me what the arresting cops had done to it when I was sixteen. Where it was broken and how badly, I didn't know, but a tangle of agitated nerve endings turned my stomach, making me think it was a compound fracture. I gritted my teeth; it couldn't stay where it was if it was bleeding. I lifted my arm out of the debris, *owww*, mother*fuck* did that hurt—

No broken skin on it, no bleeding; a snapped bone or bones somewhere in my forearm. Plus my mangled fingers and knuckles were mangled yet again. How many broken, no idea—

I was pissed, more like nuclear-option angry, but at least I was alive.

My dogs... my bounty...?

I saw nothing side to side, rocks and stones and branches still settling. Some heavy breathing started up nearby and was on the move, a dog panting, coming my way. Except maybe it wasn't a dog. The breathing got heavier the closer the animal got, creeping me out. I had only one fist to defend myself, damn it. One arm, one fist, and thirty-two original teeth if it came to that, and close in I could do considerable damage with my mouth if I could get my subconscious to quiet the hell down—

"—fisty feisty pressured gas, ruptured ass, tangled arms, pressed hams, damn it spam it, damnfuck you ass-fucks to hell!

"—tattoo..."

The beast moved to within inches of my head, sniffed away at my mouth, no growling or snapping or biting, just checking me out. Then it nuzzled my shoulder, nudged my good hand, licked my sweating face, and got back to the heavy breathing again.

"Good boy, Fungo."

Fungo dragged his wet nose across my cheek, tucked his head into my shoulder. I rubbed his face and ears. "Glad to see you too." He whined and whimpered, was so happy he was about to mount my head.

"Sit. Sit, boy, sit..."

Fungo didn't sit, instead looked past me, turned ornery. He growled, snarled, and snapped, then he hunkered down, ready to spring. He vaulted my shoulder. I heard ripping and tearing sounding as bad as a lion on a felled wildebeest. If Linkletter was down here with us, whatever was left of him Fungo was now shredding it.

It wasn't Linkletter, it was McQuarters. Or at least the top of Agent McQuarters' head, a few feet behind me to my left, his body buried but presumably still attached. Fungo was separating strips of bleeding scalp and chunks of gray matter from inside and out of what was left of McQuarters's exposed skull. Kee-rist was Fungo bringing it.

"Fungo. No. Stop, boy. No... Fungo—"

He abruptly stopped. The moon exited the fog and brightened the pit, creating shadows. In the moonlight I got a better sense of our surroundings. The sinkhole's diameter was maybe a hundred feet across. Above us I saw the rim, the din of the night sky behind it. Something was up there, struggling on all fours on the lip of the hole.

"Tess. Tess puppy. Good girl—"

Thirty feet distant it raised itself, stood tall on two legs, blotting out the moon. The silhouette of a person. *Shit.*

Linkletter peered at me in the pit.

My good arm swept the surrounding dirt and sod and rocks, warm but not hot. Nothing within reach, no guns, no phone, no flashlight, nothing. And nowhere to hide the trapped, exposed upper third of my body. I was as defenseless as McQuarters's head if Mr. Linkletter had a weapon. What he did have was my flashlight.

The beam steadied, blinded me as bad as a searchlight, then it panned to Fungo. Fungo snapped and jumped, looking for a way up and out of this massive sinkhole three stories below the surface.

"Whew," Linkletter called, loud enough for my benefit. He coughed, an exaggerated, guttural hack that ended with him doubling over to expel a stream of deeply summoned, mucous-laden expectorant. In my head now—

"Mucous," squeaked through my pursed lips.

"—lucas pukus bazooka mcdufus."

He ignored my chatter and blotted his brow with the jacket sleeve that was still intact, the other gone from Tess's takedown, that arm exposed.

"That was certainly interesting, wasn't it?" he said, touching his throat. "Christ, my skin's still hot; a powder burn. Wow. I dodged a fucking bullet at close range. Un-freakin'-believable. Some real déjà vu going on here—"

He scanned the hole with the flashlight, surveyed its height, depth, and contents. I took advantage of the sweep of the light and did the same. The view from here, scoping out the walls of dirt and jagged rock that led up to a ledge too far out of reach, was scary; a very big hole. I was lucky to be alive. But looking up from the bottom of what could become my own grave, the condition felt temporary. *Our* graves, I reminded myself. Fungo's, mine, Tess's also, painful for me to think, figuring that ship had sailed and left her tough doggie body somewhere down here with us in the sinkhole debris. And it was getting hotter down here.

"You know, you and I aren't that different," Linkletter said, going for chummy. "I'm looking for someone, you're looking for someone. We're both afflicted, you with your Tourette's, me with my cancer. But the violence... now *that's* the turn-on. No different for you as a bounty hunter, except you keep your demons bottled up. You don't want people to see the freak you really are. You send the dogs out to do your violence for you. Am I right?"

Linkletter, amateur psychologist and self-prescribed demon emancipator.

My message: "Bite me, psycho."

"Would if I could, sweetums," Linkletter said, "but I need to still do some sleuthing, and cozy up to some unsuspecting female taint over drinks at the bowling alley." He made a grand gesture of brushing off nonexistent debris from his shoulder. "'Course, a change of clothes and some Band-Aids from my car would help..."

I had to sell him on closing out his visit to Rancor right here, then take his show somewhere else, somewhere less dangerous for him.

"There are more feds, Linkletter," I managed, my voice projecting, me going for calm, but *fedletter*, *bedwetter*, and *lewdletter* queued up in my head, my epiglottis and throat muscles all dancing in anticipation of a release. I squeezed it back down with a snort and a *gaaack*.

I regrouped, breathed deeply, exhaled. "You for shit-shit-*SHIT*!-sure know there's more feds nearby. No reason to hang around in a town full of senior women with them on your tail. Be smart, get a head start—*dogfart!*

appletart!—on them. And us. Because when we get out of this hole, we're coming after you..."

"You're funny," he said, his chuckle validating his opinion. "A one-woman giggle fest. Sorry, leaving Rancor doesn't do it for me. Not until I find a former girlfriend. So let's do this. Some free association that points me in the right direction. Will only take a minute."

The beam from his flashlight panned back and forth between Fungo and me. His other hand slowly rose. Goddamn it, a gun.

"Some incentive for you to participate, sweetie. Help me out, and you'll still be alive when I leave." He steadied the flashlight on me now, blinding me. "Ready?"

"I don't live around here. I don't know anyone—"

The beam moved from me to Fungo. A trigger pull; the bullet hit a rock between my deputy and me, close to my dog. Fungo went berserk.

"That miss was me giving you credit for being honest. But local resident or not, you know more than I do. One more time, starting with the lightning round." He raised the gun at me again, followed by the flashlight. "First name, Juicy Luster. Exotic dancer."

"Never heard of her." True.

"Fair enough. Regina Briscoe."

"Don't know her. Met one Briscoe, a guy. Floyd, the bowling alley bartender. No Regina." More truth.

"Good, that was good, even convincing. How about this one: Randall Burton."

"No." True again.

"Just funnin' you. That's my real name. Not Stephen Linkletter, not Ding-a-ling Hammer, a personal favorite of mine, one I used in a skin flick once. Also not Howard Isaacs, or..."

My agitated subconscious was now reloading. Tess's takedown, his torn coat, torn shirt, his exposed arm—yes, a tattoo on his bicep...

The *women*, the prostitutes all marked, all scarred—*his* women—

A tattoo of a bunyip. *The* Bunyip. Christ—

He'd branded himself.

The torrent of verbal vomit queuing in my throat erupted. *"Demerol, clever all, suck my buns, yep, yep—pimp my buns, yep, yep—*

"Bunyip, Bunyip, Deveraux..."

He lowered the gun. I couldn't see his face above me, surprised or pissed or happy or sad, no idea what it registered, only a silhouette—

"Wow. One I haven't heard in a while. Bravo. Yes, I still have this little leader-of-the-pack tattoo here, on my arm. So you do know me. My past life. Before the attempted execution that didn't take. And the reason for me being here."

"Before—the attempted rape—of a minor," I said, grimacing. "Which is why *I'm* here. And why we'll still... come after you."

"Good for you. A paper tiger to the end. You won't survive the night down there."

An ambulance siren in the distance, faint but building. His head lifted in the siren's direction.

"How about that. An ambulance, or maybe a State cop. Change of plans then." He rubbed his crotch, where Fungo's sharp dogteeth had gripped him during the takedown. "Let's close this part out, right now."

An underground fire burning for decades for miles in all directions, a fire that never went out... the dark cave the sinkhole had exposed to my left was now glowing. Not a cave, but rather a tunnel, backlit by distant flames, and in its forefront were low-lying shadows on the tunnel's floor. The shadows advanced to become silhouettes, all shaped the same, a crowd of them, scurrying, climbing over each other as they approached the tunnel's mouth. They released into the sinkhole, the moon turning these silhouettes into a frothy-tipped, living waterfall that emptied into an advancing river of white and brown fur.

Rats, hundreds of them, headed in my direction.

"Good-bye, Miss Tourette's-afflicted bounty hunter." Linkletter's gun barrel steadied itself. "Bullets to the head. Much better than being eaten alive by rats, right? Glad I could help out. And truth be told, this is the only real cure for your affliction—"

The rat swarm overtook me, covered my head, my arms, all of my upper torso. I waited for their sharp teeth to sink into my cheeks, into my scalp, attack my eyes, my exposed arms. Instead the rats scampered lightly onto my body, gently, the same for the arm that was broken, cozying up like furry little puppies on a cold night. No malice, just comfort. The rat pile thickened, rising around my head, burying my face... my eyes needed to close. The shadowy gray and white terrain dully lit by the moon now gave way to total blackness.

Craack.

Craack craack craack.

Four gunshots. Two zipped past my ear, but the third and fourth shook the tower of rats protecting my head, blasting through fur and rat flesh and bone, with a layer of rat bodies severing into bloody chunks. Fungo barked and the horde separated, all except for the few severed dead rats left behind to bleed out, onto my face. My head was now exposed. I didn't open my eyes, there was so much blood.

Click. Click-click.

The gun was empty. A beam of light from a flashlight pierced my bloodied, closed eyelids for a pregnant few seconds. Fungo barked again and nudged my head. I stayed still, held my breath, didn't hazard moving, listening keenly. The ambulance siren was fainter; they couldn't find us. The flashlight switched off. Above me, shuffling feet rustled the leaves followed by plodding footsteps that trailed off. I opened my blood-soaked eyelids, surprised to see two eyes still peering down at me from the rim of the hole, but they weren't Linkletter's. Too closely set and not human, and glowing green from the reflective moonlight.

Tess. She was mesmerized. How long she'd been up there, taking all this in or dazed, I had no idea, but she was in doggie dreamland, her rat-chasing terrier genes paralyzing her. So many rodents, she'd either died and gone to dog heaven or she was in doggie hell, because they were so close, but short of a kamikaze dive into a fifty-foot-deep dark hole, she had no way to get at them.

The river of rats receded, silently retracing its steps, the rats scrambling over each other and scaling the pit's steep incline, a frothy waterfall in reverse. Now Tess asserted herself, barked loudly, upset at the rats leaving the sinkhole debris, upset at them climbing back into the tunnel.

But wait, inside the exposed tunnel...

What the hell was *that*?

Someone was there, standing just inside the mouth, the helmeted head a giveaway. A coal miner. Or, as I tried to keep an open mind, someone who maybe once was a coal miner but was now, at best, an apparition. It was joined by other nondescript shadows who filled in behind him, shoulder to shoulder, milling around, observant, backlit by orange flames, their safety lamps on and glowing white above their invisible faces, their helmets all facing out, facing the hole. Facing me. The river of rats flowed back upstream around and between their legs, returning to the interior of the coal mine. After the last of the rats retreated, the figures turned and peeled off to follow them, wandering deep into the rear of the tunnel, a crowd of helmeted heads disappearing into a wall of flames. A lone figure stood his ground, a guard with a safety lamp, the light like a luminous white eye in the middle of his forehead. I stared, awestruck, long enough to decide on my condition, that this was a near-death experience, not the real thing.

I was drained. I exhaled. "Fungo," I called. "Here, boy. Over here."

Fungo complied, came to my side, nudged away the few rat bodies still covering my head, was more interested in my face. He whimpered while licking me, cleaning off some of the blood. All this rat blood, soaking my head and shoulders—Linkletter had to think most of it was mine.

The bowling alley. Linkletter was headed there, which was where I needed to be. An ambulance could still be looking for us, but it should have been here by now. Other FBI too, if they were out there.

"Tess," I called. "Sit, girl." She obeyed, sat three stories up along the jagged rim of the pit, her butt wiggling, her glowing moonlit green eyes riveted on me, awaiting my next command. Only one command I could give her, and I felt silly giving it.

Timmy's fallen down the well, Lassie.

"Tess, GO."

She bolted. She'd retrace her steps and head back to home base, which was my van sitting out front of the bowling alley. After that I hoped to get lucky, have someone who knew her recognize her, maybe Andy or one of his friends. If that happened, Tess would bring someone back. Until then I was in major pain and virtually immobile, and yet, crazy as it seemed, I didn't feel in any more danger. But I didn't feel the same about Andy and the women at the bowling alley, with a psycho heading their way.

51

Rags to riches in a matter of seconds. Vicious dogs attached to his body parts. A gun under his chin. A mentally defective bounty hunter whose finger twitch should have put a bullet up into Randall's brain by way of his jaw. How the hell her bullet missed when the forest floor collapsed, he didn't know.

And those rats. Any concern Randall had about his shots missing their target wouldn't much matter. The rats would pick her bones clean.

Randall was feeling invincible.

He had the bounty hunter's flashlight, and with all his pursuers dead, his trek back through the evergreens was less dramatic and more direct. He closed in, the glow of the bowling alley's rear floodlights like a beacon. A check of his watch; eleven thirty. Prime time for some sleazy late-night cruising of the bowling alley bar, looking for his former girlfriend. Yes, he could have used a shower but there was no time for that. Time only to put on some Band-Aids, a change of clothes, and deodorant from his car, and to splash some water on his face in the men's room. Bowlers and bar patrons alike would be adequately juiced and less discerning. Should be easy pickings.

He reached the front of the bowling alley; the Cadillac had been compromised. Shattered window glass crunched underfoot. He opened the trunk. His clothes were mussed yet otherwise serviceable, but his other gun and ammo were gone. And he did need ammo.

The two drug thugs he croaked and dragged into the woods wouldn't be needing theirs or their guns. He found their bodies. Back at the Caddy, four flat tires, necessitated a need for new transportation.

* * *

Toweled off and deodorized, with a generous splash of cologne and a clean shirt, Randall felt revived. He exited the men's room and wound his way to a section of the bar patrolled by a particular bartender, one of only two still on duty at one a.m.

Minimal eye contact, hands busy at the sink underneath, his guy struck a bartender pose, cleaned a glass, waited for Randall to say what he was drinking.

"Yuengling lager. A food order too." Randall glanced at the name stitched on the bartender's bowling shirt. "You from Philly, Floyd?"

"Look, mister," Floyd said, drying his hands, "this isn't how this is going to go. You order things, I get them for you. You leave me a big tip. That's it. Limited options from the grill this late. How about some deep fried fish and chips? Not much else that's edible."

Randall nodded. Floyd topped off a beer mug for his customer. Randall dropped a fifty into Floyd's hand. "Keep it. Look, the Philly thing: I'm looking for a woman."

No pushback from Floyd feigning double-entendre familiarity, just a direct stare that was far from friendly. The fifty made its way into a miner's helmet.

"Name," Floyd said.

Randall leaned in, said in a casual voice, "Regina Briscoe. Thing is, I figure she's somehow related to you. Floyd Briscoe, right? She's owed some money. From a Philly safe deposit box. I'm Howard Isaacs, an attorney."

Floyd answered without taking his eyes off Randall, no hesitation, no emotion. "Regina was my daughter. She's gone. Heroin overdose. Excuse me." He lifted a phone from under the bar to check his texts, began walking and keying, leaving Randall to nurse his beer, unable to offer his condolences.

One of two things had just happened. Randall was either hearing news that should have shocked him, and did—Regina was young, no more than mid- to late thirties if she were alive, and a horrible thing had happened to her—or Floyd was lying.

Plus it was conflicting info. Rosie the dead Greek diner waitress, under duress, had inferred otherwise, sending him here.

Randall scanned the length of the bar. Floyd was AWOL, the bar trough unattended, until the kitchen doors swung open and he returned with Randall's fish and chips. He dropped the plate front and center for Randall, speaking past him, head-pointing.

"You see those bowlers at those two tables? Tell them about your safe deposit box money. Leave me out of it."

He eyed the two tables nearest lanes twenty and twenty-one. They abutted each other, round tables pushed together in a figure eight, accommodating six patrons, with room for maybe two more. Tonight's bowling combatants sat there in cohabitation, still dressed in either garish pink splashed with indigo blue, or in red adorned with a black longhand. Six bowling teammates, five of them women, including one in a wheelchair, and one man, plus slinky Iota Jean, the woman he'd met earlier, the only one not in a bowling shirt. They toasted each other, probably for the tenth time, and judging by the placement of the trophies, the red-shirted team had taken the championship. The smaller trophy sat in front of the tiny woman who dead Stella said was her mother, not that she was awake enough to admire it. Her head was slumped on the table, past her bedtime or passed-out drunk. The second trophy needed to sit on the floor, next to what looked like the oldest geriatric at the table, the one in the wheelchair, the trophy tall enough that it reached her seated shoulder. She was talking to it, her arm draped over it like they were the best of friends.

A server delivered a tray of tequila shots to the bowlers' tables. Heads turned toward the bar, the server pointing at the benefactor. Randall saluted them by raising his mug of beer. If Iota Jean had blabbed about his sick boasts, it didn't seem to matter, because after a tableful of stares and some whispered group discussion, they waved him over. He took his food with him.

Six people to talk to. Six people who would either tell the truth about Regina or would need to keep their stories straight while they lied.

52

Counsel was still not back, gone over two hours. The heart wanted what the heart wanted, and it wanted to see her again, but Andy was also worried.

Mr. Tequila Shots—Howard, according to Iota Jean—was on his way to their tables. Andy grabbed a chair to make room. Before he arrived, Iota Jean whispered his resume to her friends.

"Says he's a lawyer. His rap includes guns, sex, drugs, and murder." She snickered. "Might as well have said 'my dick is microscopic.'"

Howard arrived, set his wide-mouthed beer mug down, his double-paper-plated food next to it. Iota Jean officially introduced him but refrained from mentioning the ludicrous tall tales he'd attributed to himself.

"Around the table," she said, "we have Dody, Penny, and Sleeping Beauty, Myra. The heart of the Concubines mixed senior doubles team. Over there it's Andy and Charlotte, his mother, of the Fighting Cadavers. This year's league champions. Not that I pay attention to any of this bowling crap."

"Admit that you love us, Iota Jean," Dody said.

"Indeed I do, sweetie. But bowling? No."

"So. Andy, love," Dody said. "Your teammates are lightweights. A come-from-behind win like tonight's was for you, they should all be here, closing the bar down and buying shots like old Howard here just did for us."

"So saying good night and reading to grandkids, caring for sick pets, tucking in children, that's all overrated then?"

"Yes, on bowling championship night it is." Big, blonde Dody downed her shot. "Wowzers, that was good."

Howard made eye contact with each of them. "Ladies. Andy. So, Andy, let me guess. With a team name like the Fighting Cadavers, you're a nurse."

"Psych nurse. Mom here is a surgeon, retired. Fair warning, she struggles some with her memory. Iota Jean is—"

"Yes, also a nurse," he said. "I met her earlier. Lovely lady. Doesn't bowl," he said, raising his mug in salute.

The pre-Howard discussion topics resurrected quickly, degrading from kids and grandkids and pets and aged parents to ex-husbands, boring husbands, dead husbands, deadbeat husbands, boyfriends, big colorful balls of the bowling and non-bowling variety, and the joys of sex with and without a partner. Their guest took a bite from a deep fried fish fillet then stuffed some greasy fries into his mouth, chasing it all with beer.

"I saw you on the lanes earlier," Howard said to Dody. "Converted a seven-ten split. A wicked left-hand curve."

"Yes, proud of that one. But it wasn't enough. Myra, our sleepy anchor here, had an off night."

He was smooth and witty and charming and humble while the bowlers sized him up. He asked questions that were age and lifestyle and conversationally appropriate for a person sensitive to the local environment and the folks who enjoyed it. He treated them like a gentleman would. Not all of them accepted his shot-glass generosity. Dody intermittently downed the leftovers.

"You're not from around here," Dody said.

"Like I told Iota Jean. From Allentown. I'm a lawyer. Here on a case, but also some personal recon. I might relocate my practice here. Looking for good people, clean air. A less worrisome environment. I saw this news story in *People* about the town. No crime?"

"Yeah, you and everyone else, including the crazies. No crime. That's us. You a bowler?" Dody asked.

"Yes, many years," he said, adding, "I carried a two-thirty-two average. Competed professionally in the Midwest while in my twenties."

"Wow. Married?"

"A widower. She died young."

"Sorry. Natural causes?" Dody asked.

"Well, no, actually," he said, surprised at the question. "Blunt trauma. A freak home accident."

"Goodness." Dody forged ahead. "Kids? Grandkids?"

"Two kids, four grandkids. Love them all to death."

How much of his routine was true, Andy had no idea, but the odd comment about his children, and his wife's death, was unnerving.

The sleeping Myra awakened briefly, re-acclimated herself to her surroundings, showed surprise at seeing Howard seated at the table. She delivered two phrases in drunk Greek, both directed at him. The women snickered. Myra dozed off again; Dody dished. "She's my aunt, so I can translate. She said, 'At the diner with Rosie. Big dick.'"

"Guilty," he said, and tented his eyebrows in mock-embarrassment. "Very."

After chatting each of them up, a *Welcome to Rancor, Howard* chorus echoed around the table. Dody suffixed the greeting by relating how the folks of Rancor tried to be "... friendly, and good judges of character, and protective of each other, mind you, once we get to know a person, like we're getting to know you now."

A commotion at the bowling alley front entrance. Someone had trouble entering, a guy balancing on one leg while he pulled himself through the vestibule's double doors, cursing at something attached to the trouser leg of the other. The tables' occupants craned their necks.

A dog. It yanked at the guy's jeans, its feet firmly planted and backing up, tugging and growling, trying to pull him back outside. The harder the guy resisted, the more animated the dog got.

Counsel's dog Tess, Andy realized, here without Counsel. Andy pushed himself up from his chair, called to her. "Tess! Good doggie—"

The dog's floppy ears perked up, let go of the jeans, and beelined for Andy.

Andy intercepted her short of her arrival, gripped her collar with both hands. Tess calmed then stiffened, then she lunged across the table at Howard, her teeth gnashing. Andy yanked hard at her collar and scolded her.

"Tess, no—"

Tess continued to grumble, eventually relented when Andy guided her away from the table. The dog growled, now pulled at his bowling shoe.

"Andy," Dody said loud enough to better the background music. "No worries, honey. Check out why she's upset. We're fine here. Go."

* * *

Tess was in her harness but wasn't leashed. As soon as Andy exited the front door of the bowling alley the four-legged rocket bolted away from him, heading around the left corner of the building.

Andy trotted to the corner, caught sight of Tess on a full gallop toward the building's back corner, a copse of wooded pines beyond it. Exasperated, Andy screamed a command: *"About-face!"*

An educated guess, or maybe just the tone, but Tess pulled up, spun around, and returned.

Andy patted her head and cooed at her while he listened to the dog's heavy panting. He pulled her by the collar to his SUV.

"Sit." Tess complied, no restraint needed, but she kept eyeing the corner of the building, her tongue nearly on the ground.

Andy opened the tailgate, grabbed a windbreaker, slipped on a pair of Nikes. A fingerprint unlocked his handgun case. Out came the gun, then a full bullet clip. The clip went into the SIG Sauer, the SIG went into a small holster, the holster into the crook of his back.

"Let's go find your mommy."

53

"Must be a guy thing, not liking me," Randall said. "Some dogs are like that. Your friend Andy coming back?"

Dody, preoccupied with her phone, nodded in absent agreement. She finished keying a text, stole a glance past Randall, smooth, but not overlooked. "Oh, sorry. What was the question? Andy. Right. Who knows. So you're a lawyer, are you?"

Randall resisted turning around. "You just got a text from Floyd the bartender, didn't you? About his daughter, Regina Briscoe. Am I right?"

"Ah, yeah, sure, why not. Regina was my niece; Floyd's my brother. What's this about, Howard?"

Randall got into it, laid it out for them, Regina's sugar daddy in Philly, him gone for years, his will, some of his possessions, and a safe deposit box all getting settled only now. Wrapping things up, "Your brother Floyd said she's gone now. Drugs. If she had children, the money could go in their direction, via her estate."

No one spoke, the table silent, absorbing his account of Regina's Philadelphia existence. In their late-night surroundings came the white noise of intermittent pin concussions from midnight bowlers, and the clink of ice in the glasses of the remaining bar patrons. Randall pushed. "Hello? Dody? Anyone? What, did I get this all wrong?"

No refutation from any of them, only somber acceptance. Iota Jean spoke first.

"She had no children..."

Penny, mouse-quiet until now, said, parroting, "No children. She never married..."

Dody: "Found in her car. An overdose. In Philadelphia."

"Yes, terrible. In Philly," Iota Jean said, tsk-tsking. "June fourteenth. Flag Day. Five, six years, I think it's been, right, Penny?"

"Six years, Iota Jean honey. Six. Years," Penny said. "Died on her birthday."

"Her birthday, yes," Dody added.

"Terrible. So, so terrible. Yes, her birthday. My goodness," Iota Jean said, shaking her head.

They were done. Save for Sleeping Beauty and the one in the wheelchair, their concerned, expectant, and now silent looks were all aimed at Randall. Show was over; a synchronized, Stepford-like, rehearsed performance.

His turn. "Fine, I get it, it's a tragedy people want kept quiet. Sorry, but isn't anyone interested in knowing how much money is involved?"

"No one to give it to, Howard," Dody said, her answer sharp. "Unless you can get it donated to the coal miners' widows and orphans fund. And don't ask Floyd. My brother won't want it. But out of curiosity—"

"One hundred thirty thousand dollars," Randall said.

"That's a lot of money," Dody said. "Cash?"

"Cash."

The confused one in the wheelchair unwrapped herself from the bowling trophy and smoothed her skirt with the flat of her hand, her fingers long, beautiful, manicured. "She was never a bowler, but always a hard worker," she said, her eyes turning down, sad. Her hands stayed busy with her skirt.

"Charlotte, honey," Dody reached into Charlotte's lap to take her hand, "no need to get upset. She's in a better place now."

"She is sooo pretty, isn't she?" Charlotte said, continuing undeterred. "Movie-star pretty, even now that she's older."

"Charlotte," Dody said. "Charlie. Please, not now, try to focus..."

One of her lovely hands left Dody's embrace to point a finger in Dody's direction. "Now that's enough, young lady. That is a lot of money. Why shouldn't she have it, hmm? Hard as she works? That girl works her ass off..."

Dody's headshake and pay-no-attention-to-her hand gesture was meant to tell Randall that lovely old Charlotte had crossed over, was now mentally out of bounds, with Penny working Charlotte's hands back into her lap to calm her, redirecting her to the bowling trophy. Randall's facial expression feigned agreement and disinterest at the outburst, but that was far from the truth.

"Now, where were we?" Dody said. "I know. Last call."

The server brought another round of shots, a few more beers, and some nuked nachos. In the din, Dody answered her phone, listening intently, everyone else nursing their drinks. Charlotte sipped a lemonade, now engaged in deep conversation with the sleeping Myra.

Dody ended her phone call. "That was my overnight guest, Trevor, my nephew. He was in a little trouble this afternoon and just got home. He'd like his prodigal great aunt to do likewise. So tell you what, Howard, dear," she said, "why don't we do this—"

Randall noticed the glances, more like signals, that Dody gave Penny and Iota Jean. Hefty Dody stirred her glass, lowering her eyes to show a demure disinterest in the melting ice.

"The party's over, here at least," she said. "We'll head back to my place. I've been told to expect a surprise visitor. Someone you might find interesting, Howard honey. Care to join us?"

Tonight would be it for him. Maybe some torrid sex, then hopefully there'd be a meeting between the two ghosts, each of them dead to the world, and to each other, for fifteen years or more. He'd go for all the marbles, beg to meet her child—their child. His Plan B: a memorable exit should anyone get in his way, this town's no-crime record sullied up real good.

Multiple murdered women, dead FBI agents, dead drug thugs, and one dead female bounty hunter. Nationally newsworthy.

A loose end: the bounty hunter's dog that almost outted him. Another mistake on his part. He had a chance to do both dogs in the parking lot, long before his trek into the woods. Misplaced morals, at odds with what now might need to turn into a scorched-earth exit.

One last hurrah, trying to stay one step ahead of his terminal disease, coming right up.

"Your place? Sure, I'm game."

54

The ambulance gave up. At best they might have triangulated my phone signal. That could have put someone here by morning, if I was lucky. At worst, it was now considered a prank call. Down here in the dark, far enough away from the road, with broken bones and bloody rat carcasses, I was in mixed company: my dog Fungo, the dead McQuarters, and a coal miner apparition that wouldn't quit, still standing guard. I tried digging myself out. My single-hand tosses of loose dirt and stones keep sliding back in, refilling the hole.

Goddamn it. A few seconds faster tucking that gun barrel under Linkletter's chin and he'd have been executed on the spot, without due process, and I wouldn't have needed to worry about where he was or what he was doing to Andy and his friends.

I was SOL until daylight, maybe longer. Agent Van Impe would be SOL worse, dead by then if not already, wherever he was, up top or down here. No additional FBI on the scene yet either. And Linkletter...

Andy and his mom and the women bowlers at the bowling alley: these people were defenseless if Linkletter followed through on his threat.

Fungo pulled in close, was warming me, us warming each other, me guessing it was past midnight, dozing in and out, tired, cold, less pain, in shock...

No better time than the present to introduce myself to my coal miner guardian angel.

"Hey," I called, my voice shaky but with enough strength to be heard. Fungo yawned and whined at the sleep interruption. I waited for an acknowledgment, got nothing. Instead, the helmet light on the apparition in the coal tunnel shifted, lifted slightly to illuminate the rim of the ground collapse I was in, a small section of it directly above us; then the light flicked off. My ghost miner was gone. Without the helmet light the tunnel was gone too, no more than a shallow indentation against a black wall the size of a billboard. Four tall walls of blackness, all reaching up and away from me, with me at bottom, no view from here, why would there be, it was my grave—

... stay awake, I needed to stay awake...

Movement above. The patter of light feet galloping through rustling leaves, then an abrupt stop, debris kicking forward of it, fluttering over the edge of the small section that the miner's light passed over. A barking dog peered into the pit, then—

Andy's voice pierced the night air. "Counsel! *Counsel*! You down there?"

Tess, you brought help...

Some of my cobwebs cleared. A flashlight swept the contents of the cave-in, its beam finding me and my half-buried body and blood-soaked head.

"Jesus..." Andy said.

Good dog, Tess, good dog.

* * *

Fire truck. Ambulance. Far as I was concerned I was good to go now that they'd pulled me out of the pit, except Andy tricked me, had the EMTs strap me into a stretcher and give me some great meds before they hauled me up, and now I had no idea how coherent or incoherent I sounded, my awareness alighting on pillows and moonbeams and guardian angels and doggie fur...

... and Linkletter... and lanes... lucky strikes... Juicy Luster...

Rats. Caves. Maurice.

Andy listened to all of it, walking next to me, his hand lightly on my waist as they carried me to the ambulance. What I was able to process: Van Impe was alive, Fungo and Tess were fine. And Andy, too, was ever so fine as I drank him into my delirium, him smiling while he hovered, talking with his friends on his phone, and me adrift in clouds and balloons and cool breezes on a summer day.

55

They climbed into an older Ford sedan, hefty Dody at the wheel, Randall in the front passenger seat, Iota Jean and Penny pouring sloppily into the rear, their drunk schoolgirl-like giggles wafting forward. Randall was eating this up. Hot times ahead.

"It's not far," Dody said.

The car was unmistakable. A cop car in a prior life, the windshield-mounted side spotlight the giveaway. "So this is what it feels like to ride in a police car," Randall said. "Nice. This thing is huge."

Like his boner would soon be.

They reached the stop sign at the end of the parking lot. A quick tap of the brakes then a wide right turn. Too wide, a fishtailing, cinder-spreading, heavy-footed cop-driver kind of wide. A sweep of the high beams pierced the darkness beyond the shoulder. Something was there, a pair of legs in the weeds, Randall noticed, mostly because he put them there.

They settled into the main road at a high rate of speed, the fog nearly gone. "Being a former cop," Dody said loud enough to better the road whine, "has its benefits. Some late night partying and no one to give us any shit about it. Good thing, right, honey? Howard?"

Randall stayed quiet. He wasn't sure if anyone else glimpsed what the misdirected high beams showed on the side of the road. Legs and shoes in the overgrowth, toes down, far off the shoulder but not dragged as far as he'd hoped.

"Howard? Honey?"

He grunted a self-conscious yes, swiveled and draped his arm over his seat to face the women behind him, ostensibly to be playful, but wary of what the car's lights had just exposed. Iota Jean's uncovered, crossed legs looked delicious. He flashed his best lecherous smile at her before he sneaked a look out the back window into the darkness left in their wake. Headlights from a passing car illuminated the blacktop behind them. Penny's head turned, looking behind them as well.

"Anything wrong?" he asked her.

"Looks like there's some blood back there on the road, next to the shoulder."

"Just another deer strike," Dody offered. "That, or a bear. Or wolves. Maybe it was a buck taken down by a wolf pack. Rare around here, but they're out there. Any bets on that being the Park Service's report, ladies?"

* * *

The Anthracite Beer Company, 1899–1937. Fifteen lofts for Active Seniors on tap. For sales info call...

Now on foot, they stumbled past the real estate sign on the corner of the property and entered the lobby, Randall and his three horny hostesses. Dody lived here, a conversion on the third floor of what used to be a brewery. Iota Jean said she had a unit in the building too.

Dody got direct, asked if he'd ever done it in handcuffs. The women all snickered.

Ah, no, never, he said.

Like he'd ever let that happen.

When he was through with them, they'd probably never sell another unit in this building. Inside the small lobby, empty at two-thirty in the morning, they entered the elevator. Dody pressed her floor button.

One condo elevator button caught his eye. "A pool in the basement? Nice."

"It needs to be cleaned," she said.

Clear pool water turning dark crimson, rippling away from bloodied corpses... *My my my*, the visual Randall now had of this was exhilarating.

Inside Dody's condo, they went directly to her bedroom. She tossed a pair of handcuffs onto the bed, her sly grin sloppy, lopsided. Based on their alcohol consumption, Randall surmised they were about as inhibited as corpses.

Dody winked at him. "Maybe we'll change our minds about the cuffs," she said.

Fuck no, cunt. He didn't need no stinkin' handcuffs, but seeing them on the bed took him out of his game for a moment. He caught himself too late to keep the women from wandering out of the bedroom. Dody was the last to leave, her fat ass cheeks wrestling for continued cohabitation of her stretch pants.

"Be right back, hon," she said, winking. "Just getting some refreshments for the night ahead."

So be it. His wood was still seasoning anyway. He guaranteed its perkiness by dry swallowing a Viagra.

They returned with a few six-packs and some Wild Turkey. Dody had a devilish grin, her brassy hair now pulled out of the way, arranged in a ponytail, ready to play. She smelled better, too, as she got closer. How sweet was this, them getting all perfumed up just for him. Now, about that special visitor...

"Anyone else joining us?" he asked.

"I can't say. Trust me, we'll be enough for you, lover," Dody said.

Time to get down to business. Soon as he sucked down another beer. A six-pack sat at the pillow end of the mattress, near the brass bedrail. He reached for a bottle.

The handcuff snapped closed around his wrist, the bottle in his grasp. The second handcuff click was as quick and as smooth as the first. Randall's arm was now attached to the brass headboard.

"How's that feel, sweetums?" Dody said. "Oh, come on now, don't look so upset. We're still going to have fun."

He pulled at the metal bedrail, tested its strength, was sure he looked as pissed as he felt. He calmed himself into a fake smile, thought about drawing the one gun he could get at with his free hand, instead decided to play along. But once the sex on their terms was over and they let him out of the cuffs—once he had his hands on Regina again—whoa baby, were they going to suffer for this. Soon as he was back in control.

"So here's the deal then, Howard. You say you're looking for a certain someone to get in on this action?"

"Regina Briscoe. I just want to see her. After we're done here. She doesn't need join us." He was seated on the bed, his right arm extended, wrist and headboard connected.

"What if I told you," Dody said, "Regina *is* still alive, and living here in Rancor, just isn't into this kind of... fun anymore? Different name, different life, wants to forget her past..."

"I'd be ecstatic. I... I love her." A lie. This was still so easy for him. He was so good at this.

"So you say," Dody said. "So the lawyer thing is all bullshit? You're the actual sugar daddy with the money, right?"

"I'm the sugar daddy with the money," he parroted, nodding his head in agreement.

"Interesting. How about this, then? We make some calls, we track her down, we convince her to stop in. In return, you let us do our thing here, but only after we finish cuffing you to the bed—arms and legs, honey—so my friends and I get to play with this monster pecker we hear you have in your pants, and Regina gets to hear about the money. Deal?"

He was already partly immobilized, would be stuck in this room attached to this heavy bedrail until they let him out of the cuffs. Worst case, he'd enjoy some orgiastic sex then Regina never shows, which would make him no worse off than where he was now. Best case, orgy sex, then Regina, then by extension, one way or another, her kid. His progeny. What could go wrong?

"Deal."

"Excellent. Let's get you comfortable," Dody said, "and secure."

Howard struggled through one-handing the removal of his belt, the women closing the cuffs around his pant legs, the small one giggling while she lifted his fumbling hand away from his waist, snapping the last cuff around his wrist. "Leave the undressing to us, Howard, we're, like, into bodice-ripping and other raw savagery..."

"Sure, Peggy, whatever you say." He was now spread-eagle on the bed, his hands and feet attached to it at top and bottom.

"*Penny,*" Dody said while inspecting their handiwork. "Her name is Penny." She was no longer smiling. "But what do you care what her name is, right? Just like I don't much care whatever name you go by either, Howard, or Stephen, or maybe by now it's mister multiple PBA champion Norm Duke himself." Her headshake scolded him. "Two-thirty-two bowling average my ass. Norm's best year topped him out at, what was it again, Penny?"

"Two-twenty-eight, back in oh-seven."

"Right. Thanks." Dody's face brightened. "Oh. There's also this, Howard."

Wherever her gun came from, from under her bowling shirt or the bed or thin air, Randall wasn't sure, but it was now pointed at his eye socket.

"So right now," Dody offered, "you're pretty much expecting us old bitches to either fuck your brains out or do something else with you, and you'd be right. About the something else part. Let's relieve you of your hardware."

Penny carefully reached into a vest pocket in his sport coat, located a handgun and removed it, did likewise with the second, larger handgun from his other vest pocket.

"A Rhino magnum," Penny muttered, admiring it. She smelled the barrel. "And it's been fired recently. Rosie's got one like this."

"And you were with her this afternoon, weren't you, Howard?" Dody said. "Not good."

The door to the bedroom opened. He lifted his head, watched a wheelchair roll in, accompanied by a sheepish chubby kid with a bandaged nose, his eyes black as a raccoon's. The woman in the wheelchair was the decrepit bitch cheerleader from the bowling alley. She looked no less senile here than she did earlier.

"You know Charlie, Howard? Andy's mom? My nephew Trevor brought her here. Great-nephew, I should say. Trevor's got a broken nose and a swollen jaw underneath all that tape. It's from a beating he got this afternoon, so he doesn't much look like himself right now. He's here just so he could see you." Dody turned to the boy. "Trevor? Over here please."

The boy slid in front of his aunt, alongside the bed. His eyes narrowed, surveying all four sets of handcuffs. She was right; Trevor was a mess. He met Randall's stare. Randall rattled his handcuffs and lurched at him, just for grins. Trevor flinched.

The kid steeled himself and leaned into Randall's face. "That's him," Trevor said, his teeth gritted. "His hair's a different color and his beard is gone, but that's him."

"Thank you for the ID, Trevor. We're good here. Time for you to call it a night. Go get some sleep, honey."

Trevor's sweet schoolboy expression soured. He sucker-punched Randall in the face with a quick, meaty hand before his aunt could react.

"I told you they'd find you!" Trevor shrieked, his spit spraying Randall's eyes. "You are *dead*, asshole!"

Dody pulled Trevor back, admonished him for his tantrum. Randall stayed quiet, watched as the boy exited, leaving him with Dody, Penny, and Charlotte, black Iota Jean unaccounted for. He tugged at the handcuffs, same result as before. He sized Dody up again, also glared at the smaller Penny. He guessed Penny was in her midfifties, went no more than 140. Charlotte, in the wheelchair, was in her eighties if she was a day, seemed shaky as hell. Iota Jean re-entered the room, clad in what looked like a nurse's whites. Big-boned, like Dody she was large enough to give him trouble.

"This is false imprisonment," Randall said through swelling lips. "You could all go to jail for this. Why don't you sweet ladies just let me out of these cuffs and I'll find my way back to my car and leave. We'll call it even."

Dody tilted her head and pushed out her lower lip in seeming consideration of his offer. Randall tried to will her into cooperating.

Do it, bitch. Call it off. You women aren't killers. I'm the killer. Let me loose and I'll fucking show you...

Dody turned to face her friends, her finger still on the trigger of her large handgun, its cold steel barrel still rudely pressed against Randall's eye socket. When she turned back he heard a click. The gun's hammer was now cocked.

"That doesn't work for us, Howard."

Three more clicks found him facing four handguns, shaky Charlotte's included.

56

I woke up in a hospital gown in an ER bed, a familiar voice speaking to me, my head cottony.

"Hey," Andy said, hovering. "Finally awake. Feeling any better?"

"Hey," I said. Andy's face came into focus. Not sure if my foggy eyes conveyed it, but I was happy to see him. "No. Maybe. You tell me. Where am I?"

"Wayne Memorial Hospital. Carbondale."

"What time is it?"

"Three fifty-five. In the a.m., in case you're wondering."

"Your mom? My dogs?"

"Fungo and Tess are in your van. They're fine, resting as best they can without their mommy. My mom's fine too. She's in her glory. She and tonight's trophy are at Dody's place. The van, your dogs, my mom, they're all at Dody's condo."

"So your team won."

"A close match, and emotional, but yes, the Fighting Cadavers prevailed."

"Agent Van Impe?"

"He's here, in serious condition but stabilized. A gunshot wound to the head. He lost an ear but he'll survive. The other agent..."

I let him tell me about McQuarters. He didn't mention anything about Fungo's post-mortem work on his head, and I didn't bring it up. I looked at the cast on my left arm. It reached from above the elbow down almost to the tips of my fingers. "'Sup with this?"

"Three displaced fractures in your forearm. A broken thumb, some dislocated knuckles. The easiest types of fractures to fix, Counsel, so relax. A cast, some rehab, and you should be good as new. Cuts, bruises, but they found nothing else broken, no internal bleeding, no other injuries. You bitched big time about needing your clothes back on, so they compromised and put your jeans on under the hospital gown."

I wiggled my toes, then I chanced swinging my legs over the side of the bed. I sat up. "Then get me out of here, Andy. Linkletter—"

I moved too fast. No pain in the arm but I got slammed with a massive headache. I stood up anyway—a bad idea getting worse. Tough shit, Linkletter was still out there—

"Not yet, Counsel," he said, pushing at me. "You need more rest. For your own good. Just lie back down..."

I sat, closed my eyes, let the room stop spinning. "Where's my stuff? My keys, my phone? Who drove my van?"

"What they found with you in the coal mine rubble is in the bin under the bed. The feds have your guns. Your keys were in your pocket. Your phone, no, sorry. The sheriff drove your van to Dody's."

"A mine collapse? Not a sinkhole?"

"Pretty much. You might have heard," he said, a coy smile emerging, "there are a few old coal mines around here."

No guns, no dogs, and I was shakier than a jailed junkie. *Shit.* No choice but to chill here. I laid my head back on the pillow. The more it cleared, the more anxious I got. I groped for the talisman on my belt loop. It wasn't there. A shit-storm of slurred profanity was about to hit. This was going to get ugly.

Andy moved in, slid my probing hand out of the way, checked out my eyes while I tried to will the panic out of them. His big hands worked gently at my waist, where my hand was, and I heard a tiny snap, the sound recognizable, not made on my person by anyone other than by me or my husband when he was alive. Andy dropped my hand back onto my belt loop so I could feel what he'd done. Reattached there was my fuzzy dog keychain. My nerves steadied.

It was nice that he was here, the cherry on top of my soothing drug sundae, but I was also getting a different vibe while I chilled. I'd had broken bones before, but the last time I felt this woozy I was in a straitjacket, the drugs meant to incapacitate me. Plus Andy was here, with me, instead of with his mother.

Here, keeping tabs on me. I wanted him being here to mean something other than what I now thought it meant.

"What am I on?" I asked. An innocent question, delivered innocently.

"Something local so they could reset your arm. Something else for your anxiety, and something for the pain when you came to. Just go with it, Counsel."

Too much shit in me, and Andy conveniently here to let it go down that way. I focused as best I could on his face, then I formulated another question. "You drive here?"

"What? Yes. They wouldn't let me go with you in the ambulance. They wanted me out of the way."

I could relate. Before he could do anything about it I got to my feet again and concentrated, did my best to play through my wobbly legs and the spinning walls, squinting against the dizzying overhead lights.

"Counsel, listen to me, I'm a nurse..."

I found my boots, shambled to a chair and struggled with the pain of lacing them up. I struggled with my pullover, grabbed the rest of my shit from the bin under the bed.

"You're in no condition—"

"And that's why you're driving. Let's go. Linkletter's out there on a mission, looking for a woman, your friends are in the way, and he's armed. Take me to my dogs."

57

This was what it had come to for Randall. More than thirty murders over thirty years, young and old victims alike. Ten of them over the last three days. Multiple identity thefts. Rapes. Anonymous cities. Constantly on the move. The FBI, State Police, city cops, local Barney Fifes: as far as Randall knew, no one had ever gotten even remotely close to catching him. Until now. Until these women, in this small town. These *old* women.

"I have pancreatic cancer," Randall said.

"You seem pretty healthy to me," Dody said, hovering, her big gun still pointed at his head.

"It's localized. So far. I still have time. That's why I'm here."

"Not a lawyer?"

"Not a lawyer. No safe deposit box, no money."

"What you are is a bail-jumping pedophile. And a motherfucking murdering monster."

"I... I... I just want to see my kid before the cancer spreads. Regina was pregnant..."

"Sorry, no Regina. Checked out fifteen years ago. You have a real name, Howard?"

A hesitation, then a move toward some quid pro quo. "Randall. Randall Burton. No fucking way. She's here, somewhere near here."

"Not believing me is your prerogative, Randall Burton, but still no Regina."

Enough begging. Much as Randall wanted them to be, he also knew them to be wrong. Their next move—what would it be? Hold him until their Barney Fife showed?

He could stay bashful, or he could share. No law enforcement present. Time to gross the hell out of them.

"Chances are, ladies," Randall said, his charm returning, "you'll be proud of yourselves once it gets out just how difficult a person I've been over the years."

"And how's that, Randall?" Some shuffling went on behind Dody while she kept him engaged.

He was enjoying the audience; it restored some semblance of control to him. "Truth is, I did kill people. For real. And quite a bit more than I told your sexy nurse friend here."

He gave them a real number: including today's carnage, thirty-one. Only lately had he been so careless, so cavalier, too many chances, no attempt at being discreet. He'd been leaving quite a trail. All cries for help, the courtroom shrinks for sure would call it. All necessary for one final, grand stroke to his ego, this trip to Rancor being his swan song, him being sick and all. When the cancer's endgame hit, he wanted to be somewhere where something could be done about it: prison. Three hots, a cot, and unlimited medical. Not a bad place to be, medically speaking, right about now. Oh, there was also the possibility of the death penalty. The instant, permanent cure to his disease.

"Fitting that I get caught here, right? In a town with a perfect no-crime record. Only downside for you guys is, the town's record is fucked but good." He gave a sarcastic oh-well shrug. "Still, look at it this way. The media loves this shit. When they hear about it, you'll have them eating out of your hands."

And the media would hear about it, if he had to mention it himself during the questioning or profiling or whatever the authorities did to build their cases. They'd attempt to deconstruct him, and the darlings of evening cable TV and tabloid journalism would chew on his legal fight for months, would make this a media circus. He could feel the excitement even now. The overnight fame, the glory. *Wow, what a rush...*

The four women remained stone-faced. His smile dissolved a bit.

They're in shock, he decided. This had to be traumatic for them, close to giving them coronaries.

The oldest one powered her wheelchair over to the side of the bed, next to Dody. Behind them, some foot shuffling ended with the bedroom door closing. Dody helped the old woman out of her wheelchair, steadied her. She was taller than Randall realized, her permed stack of flaming red hair threatening to topple. She laid her gun, an antique-looking six-shooter, on his chest.

"Don't worry, this isn't meant to tempt you. They don't let me have bullets anymore," Charlotte said, her voice cracking. "So what will it be, dearie? Dylan, Lightfoot, Denver, or maybe some Muddy Waters?"

His face pinched. "What?"

"I'm not sure what I'm in the mood for. I'm giving you a choice. They're all such incredibly talented young men."

And two were dead, Randall knew, yet she spoke of all of them like they were newly minted and on tour. Randall reminded himself that she was the senile one. He'd humor her. "Hell, I don't like any of them. How about Metallica?"

"Dylan it is."

A pair of bookcase speakers above the bed came to life, Bob Dylan's twang now delivering the poetic, dissenting lyrics of "The Times They Are A-Changin'."

"My being here at three in the morning," Charlotte said, her smooth-skinned, pinkish cheeks dimpling into a smile, "and my probing you on your music preference presupposes your answer to the next question."

Fairly lucid comments, Randall thought. The woman must have her moments. "What the fuck are you talking about?"

"Your secrets about your indiscretions, past and present, are safe with us, mister whoever you are. You have but one more decision to make."

He grew impatient. "Look, this has been fun, but seriously, let's cut to the chase. You guys say Regina's gone. Fine; I'll need to accept that. But the only real decision I'll need to make is what my plea will be once I'm charged, and I can tell you right now it'll be not guilty. To everything. More fun that way for everyone involved, right? The media, the police, the lawyers, everyone gets a piece of the action. Everyone gets a piece of the murdering degenerate Randall Burton, aka Howard Isaacs, aka so many others. Inquiring minds will eat it up. And so will I."

He heard the click before he felt the barrel. Dody's handgun again, this time against his temple. He froze.

"Fact number one," said the hovering Charlotte, "as a reminder: Rancor has a police force of one. An elected position. A kind of figurehead who runs interference when other law enforcement types get in the way. Keeps us from having to play by the rules when it comes to dealing with violent crimes. That means no arrest, no plea, no analysis, no trial. Fact number two, about our enviable string of year after year with no reported violent crime: we do, unfortunately, suffer from crime here. Like everywhere else, we've had too many politicians doing too little about too many misdeeds. So very frustrating to us older ladies. So crimes like yours are reported, shall I say, elsewhere, off the jurisdictional radar, and have been, for many, many years."

Iota Jean, the one in the uniform, appeared alongside Charlotte. Her new nurse whites radiated brightly in the light from the bulbs affixed to the ceiling fan.

"Why just today—well, you see, someone, ah—" Charlotte faltered, her lively face pinching up. Her perky eyes became lost, apprehensive.

Dody finished for her. "Here's what you need to know about this gun against your temple. It and another one like it took out two punks in a steakhouse men's room in Scranton today, for a robbery and an assault that put a Rancor resident into a coma. Blew their heads right the fuck off. No cops. No jury. No remorse. Just bullets and body bags. The end."

Charlotte recovered, stepped into a surgical gown. Iota Jean shimmied it upward, covered the elderly woman's long legs, then her arms and shoulders. The nurse tied the gown off. Penny sidled up, joined them on the other side of the bed, rolling up the sleeves of her bowling shirt.

Charlotte lifted a hand waist-high; it shook. She narrowed her eyes and stared the tremors down, willing her hand into perfect stillness. Her smile relaxed. Her cheeks drooped to become fleshy parentheses around thin, all-business, straight lips.

"Fact three is..."

She turned her hand palm up. A sliver of surgical steel appeared there, slapped in place by her nurse assistant. Iota Jean relocated Charlotte's gun from Randall's chest, produced a pair of surgical scissors and hovered, the scissors in her hand. She and Charlotte waited.

Penny reached for his waist. Shirt fabric and love handle cinched together in her tight, two-handed grip. She pulled him to the center of the mattress, her lady nails sinking into his flesh, Randall grimacing. Held there, Iota Jean moved in with the scissors, worked her way up a pant leg from the bottom, cut away his trousers, one leg then the other, the scissors catching skin and drawing calf and thigh blood the more he resisted. His pants gone, she repeated the process with his boxers, Randall sweating, spitting, cursing, and writhing until he was naked from the waist down.

Iota Jean waited now with a syringe, next to Charlotte. Randall's engorged, Viagra-perky organ had nowhere to go but up. Yes, they were staring, Randall realized. He was too.

"You can't—no—please—"

"Fact three is, we decided to clean up the gene pool, dearie, and we do it one dirty set of genes at a time. Seems a shame, physically gifted as you are, but with monsters like you, we have no choice. So I'm thinking you'll choose my approach toward this end, which is a bit less absolute, rather than..."

Charlotte repositioned the scalpel handle to between her thumb and forefinger. The light from the ceiling fan bulbs glinted off the surgical steel, strobing Randall's face.

"... rather than, you know," she nodded at the gun against his temple, "Dody's alternative. Except I've occasionally been wrong about these things. So answer this last question for me please.

"Would you like for it all to end here, as a dead rooster, or would you like to give it a go as a live hen in a men's prison? Hmm?"

58

I melted into the passenger seat soon as I powered it to the recline position, started drifting off.

Andy's Jeep. Basic black and oversize, its SUV ride was comfortable in my altered state, but even in my haze I knew it was taking too long to get where we were going. We'd been driving close to an hour. My skepticism came from a bout of your garden-variety paranoia à la hospital anesthetic mixed with my Tourette's meds. Andy's story: he wanted me to sober up.

My eyes opened wider. I swiped at some slobber, checked my breath.

"Here. Gum," Andy said, anticipating me.

"I need mouthwash."

"You need a hazmat shower," he said, smiling. "Anything else is a waste of time."

"Give me the gum, wise guy."

My head was less fuzzy but my immobilized broken arm throbbed like it had been pounded with meat mallets. I powered the seat upright for a return to the real world. Greeting me were warm, yellow shafts of dawn reaching with beckoning arms through majestic trees, caressing my face and my heaving bosom like delicious kisses from a naked Adonis, his hot sensual breath teasing me with hints of glistening spearmint, and misty pine oil, and—

Damn it, still afloat from the meds. Shit had to stop, right now.

I went for a bottle in the cup holder, splashed some water on my face, splashed some more, dripped some on my head. I dried myself off with my terrycloth sling. Better.

Andy ended a phone chat and dropped his cell into a tray. He pulled the SUV off the road into a small parking lot that faced a large converted warehouse now full of condos. "We're here," he announced.

"Here" was a parking space next to my van. Tess sat up straight in the driver's seat, almost eye to eye with me. Her body language said that as soon as I could get close enough she'd whimper in canine ecstasy, maybe even pee the seat. Fungo's brutish head appeared next to her. My two furry deputy buddies.

"Tell me again who lives here," I asked Andy.

"Some friends of mine. Dody for one."

"You were on the phone. Anything on Linkletter?"

"And those friends and my mother are all doing fine, thanks for asking," he said, the sarcasm subtle as a hammer. "Guess the jury's still out about your bounty."

I got out, opened my van door, and lifted Tess into the crook of my good arm. I let Fungo nuzzle his head against my waist. They wanted out of the van. I redeposited Tess in the seat and apologized to them both with a smoothing of their ears, but my two warriors needed to stay here a little longer. I retrieved my pistol-grip pump shotgun, one-handing it from a gun rack on the floor behind the driver's seat. Not an ideal weapon considering my battered left arm, but tough noogies, it was all I had, so I needed to make it work. When I straightened up I faced Andy, close in. He smelled good, a clean, after-shave good, even after the night we'd had. I smelled like hospital disinfectant, sweat, and the town dump. His hands went to my shoulders, him not trusting my legs, was looking to steady me, and then... there was this kiss on my lips, less passionate than before, more delicate, and with more concern. I reopened my eyes when we finished, looked deep into his. They were pleading with me.

"Counsel, there's something more you need to know."

We were close now, his hands gripping my hips, where they'd need to be if he were ready for the start of some spirited monkey sex, but also where they'd need to be if I lost my balance. He had my complete attention, and it appeared I had his.

"That call you've been expecting from the State Police," he said, "looking for details from you about yesterday's mugging at the pharmacy... It's not coming. Calls like that never come, to anyone in Rancor, not in more than fifty years. The best anyone ever gets is a call saying we've taken care of it."

I pulled back. "What about all those cell phone pictures, pictures of me, those punk purse-snatchers, their car. Your senior friend what's-her-name took them."

"Ursula."

"Yeah, her. Why no action on it from your sheriff, or the State Police? And who's 'we'?"

"Ursula's call went to our hotline."

"*Your* hotline?"

"Yes. The Rancor Town Watch hotline. We're the 'we.'"

"Then what happens? Who do you call?"

"Each other."

An unsettling image in my head. The news story from Scranton about the gang hit in a restaurant restroom. The bloody toilets. Crime scene chalk.

Bingo chips, as mentioned by the guy at the bowling alley bar, colloquial for shell casings.

My next thought I verbalized. "Saint Possenti's in the middle of town: a Catholic bingo hall but no church. It's what? A meeting place for an NRA coven?"

"Counsel, please. It's a pistol range. It's convenient for the seniors who live close by. The name's an inside joke. It's not a secret, it's just not broadcast news."

Bullets and bingo. In Rancor, as natural as strikes and spares.

Andy took my hand, gently guided it behind him, to his lower back, where I would place it to pull him closer to me for a full body hug. It was there for a different reason, for me to feel what was tucked into the back waist of his jeans, hidden under his loose bowling shirt: a gun in a holster.

"We're armed, Counsel. All of us, soon as we're old enough to carry. All the women are, too. *Especially* the women. We protect our families and our friends. We don't arrest. We don't go to court. We punish."

An awkward moment as I looked at this sexy nurse who had suffered from an unfathomable violent act at a young age. Someone who had witnessed his father's murder, and had been wounded by it in more ways than one. An entire small town wounded in the process. His eyes pleaded to me for understanding, but beneath their plea the message was clear: it would be my loss if I didn't.

BOOM!

A gunshot from inside the rehabbed warehouse slapped us out of our interlude. I grabbed the shotgun, sprinted on wobbly legs toward the building entrance, called over my shoulder to Andy. "Floor? Unit?"

"Third floor. Unit three E. Counsel, wait..."

Fuck waiting. Fuck the elevator. I took the stairs, bounced against the stairwell walls on the way up, was doing better now, legs coming back, third floor, top, there, 3-E, unlocked door.

Fuzzy, my eyes blinking through it, but on alert. I stepped inside, raised the shotgun, grimaced as I balanced the short barrel on the cast on my broken forearm, praying I wouldn't need to use my arm or the gun.

I looked, I listened.

Living area on left, open concept, no people, windows raised, fresh air rustling the curtains. On the right, a partition wall that stretched the length of the room almost to the windows, but didn't reach up as far as the condo's tall, warehouse ceiling boasting exposed ductwork and plumbing. From around the corner, scraping noises and low-key voices, running water, and I smelled an odd combination of antiseptic, bacon, and burnt toast. On silent feet I moved to the wall, paralleled it. My shotgun and I turned the corner.

A kitchen. A woman at a double sink, the spigot water running. More scraping; she was cleaning a griddle. At a large round table and a long center island, people sat in various stages of consuming breakfast, with raised forks or coffee cups in one hand, their other hands each with a gun, and all the guns were pointed at me. I had no choice but to lower my weapon. They lowered theirs. I got a few full-mouthed "G'morning, Counsel" sentiments before they returned their interest to their plates. Andy entered the kitchen behind me.

At the sink, a senior I didn't recognize in a workout suit in rubber-ducky yellow scrubbed dishes. Seated at the center island were Al the Sheriff and Dody the retired police chief. At the table, some bowlers I remembered from last night, and the black woman I'd spoken to at the bar, plus Charlie dozing in her wheelchair.

"We thought we heard a gunshot," Andy said, catching up to me from behind.

Floyd the bartender emerged from the hallway; the attention of the entire room went to him.

"Helen's fine," he announced. "The gunshot... She's just working through some things. Whose turn is it to watch him?"

"Mine," Dody said. She thanked her condo neighbor for making them breakfast. Dody entered the hallway. Andy had me follow Dody, who opened a bedroom door.

Inside, Linkletter was strapped tightly to a queen-size mattress and cuffed top and bottom to the bed. Two IVs and a plasma bag dripped fluids into his arms. He was diapered in bandages and gauze, adhesive tape encircling his midsection. He was sedated, but he was as wide awake as I'd ever seen a sedated person, his head up, his eyes bulging. The room, the mattress, everything stank of alcohol and spilled blood, dried and drying, its heaviest concentration in the center of the mattress, under his midsection. Standing at the foot of the bed was Helen, the blue-haired fry cook, her feet squared, her arms raised, both hands wrapped around a large handgun, the barrel steady, pointed at his head.

"That was a blank," she shouted at him. "Next one, who knows."

"Easy, Helen, easy," Dody said. "They better all be blanks, young lady. We want him to be alive when we hand him over."

"Stay out of this, Aunt Dody. This asshole—ruined—my fucking life!"

Another trigger squeeze. *Boom!*

Heavy-duty recoil pushed the gun up and back, but again, it was a blank. Helen rolled her head like she was limbering her neck muscles. She raised the gun into position again.

"Helen Stovall, you stop this right now," Dody said, alongside her now. "That needs to be enough."

Dody reached in, pried the weapon from her hands. Helen started a serious cry. Dody reached her arms around her, folding her into a comforting hug.

From the bed, a voice, soft, exhausted, lost: "Regina…" Linkletter murmured. "I saved you. The baby…"

"You put me on the needle!" Helen screamed. "You made me turn tricks for you. There's no—fucking—*baby*! I terminated it! You fucking raped me, you fucking ugly—bunyip—bastard—"

"Helen," Dody pleaded, "go get yourself some breakfast. Now, please. It's my turn to watch him."

Dody, to me now, Helen gone: "Meet Randall Burton, Counsel. Aka Howard Isaacs, aka Stephen Linkletter, aka many others, or so he's boasted, along with boasting about having committed thirty-one murders. Adults and kids. He also says he's terminal. And now, by whatever name you need him to be as your bounty, he's yours."

When we'd made our acquaintance earlier in the woods, he'd been in significantly better condition. Hanging on a closet door handle within view of the bed was a clear plastic ziplock bag containing what looked like butchered raw meat, with blood pooled at the bottom. I stopped myself before I asked what it was, because I knew.

"Oh. That," Dody said, following my eyes. "Heh. The funniest thing. Helen didn't think it was him when we let her see him, because his face looks different. Reconstructed. Then she saw what was in the bag. What an egomaniac. It's got a tattoo on it."

"Let me guess. A picture of a…"

"A hand puppet. The bunyip. Same art as he's got on his arm."

Already knew about the other one. But one thing I didn't know: Helen had been another misguided runaway that this bastard had scarfed up. "So Helen… is Regina?"

"Regina Helen Stovall. My niece. She deep-sixed Regina, started using her middle name, got married, but it didn't last. Losing 'Regina' as a name helped her deal with her past, her turning tricks, her drug habit. She's been clean ever since. We're so proud, and so protective, of her. The entire town is. Here, check this out."

Dody lifted her bowling shirtsleeve, exposing her bicep. A bunyip tattoo.

"A lot of the women have one. So very, very protective, Counsel."

They should have killed him. Handling a dead body would have been easier than handling a mutilated man in this condition, needing to be kept alive.

I was finally able to formulate a comment. "So this is the new Rancor law enforcement model? Vigilantism?"

"No," Dody and Andy said in unison. "Fifty-plus years," Andy added, "hardly qualifies it as new. Most of those years, we also had a full police force. Until folks decided why bother."

I approached the bed nearly lost for words, taking in this nightmare visage that was my bounty. I managed a question for them, just to say something. "Tell me, how does the Maurice Fund fit in here?"

A moan from their prisoner. Dody produced her gun again and wandered the bed's perimeter, keen to their patient.

Andy answered. "Mostly it's like I said. For miners' families who suffered losses over the years. Then again—"

Andy's eyes shifted to Dody. My eyes followed. Dody accommodated us with a wave of her gun hand. She finished Andy's sentence.

"It also keeps us armed. Bullets, guns. All legal. Trust me, Counsel, when I say we'd abandon our approach if all the guns on the streets could magically disappear, but politics will never let that happen."

From the bed, a small, haggard plea. "Kill me," their patient said, his speech slurred. "I told them—to kill me. Whoever's here—kill me. Do it."

"We've been over this," Dody said to him, her voice firm. "It was gonna be either death or dismemberment. When we realized what you did to Rosie and Stella, you fucking monster, we overrode your decision. Good luck in prison, bitch."

Someone needed to kill him. I wanted to stick my shotgun in his mouth and let it speak for all the people who never got a chance to speak for themselves, the kids especially. I leaned over the bed, settled instead on showing him my face. This got the reaction I was looking for.

"The Tourette's woman," he said, hoarsely. "The cave-in... the rats... you're *dead*—"

"Yeah, well, fortunately for me, I'm not. Unfortunately for you, you're not either."

59

On the way back to the hospital in Carbondale, Andy was at the wheel of my van, me riding shotgun and earning the seat, my gun cradled in my arm. The barrel poked between the seats, aimed rearward. Pistol grip, short gunstock, pump action. It was manageable in my condition, good as long as I could handle the pain it would take to wield it. After my charge into the condo, my broken left arm hurt like a sonovabitch. I wanted my handguns back from the feds. And I desperately needed a soaking bath.

"There in ten minutes, twelve minutes tops. Better time," Andy said, "once we get out of Rancor."

In my head was the argument I'd lost to Andy: I don't do bounty transport, my van's not equipped for it, let the pros do it, etc. Andy's position: my cradled shotgun. That, plus Randall Burton was weak and sedated, cuffed, in leg irons, and was attached to an animal crate where my savage German Shepherd growled at him from the inside, the crate open. "Waiting for that transport," Andy said, "would only give him more time to die."

Advantage, Andy.

Deliver the bounty, retrieve my handguns from the feds, get better meds for my throbbing arm. It would all get resolved in ten minutes, twelve minutes tops, then Vonetta could pay me my bounty money.

Deep breaths needed on my part. Breathe in, breathe out. Furry keychain. Better.

We passed a feed store, post office, diner, and barbershop, and coming up at the crest of the hill, Rancor Savings and Loan. Fungo's growl was a low, threatening grumble that hadn't stopped since we'd loaded Mr. Burton in here with us, onto the van floor. No stretcher, no gurney, no strapping onto a stiff board. He was wrapped tightly in gauze and bandages, his hands cuffed, his feet in leg irons. His severed genitals-in-a-bag were attached to Fungo's crate, the crate bolted against the van wall. Prone, Burton's head abutted the crate and his feet abutted the back of the driver's seat. Iota Jean had pumped more sedatives into him at the condo, but he was slowly coming out of them, his arms and legs testing their confinement. He moaned.

"... where—the fuck—ammm I?"

"On your way to hell," I told him. "Shut the fuck up and lie still." Andy scolded my unladylike language with a sarcastic shake of his head.

"Sorry, but you guys should have gone heavier on the meds," I told him. "We don't need this chatter."

The bloody meat-bag containing his severed specimen flapped against the crate's steel bars with each bump and curve in the road, just above Randall Burton's head. It gave new meaning to the phrase "in your face."

When I asked Andy why he brought his junk with us: "No reason to clog the kitchen disposal. Hospital waste. To dispose of when nobody's looking."

Tess rested in the leg space in front of me, dozing at my feet. Randall Burton's moaning broke an otherwise quiet ride. I didn't feel like talking, and Andy wasn't pressing me.

He'd called ahead to the hospital, explained what was coming in. I had no idea how the town intended to avoid questions. Or how they intended to explain the surgery. Or how they intended to address their victim's personal account once he was able to verbalize the horror they'd perpetrated on him.

Or how much they would tell Trevor, Helen's son, about his father.

So I asked Andy about it.

"Some playful seniors and a four-hour erection," he said. "The way I see it, he was lucky my surgeon mother was there, waiting for me. But alas, her emergency surgical shunt went wrong. After that they did the best they could to save his life. The word of four senior women against a homicidal maniac. We'll make it work.

"But the Trevor thing." Andy looked in the rearview, to check on our cargo, him dozing again. "The damage that would do if Trevor ever knew... Promise me, Counsel, please, that you'll never let that out..."

"I'm good with it, Andy. All of it. You have my word."

On the record, from me, there could be no better punishment for this dehumanizing scumbag. If the authorities decided to examine Charlie, they'd rule her mentally incompetent. At times, nuttier than squirrel shit. Plus she was eighty-one years old. An elderly avenging angel. Nurses, retired law enforcement, and an entire town squaring off against a child-molesting, rapist serial killer. Risky on their part. But after decades of risky, who was I to second-guess their chances?

And for me, here was a chance I might not get again, sitting in the van right next to me.

I went for it. "Anything else of yours baggage-wise you think will shock me? As in a bad credit rating, or maybe you're a vampire?"

"No to vampirism. The B&B is paid off, and I don't owe any money to the mob. Otherwise," he said, "one man's shock may be another man's redemption. There is something else."

"And that would be...?"

"The Scranton restaurant executions." He dished: "Me. With Dody and Penny."

"Huh." My response wasn't an I'm-shocked huh or an I'm-impressed huh. It was a cumbersome, self-conscious, circle-of-life kind of huh. Not like I hadn't heard this kind of confession before. My husband, a deceased cop, had also killed people.

"You deserved to know," Andy said. "Now you need to forget I told you."

"Fine. Never heard of that Scranton restaurant. Just don't ask me to forget *you*. Because I won't."

"Maybe," he reached across, gently squeezed my shoulder, "just maybe we can work it out, Counsel. After we know it's not the meds talking, we'll schedule some time. Let's stay with a maybe for now, okay?"

At last call-in, Andy learned FBI Agent Van Impe was conscious. He and his other fed pals were eager to accept our present. We were eager to deliver him.

The van eased around another curve. The tools of my trade, snapped in place on clips around the cargo area in here with us, all jostled. Waist chains, cuffs, leg irons. Leashes, leather, Kevlar. They rattled against themselves, the metal walls, the roof. White noise to me when I was driving, me noticing it now because I wasn't behind the wheel. The equipment resettled to a gentle sway when the curve straightened.

"... kill... me..."

I glanced over my shoulder to check him out. His eyes fluttered. Spit seeped through his drooling lips, mixing with incoherent dream-speak. I wanted this monster out of here.

"Five minutes," Andy said, counting down. We leaned into another curve, this one up an incline.

"... go out... on my terms, you old cunts," he managed, slobbering. "Kill me, damn it."

He was aware, was remembering, was again grasping his desperate situation. The tires squealed a little. I watched the curve in the road, a little sharper than it looked.

"On my, *mmm,* fucking, *mmm,* terms," he said, garbled. Something had gotten into his mouth. "... mmm mmm *mmm...*"

I shifted in my seat, faced him in the rear of the van. I wanted to shut him up. "Listen, you motherless fucker you, you need to be quiet—"

Christ, his lips, they were dripping with blood. His teeth, they were clenching the plastic bag with his genitals in it—

He'd chewed the bag above his head open, chewed a hole large enough for its raw contents to slip out, onto his face, into his mouth. He spit. His butchered penis landed on his stomach, so surreal, near his cuffed hands that were—shit, he'd worked them free of the bandages—

One of his hands opened, gripped the droopy meat. He waved it, taunted, "Come 'n' get it, doggie... good poochie..."

Fungo left his open crate, was no longer growling, I could see this developing, couldn't stop it. "Fungo, *no...*"

Fungo snatched the meat, was chomping it into pieces. He slinked off with the rest of the contents of the bag, but Fungo's leash... it was unhooked, was now in Burton's hand.

I tightened my hold on the pistol grip of the shotgun, needed to raise it now, bad leverage, only one good hand—

Burton two-fisted the leather leash up, arced it over the driver's seat, over Andy's head, the leash catching under Andy's chin, lassoing his neck, the bounty jerking it into a death grip. Andy took a hand off the steering wheel, pulled at the choking leash, his neck pinned against the back of his seat. His body lifted and he arched his back, both hands on his neck now, desperate, gagging, the van nearing the crest of the hill, veering off the blacktop, leaning—

I one-handed the shotgun up. Tess jumped onto my lap, was ready to spring.

"... onnn myyy terms..."

Andy's face turned colors. Tess sprang, sank her teeth into Burton's scalp, but the leather around Andy's neck stayed tight. Tires squealed, we careened off-road and onto the cindery shoulder, sideswiped trees, still moving too fast, high elevation... the mountain skyline dropped from view—

I leaned between the seat, dragged the gun with me, lifted it, pointed it, steadied it, my broken arm, *owww,* my broken fingers, needed to will them closed around the gunstock, *agghhh*—

Tess was attached to Burton's head. "Tess! *Move*!"

No headshot there. I slapped the underside of the barrel against his chest, slid it down, jabbed it into his middle, gripped the stock tighter, pump action, shell racked, more pain, jammed it, held it there, my good hand glued to the pistol grip. A banshee yell, my fingers coiled the trigger—

The shotgun jumped. The blast shredded cloth and bandages on its way to blowing a hole through the sidewall of the van, but not the bounty. Andy was fading—fuck—shotgun empty, no weapon, I needed a fucking weapon—

I reached behind Andy's arched back, him still fighting, still strangled, still dying, into his concealed holster, his handgun there. I unholstered it, shoved the barrel into Burton's midsection—

I emptied the clip into him. Chunks of fleshy thigh and midsection and bone splinters ricocheted off the van walls, splashed up, stung my face while spattering Fungo and the floor and the roof in crimson. The van slid, left the shoulder, slammed sideways into rock, a wall, something. It teetered onto two wheels then dropped back down onto four. The engine stalled, the van coasted to a stop on a green lawn. I reached up front for Andy, pulled the loosened leash away from his neck, let it drop.

"Andy. *Andy—*"

I shook his shoulder. He slumped forward.

His phone, in here somewhere, where the fuck was his phone—

I needed to get out, needed to get Andy out. I reached for the sliding door, one-handed the handle but it didn't budge. I pulled harder, it gave a few inches, increased to a foot, enough to see outside. Through the crack I saw what stopped the van. A low, black granite wall. The coal miners' memorial. We were at the town bank. The first silver-embossed name I saw: *Maurice Prudhomme.* I reread the etched message: *The dust, the dark, the deep, and the damned. We stand tall against it all.*

A burst of sun peeked above a mountaintop, distant, across the valley separating this peak from one other. If it weren't for the granite, this memorial, this block of carved black rock no longer than a car length, in forty feet we'd have vaulted a parking lot guardrail. Another forty feet we would have been airborne, heading down the mountainside.

"*—fuck fuck fuck fuck.*

"*—fuck you, fuck you, fuck you—*"

Tess lifted my hand with her nose, licked it, licked my face, and calmed me into silence, refocusing my urgency. I climbed out through the back door and puked. I stumbled my way to the driver side door and grimaced in pain as I dragged Andy out of the van onto the grass where I delivered one-handed CPR compressions that seemed useless, worthless, hopeless... *please, please,* please—

He gasped, color returning to his face. I looped him into a one-armed hug. His arms lifted, and I got a weak, two-armed hug in return.

"You need a mint, Counsel," he said, coughing.

* * *

The van started, me driving this time, with no argument from Andy. At six a.m. the bank was closed, the town we left behind still sleeping. I shushed my dogs. Except for my pain, lessened now that I was likely in shock, we were in less of a hurry.

Andy found his phone. He reported into the hospital, got on with an ER doctor, then the FBI. "We're a few minutes out... No, Burton's dead."

One image lingered: the fucker had smiled. He mouthed a silent message then grinned, right through Tess's savage shredding of his face and head and me blowing those holes through his groin and the floor of the van, some of his ass escaping onto the blacktop underneath. I read his lips before the smile. His message was a statement. *"On my terms, fuckers."*

The next few hundred times that I would kill him in my nightmares, I hoped I would get the headshot that wouldn't leave him with the last word.

* * *

We pulled into the hospital's emergency entrance. Andy wanted me admitted. I pointed at the marks on his neck and said, "You, then me." He scolded me, exited, and strode to the van's rear doors. There he was greeted by nurses, doctors and a J. Edgar federal agent.

Fungo was back in his crate. Tess whimpered, wanted out of the van. Fungo did a nervous butt-wiggle thing, had to pee, probably more than pee considering what he just ate.

"Not now," I told my little carnivores. Tess sat on her haunches in the passenger seat, attentive, loving. I planned to keep us all out of the way while the hospital folks and the FBI did their job. The van's back door opened. In the rear view mirror I watched at least one nurse gasp, heard another say "slaughterhouse."

Yes. Good luck with the autopsy. One satisfactory outcome of the carnage: dead men didn't complain about unauthorized reassignment surgery.

I texted Vonetta on Andy's phone.

Netta you there? This is counsel

You bet counsel. sup?

Bounty is delivered. DOA. It was him or us

OMG. You ok?

Arm's fucked again. Heading into ER with Andy. He's banged up

Sorry counsel. Bad?

Could have been worse. Almost lost him

Sounds like a special person. Don't screw this one up counsel honey

I watched Andy in the side view mirror, talking to the nurses and an FBI agent. He leaned inside the rear of the van to supervise the exchange. Nearby, a car door slammed. Another agent approached, this one female, early thirties my guess, her badge clipped to the waist of her dark skirt. I exited the front seat of the van, favoring my left arm and shoulder. The agent and I arrived at the van's sliding side door together. She gave the cargo area of the van a glance, did the same with me.

"Special Agent in Charge Escobar, FBI. You're a mess, Miss—?"

"Fungo. Counsel Fungo. Pennsylvania state trooper, retired. Fugitive recovery agent. Just delivered my bounty to your men. Randall Burton, Stephen Linkletter, aka a host of other aliases. We also think he's a missing person, part of an unsolved in Philly. A sixteen-year-old cold case." The agent poked her head a little farther inside the van. I kept talking, to net it out for her. "Mr. Burton didn't make it."

"Yeah, I pretty much got that." She leaned back out. "You need medical assistance, Miss Fungo. We can take it from here."

And you can fucking have it. Excruciating pain hit my rebroken forearm like a lightning bolt. I weaved my way to the rear of the van, Andy there with Fungo, releashing him, him inside his open crate. I leaned against the rear door, needing its support or I was going down. Andy was quick to wheel around and grab me under my arm and shoulder. "Need a nurse and doctor here," he called.

Special Agent Escobar grabbed me under my other shoulder. A sudden stark, cold awareness passed between the agent and Andy, both of them with pursed lips, with me in the middle; they knew each other. They finished sitting me on the bumper then straightened themselves up.

The resemblance... *wow*—

"Dad," Agent Escobar said. "Your neck."

"I'm fine, Teddy. Just... I'm fine."

Principled, patriotic, protective. Damaged, dark, and beautiful. Andy was an enigma, with baggage that rivaled my own, maybe more of an enigma than I was.

"I'll need to ask you some questions about this," Agent Escobar said to him. "Now, preferably."

"Can't be now." Andy resettled my arm in a splint that a nurse handed him. "And I've got a few questions for you too."

A wheelchair arrived. The two of them worked together to ease me into it. Andy avoided looking at his daughter.

I remembered when I woke up in the ER before. My panic, Andy's resolution of it by way of calming, responsive, therapeutic hands. Less calm on his face now, more discomfort. I saw the pain behind his eyes, him and his daughter not the best of friends. I moved his hand from my knee to the talisman on my belt loop, wrapped my mangled paw around his, had him squeeze the fuzzy keychain, for his sake. His daughter left us to check in with another agent and give us some room.

"You and your state trooper buddy Vonetta," Andy said, his grip on the keychain gentle, like he understood it, like he needed it, "do you ever share your nightmares?"

My heart pounded for him. I wanted to sweep away whatever hurt was behind those eyes, and I wanted him to make room to let someone else in. I wanted that someone else to be me.

"She's on speed dial," I said. "We share all the time, day and night. It never fixes things, but having someone to tell it to, someone who's been on the job, been through some of the death, the horror, someone who will listen and not pass judgment—trauma's a little easier to handle when you have friends like that."

His eyes softened. "If that's all it takes..."

He retrieved his phone from me. After he keyed in a few numbers, he handed it back to show me what he did. My phone number was now number one, the pole position, numero uno on his speed dial. "Please pick up when I call," he said.

I nodded. A few tears spilled onto my cheeks. "Just don't forget to call."

He leaned into my face, kissed me, let me kiss him back. "And I'd like my own fuzzy dog keychain," he said.

"No problem. I'm on it."

A nurse interceded, wheeled me up a ramp toward the ER entrance to the hospital. Andy shadowed us. I used his phone to key in another text to Vonetta.

Andy wants a fuzzy keychain. Already I'm a bad influence

I admired the text, hit send.

You're an idiot sarge. Happy for you. Be nice to him, my friend

I will

Love you counsel

Love you netta

SCARS ON THE FACE OF GOD

Prayers sometimes land on the Devil's ears.

"*Scars on the Face of God* is a brilliant novel. Congratulations on hitting one out of the park..." **-Jonathan Maberry, NYT bestselling author and winner of multiple Bram Stoker Awards**

The year is 1964. A construction project in the town of Three Bridges, Pennsylvania unearths an ancient sewer. Inside is a mystery dating to the 19th century: the hidden skeletons of countless infants.

As the secrets of Three Bridges begin to surface, an ancient codex is discovered in the attic of a local orphanage. A bible containing writings in Lucifer's own hand.

The parish priest and a church handyman set out to discover the truth. But a series of strange visions and horrifying tragedies begin, and the darkest secret of all becomes clear:

The town of Three Bridges is marked, and the Devil is coming out to play.

ACKNOWLEDGMENTS

Kelly Linko, beta reader and cheerleader. MetLife, for severing me. Bucks County (PA) Writers Workshop. Rebel Writers of Bucks County (PA). Chris Fortunato, my former agent. Lee Dexter, creator of Bertie the Bunyip, local Philadelphia 1950s-60s children's TV show favorite. John Fogarty and CCR; I blasted "Fortunate Son" almost daily during the WIP and have done so almost every day since. Randall Klein, author and editor (randallkleinbooks.com). Marinda Valenti, copyeditor (marindaproofreads.com). Friend and memoirist Daniel H. Dorian (*Peripatetic: A Memoir*), who so wants to co-write a screenplay with me for this, and which is still so not going to happen, but our attempt to write the screenplay did improve the novel, didn't it, Daniel?

ABOUT THE AUTHOR

"The thing I write will be the thing I write."

Chris wouldn't trade his northeast Philly upbringing of street sports played on blacktop and concrete, fistfights, brick and stone row houses, and twelve years of well-intentioned Catholic school discipline for a Philadelphia minute (think New York minute but more fickle and less forgiving). Chris has had some lengthy stops as an adult in Michigan and Connecticut, and he thinks Pittsburgh is a great city even though some of his fictional characters do not. He still does most of his own stunts, and he once passed for Chip Douglas of *My Three Sons* TV fame on a Wildwood, NJ boardwalk. He's a member of International Thriller Writers, and his work has been recognized by the National Writers Association, the Writers Room of Bucks County (PA), and the Maryland Writers Association. He likes the pie more than the turkey.

severnriverbooks.com/authors/chris-bauer

Printed in the United States
by Baker & Taylor Publisher Services